KEEPING YOU

A STEAMY, SMALL TOWN ROMANCE

LENA HENDRIX

Edited by Nancy Smay, Evident Ink

Proofreads by Laetitia Treseng, Little Tweaks

Cover by Kim Bailey, Bailey Cover Boutique

ABOUT THIS BOOK

I NEVER SHOULD HAVE SLEPT with Colin McCoy.

When I moved to my sister's small town, I was looking for a fresh start—no more shallow relationships, no snotty fake friends, and definitely no charming, dirty-talking musicians.

We had a fun, red-hot night together, and we agreed that hooking up was a mistake, a one-time thing. But when my dream bakery location happens to be right next door to his bar, every day I'm forced to see that chiseled jawline and remember the feel of his incredible body on mine.

No. I'm starting over. I have rules. No more bad habits, definitely no falling in love. No matter how hard he tries to convince me, I know hooking up with him again would prove I'm the flake everyone expects me to be.

But here I am, stuck between wanting to make something of my life and wanting to grab him and make another delicious mistake.

ONE

HONEY

Okay, so maybe flipping the entire Sunday morning church crowd the bird was not one of my finest moments.

Or snatching the mimosa off that old lady's table and downing it in one gulp.

But hear me out . . .

Sunday work brunches were my least favorite part of the week. Sylvia, my boss and an actual demon from hell, thought the meetings would build team morale and, while they were "optional," it never felt that way. I sucked it up and woke up extra early on Sundays just to get ready.

Everyone who worked at Sylvia Jay PR had several expectations to live up to—impeccable fashion, full-face makeup, ruthless attitude. When I started with the company, the allure of a high-profile job and getting out of bumfuck nowhere was intoxicating. I could leave behind the cowboys and miners of Montana and use this job as a stepping stone to somewhere more exciting, like New York or L.A.

After three years of it, I was starting to realize that in order to get ahead in this company, you were forced to step on the backs of anyone in your way—including your colleagues and friends.

Sitting at brunch, I watched Sylvia drone on, again, about branding, scouting, and *using our assets*. She emphasized this by slapping her own ass.

Jesus.

"This," Sylvia drilled a hot pink lacquered nail onto the white tablecloth, "is a business. You need to do what it takes to get the job done!"

"Take Megan, for example," she continued as we all shot poor Megan tentative glances. Getting called out by Sylvia was never a good thing. "Megan? Did you meet your deadline this week?" Sylvia's eyebrow hitched up as she coolly looked down her sharp nose at Megan.

Megan cleared her throat, "I did not." She looked calm, but under the table I could see her high heel bounce up and down.

"Exactly," Sylvia stood and rested her hands on her hips. "You failed, Megan. Again."

Megan's head drooped slightly. I wanted to reach out and rest my hand on hers, but we weren't really close, so I tried to give her a look that showed her I was sorry she was put on the spot like that. God, Sylvia was such a bitch.

"So the lesson here, ladies, is that when you're a failure, you're off the team. Megan, pack up. You're fired." No one dared to gasp at the abrupt dismissal of Megan, but it was shocking. Megan led in client recruitment most weeks, and her father had recently died, which was probably why she got behind in her work. My jaw hung open.

Sylvia looked around the brunch table, daring anyone to speak. The women around the table glanced at their manicures or picked absently at their skirts and napkins.

This was team building?

Sylvia took sick joy in pitting us against each other, making everything from our numbers to our clothing a competition.

"And, Honey?"

Fuck.

I lifted my chin to meet her gaze.

"Where are we with the social media reviews for our new client?"

Clearing my throat, I stood. "Actually, I am looking to get more product into the hands of their target audience." I smoothed my pencil skirt down my thighs. "The initial reviews are less than favorable. I need to get something that we can use."

"The client expects a full social media takeover, including product reviews, next week."

"Yes, I know the deadline, and I'll meet it, but right now there's nothing coming in that I can use. People actually *hate* the product."

"I don't see the problem here."

Is she fucking serious?

"Um, well . . ."

"Make. Them. Up." Sylvia rolled her eyes so hard I was surprised they didn't get sucked into her skull.

I blinked once but recovered quickly. "I'm sorry, Syl. I can't do that." Not only was blatantly making up product reviews unethical, it was actually illegal.

"Do we have a problem here?" Her arms crossed over her large, fake breasts.

I ticked my jaw, and the words came tumbling out of me. "Yes, apparently." I leveled my eyes with hers. "I won't make up reviews. We can leave the reviews out or wait to get in some that aren't so awful, but I can't just fabricate them."

Anger flared on Sylvia's face. "Huh. I'm surprised by you, Honey. You're driven, talented. I didn't realize you were also a bleeding heart." A small chuckle rippled across the table. I looked around and saw plumped up lips pressed together, eyebrows raised. The women I had called my friends were all enjoying the show.

"I may be driven but I'm also honest. Their product sucks and everyone knows it. I can spin it to make it look a little better, but if I don't have any actual customer reviews to use, then so be it." I tossed a blond curl over my shoulder and glared at her.

I'd always been like that—back me into a corner and I stand my ground when any normal person would know it would be a great time to shut the fuck up. But I was just not wired that way.

Sylvia's eyes slitted and she looked around the table. "Anyone else have a problem with how we do things here?"

Slow, quiet murmurs and head shakes passed around the table. Sylvia raised both her palms up, as if to say, "See, you're the one not falling in line here."

I was stuck, rooted on my feet. I needed this job and the promotion I'd been working toward for over a year. Over the drone of her voice, my mind flicked back to my string of colossal fuckups.

Leave your dreams behind to chase a man. Check.

Follow him around like a lovesick puppy. Check.

Lose your ability to make a single decision for yourself. Check.

Gather the scraps of your dignity when you discover he's fucking your roommate. Check.

Shame burned hot in my cheeks. This job and its fancy office had been my fresh start. A new, serious, and independent me.

"If you think for one minute," Sylvia continued, "that you hold any value outside of my company, you're kidding yourself."

If I just sat down and shut up, I could figure out a way to make both Sylvia and the client happy.

Did I do that? Of course I fucking didn't.

Instead, I wheezed out a breath. "You know, Syl," I sipped the last of my mimosa from the champagne glass. "Working for you has been the most soul-sucking three years of my life. Go fuck yourself."

At the audible, pearl-clutching gasps from the table, I put the champagne glass down with a snap, grabbed my purse, and walked toward the door. On the way out, I saw a full mimosa at the end of a table of sweet old ladies enjoying brunch after church. I snatched up the glass and downed it all in one gulp while flipping my former employer and the rest of her Barbie-cutout minions the middle finger.

"You. Did. Not!" My sister Jo squealed on the other end of the telephone.

"Yeah, pretty much did."

"I can't believe it! What did they say? What are you going to do?"

Rolling the dough into a fresh batch of cinnamon buns, I held the phone between my ear and shoulder. "Hell if I know, sis. I didn't wake up today planning to be jobless."

"This is crazy. I can't believe you just . . . did that!" Joanna was always the level-headed older sister. She marched to the beat of her own drum—she was actually a female fishing guide several counties over—but she was reliable, steady. Unlike me, she was cautious and actually thought things out—things like having a backup plan before randomly quitting your job and losing your only source of income.

For the first time, I started to get a little nervous about what I had done at brunch. I had plenty in my savings account since my only expenses were my apartment and the clothes that I needed for work, but Butte, Montana was a small city. I was sure word was getting around quickly that I'd stormed out, made a scene, and if Sylvia had any say, she'd be calling around to blacklist my name by dinner.

Me and my damn mouth.

"I'm sure I'll figure something out." The oven creaked open as I placed the pan of cinnamon buns inside.

"Are you stress baking again?"

"Maybe," I admitted. "I thought it would make me feel better, but so far it isn't working."

"Hon, you know you can always come see Lincoln and me. We'll happily take some of whatever you're baking!"

I laughed. "I'm good. Really." I was working hard to convince myself as much as her that I was really okay with my life right now.

I changed the subject, hoping to move the focus away from me and onto her upcoming wedding plans. "Have you set up any appointments for dress shopping?"

"I don't know," she hesitated. "There's a little shop here that I wanted to look at, but I don't think I need anything too over-the-top."

"Joanna," I scolded. "Next year, you are marrying a broody, handsome, brick wall of a man that you waited a *long* time for. Don't you want him to fall to his knees?" Only part of me was teasing her—I knew she'd look amazing in whatever she chose—but sometimes Jo needed a hype woman, and I took that job very seriously.

"If I promise to let you pick it out with me, can we please stop obsessing over the dress?" Joanna's voice was laced with laughter.

"We're going to find you a dress so hot that the way he will look at you will be wildly inappropriate. The whole town will be scandalized."

Jo bubbled with laughter, and I peeked at the cinnamon buns slowly rising in the oven. I'd successfully averted more talk about the life that was crumbling around me and the stark contrast between my sister and me.

I was thrilled for her. Lincoln was her best friend's older brother, and while he was deployed overseas, Jo had written him letters. He didn't know her at the time but had kept every single one.

Joanna deserved how the pieces of her life were clicking together. She was meant to find her special someone.

I, on the other hand, tended to avoid deeply romantic relationships. Young and dumb, I'd completely abandoned my dreams of culinary school in New York to follow my high school boyfriend to state college. From that I learned the hard way that relationships have the power to change you, make you vulnerable, without you even realizing it.

Plus, serious boyfriends took up way too much time, and there were always unrealistic expectations, and meeting families, and "fixing" each other.

No thanks.

I preferred my relationships to be mutually satisfying, brief, and hot between the sheets—that was a must.

We chatted a few more minutes, and I mulled over her offer to visit her in Chikalu Falls. It was a small mountain town at the base of the Kootenai National Forest, and I was convinced there was something in the water. That place was crawling with burly, handsome men. The strong jawline of one particularly hot bar owner clicked through my mind.

Maybe a quick trip out there wouldn't be so bad after all . . .

After hanging up with Jo, I flipped through my closet and contemplated what could be next for me. Everything I owned was designer. It had to be, in order to fit in at Sylvia Jay PR. Skirts, heels, blouses, and jewelry were all luxury items. Anything less was unacceptable there. I caught my reflection in the mirror and barely recognized the always-put-together woman looking back at me.

Who even are you?

My boyfriends, college sorority sisters, even my career had changed me. Little by little, I made choices, sacrifices. Somehow I morphed into someone I barely recognized. I built my life on a superficial façade, but, secretly, one of my favorite parts of the day was coming home, whipping off my bra, and snuggling into oversized pajamas. No one ever saw me so undone, but snuggling into the plush blankets of my couch kept the tension in my jaw from compounding and helped the little, daily annoyances melt away.

Baking was the same way. I had inherited my Grandma Nana's love of baking. It calmed me, excited me, and I revelled in the thrill of taking an old recipe and enhancing it. My neighbors loved it because by the time I got done mixing and prepping and baking, I wasn't really in the mood to eat any of it.

As I waited for the cinnamon buns to finish, my phone buzzed with an incoming text.

Chad: I'm in town tonight. Busy?

Chad was a real estate attorney that made his money

traveling through Butte and surrounding small towns. We'd been sleeping together on and off for about a year, but it wasn't anything serious. He had a big dick, and he knew how to use it. Tonight I found myself more annoyed than excited.

Me: What did you have in mind?
Chad: Drinks at the Monolith hotel bar? I'll be done with dinner about 10:30.

After-dinner drinks at the hotel bar definitely meant he was looking for a hookup, and it had been months since I'd had sex. For some reason, the casual flings I'd always enjoyed just weren't doing it for me. I mulled the possibility of Chad showing me a good time. I wasn't really feeling it, but didn't have a good reason not to go either.

Me: Sure. See you then.

A little zip of unease ran through me. Maybe I could forget all about quitting my job with zero future prospects and focus on feeling something *good* tonight. I blew out a quick breath. Chad and I were going to have a great time.

CHAD WAS NOT A GREAT TIME.

I settled in at the hotel bar just after ten thirty, as we'd agreed. Forty minutes and two dirty martinis later, he finally showed up.

Tall and broad-shouldered, Chad caught the eye of every woman—and a few men—in the bar. He had a megawatt smile with straight, white teeth. It was no wonder he was so successful—he could wheel and deal and charm anyone within a fifty-mile radius. His hair was puffed and styled back away from his face, and every time he smiled, I imagined a little wink and cartoon sparkle popping around his face. The unease I felt earlier hadn't gone away, and I shifted uncomfortably in my seat.

When Chad reached my stool at the bar, he didn't bother apologizing for being late, but rather leaned over and placed a kiss on my cheek.

"Hey, gorgeous. It's been a while."

I swiveled in my seat, swapping my legs, one over the other as I turned. "Hey yourself."

Chad signaled to the bartender and ordered a top-shelf Old Fashioned. As he swirled the dark liquid in his glass, he eyed the hem of my skirt riding high on my legs. I knew exactly what he wanted.

We made unimportant small talk. He told me about his work, I avoided telling him about quitting my job. It was all surface chatter, and I struggled to stay focused on Chad. There was a nagging desire to leave the bar, go home, and cuddle under the covers with a true-crime documentary on Netflix.

Determined to salvage this day and try to have a decent time, I concentrated all my energy on appreciating his lean waist, long fingers, tight abs. After several minutes of openly gawking at him, I didn't feel a single surge of desire.

He finished his drink quickly and turned to me, licking a drop of whiskey off his lip, "You ready to go upstairs?"

Chad's directness was one of the things I typically liked about him. He wasn't interested in a relationship and neither was I. We knew exactly what the other person wanted and we were each willing to give it. Tonight, however, I was not feeling it. At all.

I suddenly felt hot. I flipped my hair off one shoulder and blew out a breath.

Why the hell am I having second thoughts about this? Go let this gorgeous man do dirty things with you.

Unfortunately, my lady bits weren't getting the message. No matter how well-fitted his dark navy suit was, it wasn't doing a thing for me tonight.

No one's done it for you for months . . . not since him.

My mind briefly jumped back to the hot-and-heavy night I spent tangled in the sheets when I visited Jo in Chikalu Falls. I buried the worrisome thought that Colin McCoy may very well have ruined me for all men forever. When he showed interest in pursuing a relationship, I had made it clear that long distance wasn't for me. I hadn't slept with anyone since, and my apparent hang-up was becoming a real problem.

"You know," I started, "I'm sorry, Chad. These martinis really got to me tonight. It's late and I think I'm going to call it a night."

He stared at me. "Are you sure? I'm only in town tonight."

Damn it, woman. Get your shit together.

"Yeah, I'm sure. I'm sorry, Chad. Next time you're in town, give me a call." I unfolded myself from the stool and grabbed my purse.

"Of course, I understand. Can I call you an Uber?" Chad was only interested in sex, but he also wasn't a total prick.

I rested my hand against the side of his clean-shaven face. "I can take care of myself but thank you. Next time." I smiled at him and walked away from the bar and into the crisp night air.

The blast of cool breeze felt good on my tacky skin. What the hell was that all about? A hot night with Chad should have been a fun distraction. I even wore my new lingerie with the black lace bodice, but I couldn't get the nagging feeling that it was *so wrong* out of my head.

I essentially cockblocked myself.

Fantastic.

Hailing an Uber from the app on my phone, I stood under the lights at the hotel entrance. Twenty-four hours ago I knew exactly where my life was headed—a well-paying job, new promotion on the horizon, a gorgeous apartment overlooking downtown Butte, a sexy man just a phone call away.

Now, none of that felt right. None of it felt like *me*.

If I was going to turn my life around, it needed to start right now. I was a total drama queen at brunch, so why stop now?

A new life. One with rules—rules designed to protect me from myself.

No shitty, meaningless job.

No fake-ass friends.

No men.

The thought of a different life rooted and bloomed deeply inside me. For my entire existence, people had seen Honey James as a pretty face without much substance to go with it . . . but not anymore.

Freshly determined to make something more of myself, I pulled out my phone and texted Jo.

Me: I think you may be right about a fresh start. You still have an open cottage?

Jo: Of course.

Jo: Eek! I am so excited. Chikalu won't know what hit 'em!

With a sharp exhale of breath, I slid into the seat of the Uber and wondered how the hell I was going to start over again.

TWO

COLIN

My fingers pressed into the strings of the guitar as I worked out the chords. I knew the song well, but figuring out the notes by ear wasn't always easy. It would probably have been a hell of a lot easier had I listened to my fifth-grade band teacher and actually learned how to read music. You win some, you lose some, I guess.

I had fumbled throughout most of the song and was getting a feel for the bridge when my sister Avery walked up to the empty stage.

"Hey. I was in town getting groceries for dinner. Six o'clock at Mom and Dad's, yeah?"

I looked up into the kind, anxious eyes of my sister. We were twins but couldn't be more different, and her crazy-ass brown curls made her look insane. She tamped down a curl behind her ear, and it sprang back out as soon as she moved her hand.

"Yeah, of course. Do I need to bring anything?"

She shrugged, "Nah. Maybe a couple bottles of wine. I think I have the food covered."

"Sounds good," I refocused my attention on the acoustic

guitar. I didn't really want to think too hard about why we were getting together tonight. I finally asked, "How is she?"

Avery lifted a shoulder but looked away, "You know Mom. She has good days and hard days. Nate's birthday makes it an extra hard day.

"Yeah," I croaked around the tightness I felt in my throat.

"Time just goes too fast," she blew out a breath, and her deep brown eyes had filled with tears.

Fuck. I did not want her to cry right now, or I was going to lose it too.

I cleared the hard lump that formed in my throat but couldn't look at Avery.

"Yeah, it does."

"We'll see you tonight. Love you, Col."

"Love you too."

When I knew she had turned to leave, I looked up at her and watched her walk out. It was early on a Tuesday morning, and my bar wasn't open for customers yet. She slipped out the side door to the parking lot, and after the whomp of the door, the large, open space filled with fresh air.

Losing steam and feeling an unwelcome buzzing behind my eyes, I set the guitar down and moved behind the bar. It may have been only nine in the morning but fuck that. Tonight I had to face my family for Nate's birthday, and I needed a drink.

I poured a healthy shot of whiskey into a glass and felt it burn through me on the way down. The years were ticking by, and we still got together every year for his birthday, but the sting of his absence still felt fresh. Raw.

Thoughts of him cropped up every day—a song he liked, the Thompson kid driving his old Jeep around town, his favorite T-shirt on the bottom of my dresser drawer.

Most days I tried not to think about how or why he left us. On bad days, it was hard to shake the reality that it was my fault.

I should have called. I should have been home. I should have answered the fucking phone.

In the aftermath they all said it was no one's fault but I knew. Nate would still be here if it weren't for me leaving to chase my dreams of becoming a musician.

Throwing back one last shot to drown out those thoughts, I cleaned up and headed into my office. I had successfully turned an old bar into a honky-tonk that did great business but I couldn't slack. If I was ever going to make up for what I had done, I needed to make sure I could take care of my family. I had plans to expand to the space next door. Bills needed to be paid, bands needed to be booked, and I needed to keep my shit together if I was going to survive tonight's dinner with my family.

"ARE you gonna ante up or what?" Deck tossed chips into the pile and glared at me as he took a gulp of his beer.

Cole Decker was a local cop and one of my best friends since high school. Him and our buddy Lincoln Scott started poker nights years ago, and after the dinner with my family, I needed an escape.

"Yeah," I grumbled. I peeked again at my cards—I didn't have jack shit—and tossed some chips into the pile. Hopefully, I could bullshit my way through this hand.

Lincoln sat next to me. He was a Marine and fit the bill —quiet, broody, and scary as fuck. I sized him up as he considered his hand. "Glad you could make it out tonight," I said.

A nod was his only response, and it made me appreciate my steadfast friend. It wasn't often that he came out to poker night, but since getting together with his fiancée Jo, he'd become a regular again. She was great for him, and he was opening back up more and more. The old Lincoln was slowly coming back to us, and that was cool as shit.

I let my mind wander to Jo's sister, Honey.

Damn, if she isn't the one who slipped away.

"Well, fuck. I'm out." Finn, Lincoln's younger brother, flipped his cards down in front of him. "Beers?" He unwound himself from the backwards chair and ducked behind the wooden bar. The three of us raised our mostly empty glasses to him, and he started pouring fresh ones.

We finished the hand, and I scooped up my winnings, laughing.

"You rat bastard." Deck finished the last gulp of his beer.

I smirked at him.

"That. There. It's that shit-eating grin. You can't trust that shit," Lincoln said to Deck, tipping his glass in my direction.

Deck collected the cards and started shuffling them for another hand.

Mid-deal he said, "Things go okay tonight?" His eyes flicked up to mine briefly but he went back to dealing.

An uncomfortable tightness pinched the center of my chest. "Yeah. It was fine."

"Man I can't believe Nate would be twenty-eight. He was such a *kid*, you know?" Decker talked while dealing our cards.

"He was a great kid," Lincoln added and the pinch in my chest grew to an ache. "Do you remember that time I was home on leave, and we had to yank his Jeep out of the ditch? Man, I thought he was gonna shit his pants."

We all laughed at the memory. One night in high school, Nate was out with his friends spinning a brodie in the parking lot when he lost control of the Jeep. His tight circles spun wide, and he took out a sign before landing nearly sideways in the ditch. He freaked out and called me at 3:00 a.m. I loaded up the boys, and we winched him out.

Nate was always doing harmless small-town shit like that, but the kid had zero luck. If there was a chance he was going to get caught doing something, he got caught. Every fucking time.

"Mr. Richardson was so pissed we took out his sign. We bagged groceries for him for a month." Finn's hearty laugh filled the thick air in the bar. He was there that night, and although Lincoln gave him a hard talking-to about hanging out with the older boys, it didn't stop him from always finding trouble with Nate.

It got quiet and I felt uneasy. I liked when they talked about my little brother—it felt good to share happy memories about him—but it was also really fucking hard.

"All right, let's go." Lincoln's gruff voice broke the heavy silence and we shifted our attention back to the game.

My thoughts drifted to Nate and how I was his phone call when he needed me that night with his Jeep.

If I hadn't left to chase a stupid fucking rock star dream, everything might be different. I would have been around to answer when called me the night he died.

THREE

HONEY

Two WEEKS after I gave the one-finger salute to my former boss, I pulled my vintage matte black Chevelle onto Main Street of Chikalu Falls, Montana. The ninety-minute drive left behind the flats and wound through beautiful mountain highways.

Chikalu Falls was nestled at the base of the mountains, and from the church on the corner to the grocer on the right, it always felt slower and a little like stepping back in time. Childhood memories of the summers Jo and I spent with Grandma Nana and Pop flooded back to me.

A bubble of excited energy squirmed in my chest. Nearly every person I passed raised their hand in greeting, and whether they knew me or not, I waved back enthusiastically. I peered over the steering wheel as I entered town to watch someone rolling white paint high on the town's water tower.

Are they painting over a drawing of a dick?

I shook my head and laughed about this quirky town— Jo always had great stories about it. I passed the town bar and dance hall, The Dirty Pigeon, and fractionally slowed my car. Willing myself to look straight ahead, I still managed to sneak a side-eyed peek at the front door.

My palms felt sweaty against the steering wheel. It wasn't all that long ago I spent the most incredible, panty-melting night of my life with the bar's owner, Colin. My chest warmed just thinking about it, and a tingle settled between my legs.

Get it together. You both knew it was just one hot night.

Squashing the thought, I pressed the gas harder and cruised forward, leaving behind all thoughts of Colin's thickly roped arms pulling me close and the scrape of his stubble against the sensitive skin of my neck.

Four turns later, I pulled into the hidden driveway of Joanna's farm property. The long and winding gravel path opened up to a stunning piece of land.

Off the road, the Big House was a gorgeous white home with black shutters and a huge wraparound porch. A small river cut through the landscape, and near it were several little cottages. I wasn't sure where Jo wanted me to stay, so I parked near the house and found her sitting on the veranda, waiting for me.

"There's my girl!" I called up to Jo. The excitement expanded in my chest at seeing my sister after so long. I felt overwhelmed with gratitude and a sense of relief.

She pulled me into a tight hug, "I've missed you!" Jo and I used to share an apartment, but with her now living in Chikalu Falls, it felt like an eternity since we'd been together.

"Mmmm," she replied, squeezing me a little harder. "I just still can't believe you're really here."

"It didn't take too long to sublease my apartment, and I *need* a change of scenery."

"Well," she moved away from me to sweep a wide arm

around the impressive, rural land, "this is definitely a change!"

We both laughed and held each other tightly.

It was fantastic to see Jo's face so full of life and happiness. I shooed away the brief pang of jealousy. She deserved this life and it suited her.

"You're welcome to stay for however long you need. Mr. Bailey is in Cottage Four, but all the others are open. I think the best view is from Cottage Two."

"Cottage Two it is! Help me unpack?"

Jo looked past me to see my car practically bursting at the seams with bags and luggage. She didn't know it, but the trunk was full too.

"How is it possible you have so much shit?"

"Well," I answered, "a girl's gotta look her best." I winked at her and lifted a shoulder.

"Honestly, Honey. If you're going to survive here, you at least need *one* pair of good work boots." She eyed my ankle booties and their sharp heels warily, but then we got to unpacking.

It only took a few—okay, fine, several—trips for Joanna and me to lug my clothes into the cottage, but we managed to get it all in. After she helped me put some things away and stack the suitcases in the closet, we stood together in the dimly lit kitchen. Jo wrapped her arm around my shoulders and squeezed as we both looked out the large picture window overlooking the riverbank.

"You did what so many people are afraid to," she whispered in my ear. "You started over."

My eyes misted and a small, scratchy lump formed in the back of my throat. I pressed my tongue to the roof of my mouth and willed the tears away.

I cleared my throat and took a deep breath. "Thanks, Jo."

I hoped with every fiber of my being that I could get it right this time.

∾

AFTER GETTING CLEANED UP, Joanna and I decided to meet her fiancé, Lincoln, at The Pidge. A flutter danced in my stomach at the possibility of running into Colin. He was Lincoln's best friend and *hot as fuck.* I glanced around to see if I would spot him. Bumping into someone I'd slept with had never been a big deal before, but Colin just *did* something to my insides.

Since he was Lincoln's best friend, Colin and I had been thrown together to help with Jo's fundraiser. At the time, she hosted a fishing event for veterans, and he insisted that the bar cater it. The food was spectacular, and his generosity did not go unnoticed. Neither did his thick arms, hazel eyes, or that tight ass.

I needed to think about something—anything—else.

"Can you believe this place?" Jo was perched on a stool across the high-top table.

"It is pretty incredible," I admitted. The walls were covered with old photographs of life in Chikalu Falls mixed with posters for local bands. It had a real honky-tonk vibe but with an upscale flair to it. The name might suggest it was a dive, but the parts of my brain trained in marketing knew it was intentional. My eyes swooped across the stage and dance floor, still secretly hoping to catch a glimpse of Colin.

No. Remember the rules? No men. Especially men who make you tingle straight down to your toes.

"Well aren't you two a sight for sore eyes," Lincoln's deep, rumbling voice had us looking behind us. He wrapped both arms around Jo and left a trail of kisses up her neck. She giggled and tried to move away, but it was obvious she loved the attention of her man.

"Hey, Linc," I said between sips of my vodka gimlet.

"I heard you stepped away from your old job. Planning to stay a while?"

"More like lit my old life on fire and danced on the ashes. But yeah. You're stuck with me now."

We all laughed but a heaviness lingered around my shoulders. I took another sip of my drink and added, "I still need to figure out what the fuck I'm going to do about a job. But that," I finished my drink in a burning gulp, "is a worry for another night. Who needs another?"

Jo lifted her glass, and Lincoln unwound himself from her. "I got this, ladies. You just sit back and enjoy."

Joanna's gaze wandered over her fiancé's muscled back as he walked up to the bar.

"You going to eye fuck him all night or what?" I teased. A blush immediately rose to her cheeks.

"Cut it out." She slapped her napkin against my arm, but not before I caught her sneaking another peek and drooling over him again.

When I followed her gaze to the bar, my heart sputtered and my mouth went dry. Colin McCoy was behind the old wooden bar, filling glasses from the tap with beer in beautiful shades from dark amber to gold.

"You know," Jo added hopefully, "now that you're in town again, maybe you and Colin could pick up where you left off."

I tried to sound as indifferent as I could manage despite

the warmth feathering across my chest. "Nah. I think it was just a one-time thing." Over my drink, I took a peek at him again.

Fuck. That man is a walking orgasm.

"We agreed it would be better to be friends—especially with you and Lincoln now back together. Your friend group doesn't need us tangled together and complicating matters. Plus, we were separated by ninety miles." I shrugged my shoulders and flicked my eyes to the dance floor and hoped to look confidently unaffected by his presence.

"Well, not anymore. He's right here." Jo bumped my shoulder and winked. Since getting together with Lincoln she'd become a hopeless romantic.

I can't even handle being around him—he's too tempting and my life is a literal train wreck right now.

As if my thoughts wound through the crowded bar and tapped him on the shoulder, his eyes flicked up and locked onto mine. The familiar thrum of desire bloomed in my chest, sinking lower into my belly.

It really was a fucking shame that I had sworn off meaningless sex—all sex for that matter—before getting to see Colin McCoy naked again.

Damn, the things I would do to you.

Colin's eyes didn't leave mine, but a smile quirked his lip up, and that lopsided grin was nearly my undoing. I pressed my thighs together and felt the familiar hot throb of my clit.

Holy shit.

In that moment, I forgot all about my new life and the new rules meant to save me from myself. I didn't give a *fuck*.

He was quite the snack in a tight black tee that stretched over his broad chest. I only wished I could get a better view, but the bar and crowd blocked any chance I had of getting another peek at his jeans, slung low on his hips. His hair was cropped short on the sides but longer on top—it looked like he'd dragged his hands through it, and I had to stop myself from recalling what it felt like to run *my* fingers through it while he kissed me.

Clearing my throat, I tore my eyes from his and refocused on whatever Joanna was pointing out on the dance floor.

I would not, could not, fantasize about that man. His memory had gotten *plenty* of attention when I had returned to my apartment in the city. I probably should have named my vibrator after him after all the late nights I spent thinking about our single night together.

I needed to be serious and figure out how I was going to be an actual adult and earn a living. Would I stay in this small town or start again in a new city? The uncertainty had me uncharacteristically rattled, and that feeling had annoyance bouncing through my legs.

"Don't you think?" Jo's voice pulled me out of my own head, and I was left blinking at her.

"Honey, c'mon. It's perfect!" When she realized I had no clue what she was talking about, she rolled her eyes and started again. "The cafe! You should talk with Mrs. Coulson and see about getting a job at the cafe. You are an *amazing* baker, and I haven't forgotten you almost went to culinary school. I guarantee they'd hire you."

A smile pulled at my lips. The last time I was in town, Mrs. Coulson called me an attention whore, in not so many words. The little old lady had zero filter, and I found her amusing. Working at the cafe wasn't the worst idea Jo had ever had.

"I might be able to make that work." I tapped a finger against my bottom lip as the idea took root in my mind. Jo's mention of culinary school had my thoughts swirling back to old, entombed memories. For so long, I'd been determined to make up for the left turn my life took when I'd chosen someone else's path instead of my own.

A job at the cafe wouldn't be horrible, but it also didn't spark overwhelming excitement. I could feel something bigger inside of me, pulling at me. I couldn't name it yet, but I knew I hadn't landed on exactly what I was meant to do with my life.

I hoped *something* ignited soon, or I was going to die a shriveled-up shell of a woman who tried to listen to her gut instead of waiting tables to put food in the fridge.

A brief, but highly comical, thought of my shriveled-up old lady corpse clutching a wineglass and still in Louboutin heels forced a gush of giggles out of me.

"I think I might give old Mrs. Coulson a run for her money," I whispered as I leaned into Jo. "C'mon. Let's dance!"

Lincoln returned with fresh drinks as I pulled a reluctant Jo out onto the dance floor.

AN HOUR of shaking my ass later, Jo and I decided to call it quits. She had an early day in the field.

"You sure you don't want me to stay?" she asked, stifling a yawn.

"Totally sure. I'm just going to listen to the band for a while, and then I'll head back."

I was still amped up and digging the bluesy rock of the

house band, so I hugged her tightly and pocketed my car keys.

"Let Colin know if you need anything," Lincoln said as he tipped his head toward the bar. "He'll take care of you."

I followed his gaze to see Colin lift a chin to Lincoln in some bro-code acknowledgment that I didn't totally understand.

Oh, he can take care of me all right—shit. No.

"You bet." I smiled up at Lincoln.

He leaned in, his large frame stiff as he tried to give me a hug.

I patted his back and stifled a small laugh. "All right, big guy. I'll see you two tomorrow." Lincoln was such a stoic man, but he definitely had gooey insides. He was really leaning into his new role as big brother-in-law, and it made him adorably awkward. I loved him all the more for it.

After reassuring them—again—that I was completely fine to hang out by myself for a while, I squared my shoulders to the bar at the back of the room.

If I sit at another bar, if I don't see his handsome face, maybe I won't jump his bones.

I looked around. The small bar to the side was packed, not a single space to sit. I chewed the inside of my lip. Too keyed up to go home, I gave myself a pep talk to steady the nerves bubbling inside me.

Colin is just a man. Lincoln's friend and nothing more. Sure, you know what the spot on his hip, just below his belly button, tastes like, but, fine. It's fine.

I huffed out a breath and ignored the way my nipples tightened and pushed against the lace in my bra at the memory.

What's the harm in a little flirty fun?

Instead of making the smart choice and heading home, I

made my way back to the bar where Colin was clearing two glasses from in front of an open barstool.

He wiped the smooth lacquered wood with a wet rag, looked at me with his lopsided smirk, and winked. "Well, saddle up here, sweetheart."

Fuck. I am in so much trouble.

FOUR

COLIN

UP CLOSE, Honey was twice as gorgeous as I'd remembered. I had only met her once, at Jo's first Project Eir event —a collaborative project she had started to help veterans make community connections through outdoor fishing guides. It had absolutely exploded in popularity, and everyone around town was proud of our girl.

Honey managed the entire event from set up to take down, and I watched the swing of her hips all fucking day, just working up the balls to talk to her. After a brief introduction and one too many celebratory beers later, we were tangled in each other until the sun started peeking over the mountain the next morning. She lived over an hour away, and we knew that would be tough. At the time, neither of us were ready for promises, so we parted on friendly terms.

I was surprised when Linc and Jo left without her tonight, but as she perched herself in front of my bar, I was grateful.

"What'll it be? Another vodka gimlet?"

Honey moved her shoulder, and I watched her golden blond hair tumble behind her. Over the din and musk of the bar, I could smell her intoxicating mix of apricot and something spicy.

With a little pout, she pursed her full lips, and I couldn't help but lock my eyes onto them. That girl was so fucking kissable.

"Nah. I think maybe I'll try a beer." She scanned the taps to my left. "Cold Smoked Scotch Ale," she said with a resolute nod of her head. "Definitely."

My eyebrow ticked up. "Impressive." I reached for a clean glass and started filling it with the deep walnut-colored beer. "I pegged you for a light ale kind of girl."

I slid the pint glass in front of her but let my hand linger on the glass.

"Well, I guess there's a lot you don't know about me yet."

Yet.

Desire spiraled up my spine at hearing she hadn't quite slammed the door on the possibility of more between us.

I know plenty about you. I know you like it when I grab your ass, and I can learn whatever you let me, darling.

Honey winked and the flash of a single dimple had the bottom of my stomach dropping out. As she reached for the glass, her soft hand brushed against mine. Heat curled in my gut, and I subtly moved my leg to adjust the growing heaviness I felt between my thighs.

She swiveled in her stool, crossing one leg over the other in a fluid movement that put a sexy little arch in her back. She focused on the house band and the Outlaw Country sound, and all I could do was stare, slack-jawed, at the sway of her pretty head as she moved in time with the music.

I was used to getting hit on and had even mastered the art of deflecting the unwelcome come-ons, but one flirtatious wink from her and I felt a tingle creep up my neck.

That was new. I thought about Honey a lot in the months after we had hooked up. It always felt like our time together was cut short, but when she left there was nothing I could do about it. We both moved on and that was that.

But she's here now.

I felt a tick in my jaw as I wondered how long she would stay this time. Annoyed at the thought, I went back to helping behind the bar but couldn't resist keeping an eye on Honey as she chatted with the people around her. She clearly never met a stranger in her life. She talked to every person near her, arms raised during an animated story.

" . . . and before I knew what was happening, my heel snapped off, and I was tumbling into the bike courier. *His* bag went flying . . ." The group of new friends she was talking to was completely engrossed in her story. It was like the entire room was tuned into this tiny spitfire of a woman.

"Hey, Boss," Isabel, one of my servers, called to me, cradling the phone between her ear and shoulder. "For you."

Wiping my hands on a bar towel, I reluctantly moved away from Honey and strode toward the privacy of my office.

Isabel patched in the call to my desk phone. "This is Colin."

"Colin, Ray Shaw. I apologize for the late call, but I have interesting news about the space next door."

He had my attention.

Ray, my real estate agent, knew I had been looking to expand The Pidge again. Together we'd been weighing the options of opening a second location or waiting out the neighbors in the existing building. While I had expanded once, pushing out the back wall to include a stage and space for dancing, I hoped to gain a little more square footage. My office was a shoebox, and in the past year, we had been getting more requests for catering. The kitchen was in desperate need of a complete overhaul.

"I'm listening."

"The previous deal fell through." Ray's voice ticked up with a hint of excitement. "Apparently, Mr. Stevens refuses to sell to, and I quote, 'some out-of-town, LA yuppie.'"

I could feel a buzz run down my arm. I scrubbed a palm over the stubble on my jaw.

"Well, that is interesting news."

Over the winter, the ice cream shop had moved to a bigger location, and Mr. Stevens was holding onto the old space. The old ice cream parlor shared a wall with my current office and the entire north wall of the bar. I wanted it . . . bad.

I had been trying to talk him into selling when some slick investor with deep pockets swooped in and made an offer that outbid mine by several zeroes.

Fucking suits.

"There's a hiccup, though. His son is in charge of the business side of things and feels it would be beneficial to lease the property instead of sell. He's hired some big-gun leasing company to manage the listing. My sources tell me that the plan is to rent the space out before he sells it to reduce his taxes."

"So I'll rent it, and then we'll buy it when he's ready." I wasn't sure why Ray was seeing a problem.

"That's the hiccup," Ray continued. "Apparently he's got some backwoods bug up his ass that his precious shop can't go to just anyone. Stevens wants to *personally* choose the tenant."

My thoughts mulled over Ray's news, and I felt an irritated ache at the base of my skull. I had an indescribable need to continually level up—to grow and expand my business. I could succeed in business where I failed in music. I was determined to tether myself to this town and prove to my mother that I wasn't a fuckup.

"As long as no one else weasels their way in there," Ray added, "I think this could be a done deal. Say the word and I can have the paperwork drawn up in a week or so. With your reputation we might even get a lower price on the buyout, but I'll strong-arm him if I have to."

"Move forward with a buyout following the rental agreement period, but with the original offer. I'm not interested in pulling one over on the old man. Our offer is more than fair. Just make it happen."

I thanked Ray, hung up, and blew out a deep breath I didn't realize I was holding. A bottle of fifteen-year-old wheated bourbon clanked against the desk drawer as I slid it open. I poured myself two fingers and sat on the desk in my office. After the first smoky sip, warmth bloomed across my chest. I looked around at the cramped office space. I thought back to when I was only twenty and left everything—and everyone—in the rearview. With a backpack stuffed with clothes and my secondhand guitar, I was convinced I was going to make it big.

As the dull haze of the bourbon swirled through my body, memories bled into one another—my mother's sobs, screaming fans calling *my* name, Avery's haunted eyes, cleaning a dirty apartment and ignoring the square of blood-stained carpet someone attempted to cut out. Only five years on the road and I was so close before it all came crashing down around me.

Then I found myself back in this small town, and I picked up the pieces the only way I knew how—starting over and living with the weight of my brother's death.

I used the money I had made in music to buy the run-down townie bar and turn it into a place to share good food and great music with your neighbors. Within the last three years, bigger names had started to book gigs, and expanding was the next logical step.

I rapped a knuckle on the hardwood of my desk and thought about my brother. Nate might be gone because of me, but I was damn sure trying to do something that would've made him proud.

THE LAST BAND of the night was on the tail end of their final set, and I gave my sound manager a nod as I walked past him. The crowd was dwindling, and I could see that Honey was sipping a tall glass of water.

Her back was to me, and I got a full view of her incredible body. She was small, with curves in all the right places. She reminded me of an old-school pinup with a tiny waist and a full swell of tits and ass. In the short time I'd been around her, I'd learned she was a walking contradiction—a hot-as-sin city girl, funny as hell, with the mouth of a trucker, and an even bigger heart, from the way Jo talked about her.

A jolt of disappointment hit me when she moved to leave the stool, and I was determined to catch her before she was gone.

Next to her, I settled one hip against the bar and leaned forward.

"Kiss me in the dark," I dipped my voice low and whispered into her ear. I could see her skin prickle, and the pulse in her neck seemed to quicken as my breath moved over her ear.

Surprised, she turned toward me, her chest pressed against the outside edge of my bicep, and I was rewarded with feeling the tight buds of her nipples beneath the silk shirt she wore. Her eyes went wide and her pupils expanded.

Goddamn, she smells good.

"The song." I couldn't help but enjoy her surprised expression, the closeness of our bodies. My dick ached in response to her. A slow smile bloomed over her face, and her one dimple flashed.

Something was shifting and I didn't know what it was—I didn't care. Without a second thought, I lifted my finger to move a stray piece of her hair away from her eyes. I wanted to lean forward, take her face in my hands and devour her, but as quickly and intensely as the moment came, it was gone when she turned.

Honey flitted her rich blue eyes away from me and grabbed her purse from the hook underneath the bar.

The smile still played on her lips as she reached into her purse for cash.

"Tonight's on me." I gently placed my hand on her forearm to stop her from taking out the bills.

One eyebrow raised, she shot back, "Then I guess I'll have to figure out a way to pay you back."

Her flirtatious smirk had my cock pushing against the denim of my jeans. She turned and I watched her the entire way to the front door. I tipped my chin at her when she gave one last look over her shoulder.

Game on, sweetheart.

FIVE

CHIKALU CHATTER

NEW IN TOWN

THURSDAY PROVED to be an interesting day in our small town. As the storm clouds rolled out, an impressive classic car rolled in. Behind the wheel was the sister of Chikalu Falls' own recent adoptee, Joanna James.

Ms. Honey James was spotted cruising down Main Street, and several reports indicate the car was brimming with boxes, leaving many to wonder if she is in town for a brief visit to help with upcoming wedding plans or perhaps relocating to be closer to Joanna. At the time of this writing, it has not been confirmed.

You may recall Honey helped coordinate the wildly successful Project Eir to bring together our community and others throughout Macon county. A breath of fresh air, Honey's arrival may indicate the turning of a new season for Chikalu Falls.

SIX

HONEY

"I STILL DON'T UNDERSTAND what you two see in that town." My mother let out an exasperated sigh through the telephone.

"Aw, come on. It's cute here." It was a beautiful, sunny day, and I had been on a run when my mom called to check in. Slowing my pace to a brisk walk, I chatted with her and got her all caught up on what Jo and I had been doing the past few days.

My mom continued her assault against Chikalu Falls. "It may be quaint, but there's absolutely no anonymity. Everyone tries to know everything about *everything*. Whatever you do, do not read the town newspaper—it's nothing but a gossip rag. And don't get me started on the lack of progressive thinking . . ."

I couldn't help but laugh. My parents both tried to outrun their small-town upbringing. They were academics —college professors—and each felt they were too cultured to be appropriately stimulated in a town as set in its ways as Chikalu Falls.

I thought back to the lavish parties and fancy dinners

with my friends and colleagues back in the city. I did miss a good cocktail dress. I also missed the women I'd called my friends. Most of them had been friends I'd made at work, and since my grand departure, we hadn't exchanged more than a few sporadic texts. It was hard to not feel completely forgotten.

"Well, I need to do something new. Start over. Here is as good a place as any, and I get to see Jo every day."

"It's a shame your degree will be all but wasted. I just hope, whatever it is, you take it seriously."

I couldn't help but roll my eyes. "I am serious, Mom."

"Serious like culinary school?"

She hit a nerve with that one. "One time. It was *one time* I balked at a responsibility."

She tutted her tongue at me. "You walked away from a prestigious scholarship to attend culinary school in New York to stay in Montana. For a boy." Her words dripped with derision as she openly disapproved of the decisions I made when I was nineteen years old.

Fine, yes. It had been to stay behind for my then-boyfriend and attend state school. But after our relationship fizzled and he found my replacement, I had learned a valuable lesson. Times like these, she didn't let me forget it.

"I remember, Mom." I pinched the bridge of my nose and calmed my breathing. The reality was, she wasn't wrong—I had made an impulsive decision fueled by hormones and had to face the consequences.

I might have been the younger daughter, but after that disastrous decision, I had *always* been serious about the things I went after. Moving to Chikalu Falls was a departure from what they thought I should be doing, but that didn't mean that I wasn't taking it seriously.

"It all worked out in the end, I suppose—a degree, lots of

friends, fancy clothes. You'll land on your feet, dear," she reassured.

It was beyond frustrating to feel like no one believed that I could be anything other than a pretty office girl. I wasn't even sure I even wanted to *do* that anymore. So what if in the meantime I waited tables at the cafe? I loved baking and I was good at it. Plus, the idea of serving up freshly made pastries to the Coffee Clutch in town could be fun.

After changing the subject and providing a few brief updates to Mom, I ended the call. Feeling frustrated, I switched my music back on and picked up the pace of my jog. As I turned onto the downtown sidewalk, my eyes immediately scanned far ahead to Colin's bar. It was too early to be open, but from the side I could just see the tailgate of his truck parked in the front. I felt a deep pull in my belly and pushed my legs to move harder, faster, in an effort to ignore the pang of desire.

I did not need to focus on the way he leaned in so closely to me and made my heart beat faster. I definitely did not need to think about how he smelled like lemon and something earthy, or how I'd gone into the boutique on the corner, sniffing candles just to see if I could find one that smelled a little bit like him.

As I ran in front of the wide glass window of the cafe, I tried to ignore the sea of eyeballs that followed me past the window. Mom did have a point—in a town like Chikalu Falls, everyone's business was public knowledge. Sleeping with the town's most eligible bachelor would be the fastest way to peg me as a flighty city girl who was clearly unreliable. A cliché, or worse, an outsider.

My breath heaved out of me with force, and my lungs burned as I pushed my run harder. I thought about all the times I was underestimated—assumed to be unintelligent or crass or contradictory.

If you think for one minute that you hold any value outside of my company, you're kidding yourself.

Sylvia's words burned in my gut.

Nothing's really changed since you quit work.

The women I thought were my friends didn't even care about me. I hadn't gotten a single text that I didn't initiate, and those were sporadic at best.

I just hope, whatever it is, you take it seriously.

Not even my own mother was being supportive.

With each memory, the anger stacked, building inside of me as I ran down the sidewalk. My nose burned as tears threatened to tumble down my face. I swiped the back of my hand across my eyes.

Without notice, a brick wall of a man stepped backward into my path, and I shifted to avoid hitting him. I stumbled on my feet and fell flat on my ass.

"What the fuck?!" I tore my earbuds from my ears, dusted the little pieces of dirt and gravel that bit into my palms, and rubbed my very sore butt. "Ow . . ."

The brick wall turned out to be a very concerned-looking Colin and another man in a suit. Colin scooped me up by the elbows as I struggled to regain my breath and balance.

Without releasing me, he held me closer. "Are you hurt?" His brow was creased, and I felt his calloused palms gripping my arms. My breasts pushed against his broad chest, and warmth pooled between my legs.

His eyes roamed over my body, making me feel completely naked in the middle of Main Street. I suddenly became hyper-aware of my sweaty ponytail and wiggled an arm out of his grasp to smooth it back.

A pitiful groan escaped me. "Yeah, I'm fine," I said as I continued to rub my right ass cheek. "I was kind of lost in thought. I didn't see you."

"You came barreling down the sidewalk. And you looked pissed as hell. I thought you were coming after me.

I chuckled and took another step backward but not before I got a fresh hit of his lemon and cedar scent.

Please don't also have a sense of humor. I'm already trying not to dry-hump you right now.

"Are you used to strangely aggressive women running after you?" I teased.

Colin's caramel eyes seemed to deepen to a warm coppery green as his lip tipped up in a small smile. "Wishful thinking, I guess."

I felt a blush creep up my neck as I looked from him to the other man.

Colin cleared his throat. "Honey, this is Ray Shaw, my real estate agent."

"Nice to meet you, Ray." I wiped a hand on my running tights and stretched my hand in greeting. He shook it with a nod and turned his body back toward the building.

Following his gaze, I shielded my eyes from the sun and squinted at the small, open storefront that was attached to The Dirty Pigeon.

"Is this your place?" I asked, still evening my breath and trying to calm the thrum of my heartbeat at the closeness of Colin McCoy.

Colin rubbed his wide palm across the scruff on his jaw. "Not exactly. Ray and I were talking about options—expansion." He shrugged. "But Mr. Stevens is old-school. He's very *particular* about who he sells to."

"Doesn't want his place overrun by ruffians and thugs?" I smirked and bumped my shoulder into Colin's solid bicep.

I was rewarded with a hearty laugh and his bright, wide-toothed smile. "Something like that." He shrugged one hard, sculpted shoulder and put both his hands in his back pockets. "He declined our offer this morning."

"Huh" was all I could manage, and Ray's eyes squinted fractionally in my direction. It was like he could see it happening as I felt it. I studied the empty ice cream parlor. My mind was turning, and the pieces tumbled and clicked into place.

This could be it.

Holy shit.

This is it.

A WEEK WENT by as I tried to gather intel on Mr. Stevens. With my business background, I knew that with enough research, I could have him eating—quite literally—out of the palm of my hand. Most of the residents of Chikalu Falls were all too eager to spill any gossip they had.

On the following Thursday, I gathered a basket of homemade buttermilk biscuits with a jar of vanilla fig jam and walked next door to my grumpy neighbor, Mr. Bailey's cottage. He was sitting on a small black bench, looking out over the riverbank when I came strolling up.

"Morning, neighbor!" I chirped. I was rewarded with only a "harrumph."

A second later, his face softened a fraction, and he turned to me. "You always this bright before 8:00 a.m.?"

"Usually, yeah." I smiled. "But if I'm bothering you, I'll just take these biscuits down to the water and feed the ducks." I started to walk away but counted in my head.

One. Two. Three. Four—

"Be a shame for them to go to waste. You might as well sit down."

A slow smile spread across my face. Mr. Bailey might have been a hardened retired Marine but he had a soft side, and, like most men I knew, he couldn't resist fresh-baked biscuits.

I sat next to him on the bench, the basket perched on my knees, and unwrapped the biscuits. I let their hot steam waft up in his direction.

His eyebrows tipped up.

Got him.

I knew I had his attention. "Homemade jam?"

He nodded once and I slathered the jam over the flaky biscuit. After handing it to him, Mr. Bailey took a hearty bite. I made one for myself and nibbled the corner. We sat in silence for a long while, enjoying the warmth of the morning sun chase away the chill of the waterfront.

Mr. Bailey stood and, without a word, walked back into his cottage.

Shit.

Thinking I had missed my opening to ask about Mr. Stevens, I was about to leave. Then, slowly, he came walking back out with a second steaming coffee cup in his hand.

He handed me the cup. "Black's all I got."

I thanked him and my heart swelled for this sweet, cantankerous old man. We chatted about Jo and Linc's wedding plans, my life in Butte, and starting over in Chikalu Falls.

"Chikalu."

When I looked at him with confusion, Mr. Bailey continued. "Locals only call it Chikalu Falls if we're trying to find it on a map. 'Round here it's just Chikalu. If you want to be one of us, you gotta be one of us."

"Yes, sir." I smiled up at him and met his crinkled green eyes. Then, I saw my opening, and I went for it.

"You must have known Mr. Stevens for a long time. What's he like?"

"He ain't got money if you're thinking that you can get his sorry ass to marry you," Mr. Bailey grumbled.

I was too amused to be offended. With a laugh I replied, "While I appreciate your faith in me, I promise that I'm not trying to marry Mr. Stevens."

"Then what do you want to know?"

"Well," I nibbled another corner of the biscuit. I hadn't told anyone outside of Jo my plans yet, and it felt all too real to say them out loud . . . but I needed to know exactly how to get Mr. Stevens to agree.

"I want to use his old ice cream parlor as a bakery." The truth whooshed out of me before I could chicken out of saying it. "I have the money for rent and the bank pre-approved me for a loan. Now I just need to get him to agree to lease it to me."

Mr. Bailey's cool, mossy eyes looked at me for a beat. "You seem like a smart woman. You'll figure it out."

Mr. Bailey stood and took two jerky steps toward his cottage before he turned, "Make a decent pasty. It'll help."

"ARE you fucking kidding me with these?" Finn, Jo's best friend and Lincoln's younger brother, said around a mouthful of version nineteen of the Irish Butte Pasty.

A trill of excitement ran up my spine at his words. "Better with the butter in the crust, right?"

"Honey, these are *insane.*" Jo reached for another small, savory hand pie and bit off the corner.

I pushed out a deep, satisfied sigh, and the front of my hair lifted up. I was exhausted.

Without a word, Lincoln grabbed his third half-moon pasty, and a slow grin spread across my face. Feeding people was my love language, and it felt pretty damn good to nail it.

All week I had been working to get the correct proportions and hammer out a million different options. For such a simple country recipe, it was a real pain in my ass.

Ground beef or sirloin? Chopped veggies or sliced? Lard gives a flakier crust, but butter tastes better. The options were literally endless, and I had spent the better part of the week making every variation I could think of.

With my hands on my hips, I watched my friends devour the small plate of food. I flipped the dish towel back over my shoulder and couldn't resist a happy little shimmy.

I fucking nailed it.

SEVEN

CHIKALU CHATTER

WHO WILL TAKE OVER STEVENS'S PARLOR?

THIS WEEK MARKS *the end of an era in Chikalu Falls, Montana. With the closing of Neville Stevens's beloved ice cream parlor, Neville's Dairy Palace, the premier shop will no longer be found at the corner of Henley & Main Street. Looking to expand the seating and service options, Neville's Dairy Palace is now located three blocks west. The new space boasts a drive-thru service, expanded indoor seating, a back patio with social tables and inviting seating arrangements. Local carpenter Devin Miller also plans to build a large play structure for the children.*

While the much-anticipated improvements call for the delighted giggles of our children, one question remains: Who will take over the ice cream parlor's Main Street retail space? Rumors of The Dirty Pigeon expansion abound while others are calling for a more family-friendly business to take its place.

EIGHT

HONEY

"Jo, I think I'm gonna puke."

"Honey, this is the most incredible thing *ever!*" Jo was beaming at me. "You're *really* doing this! You are opening your very own bakery . . . right here." Joanna's arms spread out wide in front of her, gesturing toward the dark, empty storefront.

I hissed out a breath as I doubled over, hands on my hips. "Yep, definitely puking."

She rubbed a hand up my back. "You always tell me to grab life by the balls. Well . . . this is your chance. Grab those balls, or, well . . . you know what I mean."

I turned my head to eye my older sister. Her lips were tipped up in a smile, eyebrows raised. Hearing my crass words tumble out of her mouth had her joy spreading to me, and we both dissolved into a fit of giggles.

I *was* doing it.

Opening a real bakery had always been in the back of my mind, but it never seemed feasible. After signing my name on the rental paperwork eight billion times, it was definitely real. For the next year, the space would be my

bakery. The opportunity to prove mys ~~~
dusty and abandoned, at my feet.

"Come on. It's Friday night and e ~~~
here. We have to celebrate!" Jo pulled ~~~
bar next door.

Walking into The Pidge, I could see why ~~ ~~~
most popular honky-tonk in the county. A band was already
deep into a set, and a sizable crowd was gathered on the
dance floor.

From older couples two-stepping to single ladies trying
to catch the eye of a cowboy, all walks of life were gathered
there. Groups of college guys on the prowl clung to the
edges of the dance floor, watching and bumping their
friends to nod in the direction of boots stomping and hips
swinging.

The vibe was high-energy and frenetic. I immediately
felt a buzz of excitement.

Joanna and I slithered our way through the crowd,
winding and ducking around bodies. We found our group,
sitting at a large semicircle table that overlooked the
dancers. Lincoln and Finn were already there, along with
Cole Decker.

As if he could sense her, Lincoln stood as soon as we
moved past the man with shined boots and wide black
cowboy hat. She squeezed my hand, and her face split open
into a grin.

"Babes!" Finn shouted as we came into view. He placed
a hand over his heart. "Oh, your combined beauty kills me.
Come here!" He pushed past Lincoln and pulled Jo and I
into a big hug, squishing us together.

"Hands off," Lincoln growled but Finn playfully
punched his shoulder as he released us. Linc wrapped Jo

↳ intimate embrace, and I looked away, but not ↳out pinching her butt first.

"Deck, you've met Jo's sister, Honey, right?" Finn asked.

Cole Decker stood to shake my hand. "Yeah, at Jo's event thing, right? How are ya?"

Deck was clearly a gentleman and supremely handsome with his dark eyes and broad shoulders.

What the fuck is in the water around here?

We shook hands and everyone scooted to allow room for Jo and me to sit. A server came around, and we all ordered a drink. Vodka soda with lime for me. I scolded myself for looking around and feeling a dull pang of disappointment that Colin wasn't sitting with us.

Do not bring him up. Do NOT.

"So chickies," Finn cut in before I was able to make a fool of myself, "what's new?"

Jo looked at me, expectantly nodding her head. When I didn't attempt to speak, she chimed in. "It's a *big* day. Honey's leasing the place next door. She's opening a bakery!"

I was jostled around by a shoulder bump, a high five, and a pat on the back.

Finn whooped once and scooped me up, flipping me over his shoulder like a caveman. He took the three steps down to the dance floor and placed me on the worn wooden floor with a twirl.

"Time to celebrate, sweetheart!" he shouted.

I laughed a deep belly laugh as we swayed to the music. I didn't really know the steps, but Finn did, and I was able to learn the line dance pretty quickly. The people dancing were kind and helpful. If someone saw you were a little lost, they would intentionally slow a bit so you could catch up.

The sense of fun and community on the dance floor was

contagious. Something swelled in my chest, and I realized that I'd never felt more at home and at ease than in this moment in a dusky honky-tonk, of all places.

This was my chance. A fresh start and I was damn sure taking it.

NINE

COLIN

I ZEROED in on her as soon as she pushed open the heavy wooden door to the bar.

Tucked behind the stage, I had a good view of Honey and Joanna as they wove their way through the crowd toward the table of my closest friends.

She was stunning.

Her pale eyes were wide and blond hair was in a braid that cascaded down one shoulder. The thought of me wrapping that braid around my wrist as I licked up the side of her pretty neck had my dick stirring.

From the cloaked darkness of the stage, I watched the sway of her ass as she walked up to the table. I licked my bottom lip and thought back to how incredible a handful of that ass felt as I buried my face between her thighs.

Goddamn.

I sucked a breath in at the memory.

Friday nights were some of our busiest, and I had already agreed to sit in and play tonight. I would have rather been off the stage with my friends, working my ass off to flirt with Honey, but that didn't pay the bills.

I resigned myself to the fact that I was working but hoped like hell she would be around at the end of the night when the crowd thinned.

As the first band closed out their set, I greeted them backstage.

"Fuckin' A, man!" the drummer shouted, as they ducked into the corner of the stage. "That was incredible!"

The singer and his bandmates high-fived and hugged as the adrenaline of a great set thrummed through their veins. It was a feeling I knew well, and there wasn't anything like it. The young musicians were talented, and if they could manage to stay focused on the music, they would actually have a shot in the business.

The eager looks they exchanged as they walked toward the line of band bunnies told me they were in for a rude awakening. Not all the girls were trashy—and, once upon a time, I was into that kind of thing—but as the years wore on, I got less and less satisfaction from random hookups. Plus, a particular pinup-esque blond had been consuming my thoughts.

Fuck it.

I pulled out my phone and texted the DJ to play another few songs to buy me some time. I could push back our set for a few minutes.

I moved down through the crowded room, stopping only to shake hands or nod hello. I was laser-focused on stealing as much time with Honey as I could.

When I got to the table, she was still out on the dance floor.

Deck was the first to see me and stood to shake my hand. "Hey, man, thought you were playing tonight?"

"Up next. Just thought I'd have a beer with everyone before we start."

I looked up at Honey dancing, and Deck saw my eyes linger just a little too long. He pushed a small laugh out of his nose. "Sure."

"Stop busting my balls." I pushed into his arm. "Besides, don't act like you didn't see Maggie walk in an hour ago."

That got a rare rise out of Lincoln. "Ooh, ha ha. Got him."

"You know what? Fuck the both of you." Deck took a long pull from his beer bottle.

Maggie went to high school with us, and she and Deck had been really close. Poor guy held a torch for her and never told her how he felt. She had a kid with someone we went to school with but they never married. He died a few years back, and when we encouraged Decker to ask Maggie out, he only grumbled and changed the subject. Most of the time he looked pissed off when she was around, but we all saw how he stared at her when she wasn't looking.

Deciding to give him a break tonight, I refocused on my goddess on the dance floor. The dim lights did nothing to hide the wild-eyed joy that radiated out of her. She giggled at herself when she bumbled the steps, and her laughter floated above the music. When the music slowed, and Finn held his hand to her, I had to remind myself that he was gay —a fact that I'd long suspected but he only recently confirmed.

Still, the animalistic part of my brain did *not* like seeing Honey wrapped in another man's arms. Downing my beer in a hard gulp, I rapped the bottle on the table and moved toward Honey and Finn.

I stepped up to their swaying bodies. "Mind if I cut in?"

Honey looked up at me with wide, wondering eyes.

"It's all you, man. Watch your toes with this one," he teased but moved away and walked back to the table.

I slipped into her space. Honey's arms wound themselves around my neck. I could smell her mix of apricots and spice, and I pulled her closer to me. The slow music and low lighting made every step toward her feel more intimate.

I lowered my lips to her ear. "Hope you don't mind."

She swallowed hard but answered on a breath. "No."

I could feel the drumming of her heartbeat as I ran one hand up her back. Her arms tightened around my neck. Our bodies were flush, and I couldn't help but feel my cock harden between us. She smelled so damn good.

"I heard you charmed Mr. Stevens. Looks like we'll be neighbors."

"Well, I had some insider information and he couldn't resist." A mischievous smile laced in her voice. "I hope you don't feel like I stole it out from under you . . . but it is the only open space in town." She pulled back to look me in the eyes. The concern that flooded her expression was endearing.

"Nah." I shrugged. "Mr. Stevens wasn't ready to sell it to me. Besides, I think I like the idea of having you around."

I meant it completely.

But what I didn't mention was that I had spoken to Mr. Stevens and his son, Charles, earlier that week. We had worked out a purchase agreement for after his father's agreed-upon lease arrangement. We had a handshake agreement that whenever Mr. Stevens was ready to sell—whether that be a year or five years from now—the parlor space would be mine. At the time of our meeting, I had no idea that Honey was the new tenant, and now that information nagged at me.

Instead of killing the mood, I pulled her close again and hummed the melody of the song into her ear.

We swayed to the music, and when the song ended, I

couldn't let her go. Instead, I leaned away, brushing a strand of hair away from her face, trailing my finger across her jawline.

My chest pinched and it physically hurt to move away from her. We stared at each other for a beat. Honey's mouth separated and her gaze fell to my lips. I leaned my head forward.

"Hey, man, we gotta get moving." A hard hand clamped on my shoulder, and I was snapped back to reality. The lead guitarist of the house band was looking at me like I'd lost my fucking mind.

Without a word, Honey ducked her head and slipped past us to join our friends at the table. I watched her walk away, and she grabbed a beer from the bucket, drinking down three long gulps. Jo whispered something in her ear, and I watched her throat bob as she swallowed. I had to rip my eyes from her.

Scrubbing my palms over my face, I heaved out a breath.

Fucking showtime.

THE LIGHTS DIMMED and I sat on a wooden stool on stage. Once upon a time, I was *this close* to making a shit ton of money in music.

In eighth grade, I realized that girls thought a guitar was cooler than a trombone, so I quit the school band and taught myself to play on a thrift store acoustic. It was cheap and sounded awful, but it started my path toward country music superstardom. As it turned out, buying that guitar was the best seventeen dollars I had ever spent.

The night that Nate died, my band and I were on a tour,

opening up for a big name in Texas country music. It was the huge break we had been waiting for. I got the phone call from a heartsick Avery at 5:00 a.m. on a Monday, packed it all up, and never looked back.

The hard truth is, Nate called me the night he died, and I was too selfish to pick up the fucking phone. A thousand nights I wished that I could blame it on a show, or being tired, or being too drunk. But I knew the truth—I was partying when he called. I looked at my phone, saw it was him, and decided that I could call him back in the morning.

Three hours later, my sister found Nate dead in his apartment bedroom.

Sitting on the stage of the small-town bar I owned was the only time I allowed myself to enjoy a piece of the man I used to be.

The house band and I wrapped our eight-song set on a country classic that Joanna loved. It was also a crowd favorite and set the stage for the rest of the night to be handled by the DJ.

While we played, I watched our table—more specifically, I watched Honey. She had never heard me sing, that I knew. When I started, her eyes were locked on mine.

The intensity of her watching me on stage was overwhelming. It felt like the band and the crowd dissolved, and I was pouring myself out to her in a way that I hadn't done for anyone before her. Desire swirled with something unfamiliar, and I held onto the feeling, infusing it into the lyrics.

Once we finished, I was eager to get back down to their table.

"Incredible as always, man!" Finn shouted above the music as I walked back to the table.

I shook his hand and took the beer he offered.

"Oh," Jo leaned in to hug me tightly. "I love it when you sing the George Strait song! It reminds me so much of Pop."

"I remember. I try to play that one for you when I can—the crowd loves the old favorites anyway." I winked.

The group chatted idly for another few minutes until the late night began to settle around everyone's shoulders. Somehow, throughout the conversation, Honey and I had slowly moved toward each other. It was like gravity—an invisible tether that drew us closer together until we were elbow-to-elbow at the table.

"So did you like the set?" I asked. My heart was rabbiting in my chest like a fucking kid, but I had an indescribable need for her approval.

"Eh," she shrugged her slim shoulder. "It was all right."

Her cool eyes lowered, but then swept up to mine. Unable to keep a straight face, a bubble of playful laughter rose out of her.

"I knew you could sing, but I was *not* expecting that! It was really, *really* good." I was rewarded with a full, one-dimpled smile and the bubbling warmth of her laughter. I felt my heart *thump-hop* in my chest.

Testing my limits, I lowered my hand off the table. Without drawing attention to it, I brushed the back of my knuckle across Honey's hand.

She didn't miss a beat, still wrapped in conversation with Deck and Jo, but she did stiffen fractionally. A smile widened on my face as I brushed her hand again, lingering a bit longer this time.

I casually drank my beer and nodded along, adding to the group's conversation. A third time I brushed my knuckle against her but then twined my pinkie finger with hers. A hot, heavy need settled between my thighs as I saw goosebumps erupt across the delicate skin just below her neck.

Satisfied that I hadn't imagined her earlier reaction to me, I slowly released her hand. She smoothed back her braid and shot me a single hot glance.

It had been months since I'd had Honey beneath me, but if she was game, my cold streak was ending.

Tonight.

Ever the detective, but a shitty actor, Deck stretched his arms above his head with a dramatic yawn. "Well, kids, I'm calling it night. I have an early morning questioning some punks about the park."

"Someone still drawing dicks with little top hats around town?" Lincoln chuckled and winked at Finn.

Deck rose. "Fuckin' A, man. I swear, if I find out this is one of you assholes, I'll arrest you myself!"

Deck threw Finn in a playful headlock. They wrestled a bit, bumping into the table behind them and laughing.

"Chikalu has a Dick Bandit in town?" Honey's cool blue eyes danced with the stage lights in the room.

"I can't believe I didn't tell you that," Jo added with a laugh. "You have to watch the bakery. It could be a new target!"

Deck released Finn and squared himself to Honey. "We'll make sure that doesn't happen, but if you see anyone around that makes you suspicious, let me know."

"Yes, Officer." Honey stood at attention and saluted him.

One by one, the group peeled off, saying their good-nights. Finn and Deck continued taking playful punches. Joanna wound herself around an eager Lincoln as he whispered something in her ear that had her blushing and giggling.

Honey went to grab her denim jacket, so I pulled it off the chair and held it for her.

"Are you always such a gentleman?" she teased.

Slipping her jacket onto her shoulders, I moved my mouth closer to her ear and let my voice dip low. "Not always." There was enough gravel in my voice to let her know exactly what I meant.

Honey's lip tipped up in a smirk, and her blue eyes held mine over her shoulder.

"Jo," she brightened without breaking our eye contact. "I'll see you tomorrow. I'm going to look at a few things next door—figure out what I'm going to need to get the remodel started right away."

"You sure?" Jo's brow wrinkled with concern. "It's pretty late."

"I'm sure." Honey smiled sweetly at her and blinked twice.

For such a smart woman, Joanna was *not* getting any of Honey's signals. Thankfully, Lincoln knew what she was throwing down, and he gently pushed Jo forward, keeping his arms securely around her shoulders.

"All right." He added, "Just be careful. Call if you need anything." Lincoln shook my hand just a fraction too hard. I knew a warning when I felt it.

Once the group was gone, I took one last sip of my beer. Honey grabbed my hand and led me toward the back exit door. "Come on, cowboy."

TEN

HONEY

THE ENVIOUS, dagger-filled looks thrown at me as I grabbed Colin's hand and headed toward the door were plentiful. I smiled—a cocky grin that grew by the second.

That's right ladies, back it up. This one's mine.

The truth was, I still had my rules and knew that hooking up with Colin was a terrible idea. But fuck.

Seeing Colin perched on a rickety wooden stool, his arms wrapped around an old guitar was H-O-T, *hot*. He wore a tight gray T-shirt, and his jeans stretched over his muscular thighs. At one point he adjusted his pant leg, and I thought I would melt into goo, seeping out onto the dance floor. The entire time he sang, I fought away thoughts of straddling him and feeling his hard length press against my pussy while he sang low in my ear.

The sound that came out of that mouth was rich, bluesy, and soulful—like Chris Stapleton and Luke Combs had a six-foot-two-inch love child. I was *not* expecting that. Watching him sing was the most incredible foreplay I never knew I needed. Rules be damned, because Colin McCoy was sex on a stick.

"You kidnapping me?" He squeezed my hand once.

"You wish. I really do want to check out the bakery again and Jo is right. It's late. You're my bodyguard."

We pushed past the crowd and slipped out the back door into the alleyway. We rounded the pavement, and as I dug the key from my purse, Colin leaned his body forward.

My back was flat against his broad chest, and I couldn't help but lean my head back and to the side on a sigh. "Mmmm." A moan escaped my lips. "You need to stop doing that."

"Get that door open, baby," he ground out and nipped at the thin skin just underneath my ear.

I pushed the door open, and the heavy darkness enveloped us. A moment of panic skittered through me until Colin moved his wide palms up my arms.

A nervous laugh escaped me.

"I've got you." His deep, warm voice comforted me.

An overhead, fluorescent light blinked to life, and I let out a sigh of relief. Colin didn't move from behind me, but we both looked around the small kitchen space.

A tingle from my legs to my chest fanned out, reaching my fingers and toes.

This is my kitchen.

"Tell me about it," Colin urged.

I took a deep, cleansing breath and moved forward. I hoisted myself up on the metal island table in the center of the space. Colin stood next to me, his hip leaned up against the cool metal.

"Well," I started. "I have no fucking clue what I'm doing . . . so there's that."

We both laughed. His eyes crinkled at the corners and his deep, sensual chuckle moved over my skin. I felt a pinch in my chest and did my best to ignore it.

"You are a smart," Colin tucked a hair behind my ear, "beautiful," ran his hand down my arm, "extraordinary woman," moved his palm down my leg to my knee. "I have no doubt that you can do amazing things with this bakery."

I swallowed hard. His words, combined with the sensual touches on my body, were dual waves crashing inside my chest. No one besides Jo had ever so completely and automatically believed in me. The feeling of his fingertips against my skin blazed a fire in their wake, and my head felt like it was swimming.

"I never thought I would be here," I admitted, "sitting in an empty kitchen, just waiting for me to bake whatever I want. It's exciting and mind-blowing but a little overwhelming too." I chewed the inside of my bottom lip.

Colin shifted to center himself and faced me. My heartbeat ticked upward. Standing in front of me, he placed his palms on my knees, gently pushing them apart as he settled his body between my legs. Warmth pooled at my core, and I felt my pussy pulse in anticipation. I wanted nothing more than for Colin to keep talking, keep touching my body and lighting it on fire.

His hands moved up my thighs and around to the outside swell of my hips. He leaned down and placed a soft, gentle kiss at the base of my neck.

"Tell me what you'll make," he whispered.

"Oh fuck," I breathed. "Who gives a shit about baking right now? I can't focus when you're . . . doing . . . *that*."

Colin burned a path of kisses up my neck. A soft peck. A scrape of his teeth. A drag of his tongue. I hissed in another breath.

"I think what you're doing is incredible." Colin's gravelly voice vibrated through me. My pussy ached with need. I pressed my hips forward, desperately trying to feel friction between my legs. I was rewarded when I felt his steel erection press into me.

"Tell me one thing you'll make," he repeated as he took my braid in his hands and loosened it. He ran his fingers through my hair.

My breath was light, barely above a whisper as Colin continued his assault on my senses.

"I make cinnamon buns and—" My head lolled back, melting into every warm, wet swipe of his mouth. His broad hands moved up my back, pulling me harder against him. He slanted his mouth over my ear, sucking the lobe and biting it softly. I arched and pressed my breasts into him.

"Mmm. Will you let me lick the icing off you?"

My eyes flew open. Colin McCoy was a dirty-talking, guitar-playing sex god.

Oh hell yes.

My internal sex freak was cartwheeling and backflipping across the kitchen.

Game on, dude.

I touched a finger to the base of my neck. "Only if you lick it off here," I trailed the finger across my neck and moved down my chest. "And here," I arched again, jutting my tits out and circling my hard nipple through my shirt.

On a growl, Colin nipped at my neck and pushed me back onto the large metal island, mounting me in the process. The cold of the metal bit at my back, and the warmth of his mouth consumed me. I felt the hard length of his body press into me.

"I am so fucking hard for you right now, Honey."

My hands moved lower, tugging his shirt up. My fingers traced the cut lines of his abs, and my fingers fumbled at his belt.

"I want to feel this cock inside me again." Our mouths

crashed together as I worked his zipper down. Colin's hands were tangled in my long hair, pulling my head to the side to gain access to my neck.

"I haven't forgotten how it felt when I split your pussy open. I need that again." His right hand moved lower, brushing a thumb against the peak of my nipple. A sizzle of pleasure shot straight down to my core.

"Yes. Colin. Fuck, yes. I want you to fill me."

I moved my hands under the back waistband of his boxer briefs to grab his firm, round ass. I pulled him into me and felt my clit buzz at the pressure.

"Wait, wait. Hang on," Colin breathed heavily.

He leaned his body weight to one side and lifted to look at me carefully. His hazel eyes looked at me as if I were the most precious thing they'd ever seen. He traced the bottom of my lip with the pad of his thumb. Our breaths were ragged, and I could feel our pulses fighting through the fabric of my top.

"What? Why'd you stop?" I pulled him closer and wound my legs around the backs of his thighs.

"I don't have any condoms," he said, searching my eyes.

"Are you serious?" My mind raced in a thousand different directions. "You're a musician," I exhaled. "You're supposed to be a slut."

He chuckled. "Maybe a lifetime ago but not anymore."

My mouth dropped open. I literally had no words.

"*Fuck*," he snarled. "I'd give my right arm to be inside you right now."

My heart danced at his words. I should not be feeling this level of excitement for a reformed playboy, but knowing I was driving him as wild as he was driving me was powerful.

"No, no. It's okay." My voice was laced with disappointment. "It's not just the guy's responsibility. I get that but I don't have anything either."

I meant the words I said, but I had to fight the urge to pout. A moment ticked by as a war raged inside of me. I'd never had sex without a condom, and that wasn't a rule I was *ever* willing to break.

I brushed a hand through his hair, leaving it splayed out in different directions. He looked cute and horny and a little bit sad. My heart tumbled, just slightly, for Colin.

"I'm sorry," I said.

"Hey," he looked far less amused than I was. "You have nothing to be sorry for."

This is why you have rules in the first place. Get your shit together.

Colin lowered himself to kiss me again, but I moved my head to the side, forcing his kiss to land on my neck. I gently pushed up, and he moved in tune with my body, peeling himself off of me and standing again in front of the kitchen island.

"Look," I started, "this isn't a good idea. We got carried away. I'm sorry I dragged you over here."

Colin's brow creased. "I'm not sorry but you're right. It's just not the right time."

I blew a breath out and tucked my rumpled hair behind my ears. I'm sure it had that just-fucked look, and it was a damn shame that wasn't the case. Colin adjusted his dick back into his jeans, and my traitorous insides clenched.

But rules were rules.

"I just think I have a lot going on right now. This bakery is going to take up a lot of my time." I knew I started to ramble, but my unsatisfied lust and a bundle of nerves were making the words tumble out of me. "Plus, you know how this town is . . . I don't need people talking shit about me."

He looked at me, but his eyes were hard, unconvinced. After a moment he nodded his head once. "Okay then. Let me walk you to your car."

Colin turned and exited the same door we entered, leaving me a jumbled mess of heat and confusion. I'd been the one to shut it down, but something inside of me hated it just as much as he did.

I dragged my hands through my hair, pulling it back into a low ponytail. I flipped off the lights and locked the door to the bakery behind me. Colin was waiting for me outside, and he grabbed my hand, walking me to the side parking lot.

I took the lead, stepping up to my car.

"Are you fucking serious?" His eyes scanned my vintage ride and I smiled widely. I loved the reaction I got anytime someone else appreciated my car.

"What?" I blinked at him innocently.

"Oh, you know what." Colin ran his hand across the matte black paint. "A vintage Chevelle? What year is this?"

"'69. You can tell by the center bar in the grille. The taillights are different too."

Colin pushed his hips into me, leaning me into the car. "You are something else, sweetheart." His arms caged me in, and I couldn't help but run my hands across his muscular biceps and into his shirtsleeves.

"I thought we said we weren't doing this." My voice came out breathy and tight.

"All I said was, not tonight. Because when I fuck you, it isn't going to be rushed and in the middle of some dusty kitchen. I'm going to lay you down and take my time worshipping every curve of your body."

His words had me seriously reconsidering my rules— even the no condom rule.

Oh yeah, pull him into your car and bang him under this streetlight. Real smooth. That will definitely keep people from talking about you. Idiot.

"Thank you for walking me to my car."

Colin's hand wound around my neck and into my hair. He leaned forward, pressing his hips into me again as his lips moved over mine. I could feel the bass of his heartbeat push against me as his tongue moved over mine. Instinctively, I hitched a leg up, pulling him tightly against me.

Breaking the kiss, he brushed his nose against mine. "Give me your phone," he whispered.

In a haze of sexual bliss, I pulled it out of my purse, unlocked and handed it to him. A serious expression settled on his face as he typed something into my phone.

"There. I put my number in there. Text me when you get home safely."

"Okay, but—" I started.

"I'm serious, Honey. I need to know you made it back okay." His stern tone had my sex goddess perking up again, but I shoved those feelings to the side as I opened the car door.

"Yes, boss," I teased and as I turned to get in, Colin slapped my ass.

"That's right," he winked and I nearly came right there. Colin helped close my door and stood there, beneath the streetlight, as I pulled away.

I watched him from my side mirror and fought a battle to not turn around.

You can either be the old you or the new you. You don't get both. So what is it, girlie?

Thoughts of a new life tumbled before me as I followed the winding roads toward Jo's property and the tiny cottage that waited for me. For a brief moment, I wished that a new me included Colin, but there was no way around it.

If I was going to course correct, do better and live my life as my authentic self, then any chance of a fling with him couldn't happen. I would need to do something drastic—for myself and by myself.

A swell of disappointment filled me as I traced my kiss-swollen lip.

Friends. Friends with your hot as fuck neighbor.

After arriving home at the cottage, I sent a quick, impersonal text to Colin and snatched a pad of paper and pen from the kitchen counter. If I couldn't trust myself to make the best decisions, then I had to write it all down. If I was going to be serious, to live the life I should have started before I let other people change me, then I *needed* new rules.

HONEY'S RULES FOR A BETTER LIFE:
No fake, shallow friends
No hookups {no matter how hot}
No swooning
<u>Definitely</u> no falling in love
No deviating from the plan

ELEVEN

CHIKALU CHATTER

CHIKALU FALLS: SMALL-TOWN LIFE PROVES IRRESISTIBLE

AFTER SEVENTEEN DAYS IN CHIKALU, *it seems that Honey James may be extending her visit. Eyewitnesses report Ms. James called upon our very own Mr. Stevens last week with a small package. Could this mean that Honey is considering bringing a new business to our hometown and wants to get in the good graces of one of our town elders? If so, are rumors of a bakery to be believed? Not all are convinced.*

"She has the most gorgeous clothes," Beth-Ann Harding noted. "I sure hope it's a new clothing boutique!"

Bobby Prince commented that she passed Honey on her way to Stevens's place and stated, "Whatever she had smelled better than anything I've made in the past month. If she's cookin', I'm eatin'." Perhaps Honey is considering giving the cafe a run for its money? Whatever the endeavor, this reporter will bring you the latest updates as they unfold.

TWELVE
COLIN

FOUR DAYS. Four days had passed since I got the stupidest fucking text ever:

Honey: Made it home. Thanks.

Thanks? Fucking *thanks?!* I was coming apart at the seams over this woman, and she acted like it was no big deal.

I swear to Christ, I am carrying a dozen condoms with me at all times. I don't give a shit if I'm going to Richardson's grocery store, they're coming with me.

Shaking my head, I dragged a hand through my hair. I couldn't concentrate on anything lately. Thoughts of Honey and her laughter, smile, that tight little body, pushed their way to the surface no matter how I tried to ignore them. I swear, the smell of her—apricot and spice, always—was permeating the wall of my office from the bakery next door.

I heard her voice drift through those walls, and I caught myself leaning an ear against it like a fucking lunatic.

A tremor of panic rippled through me anytime I thought about my side deal with Mr. Stevens's son. I would have to tell Honey eventually, and I didn't want to piss her off before I had the chance to explain myself—that I truly didn't know she was renting it before I made the purchase agreement with Charles, and it would likely be years before he was ready to sell.

Damn it. Add it to the running list of things you have managed to fuck up in this lifetime.

The monotonous drone of voices had me moving from behind my desk. I had to figure out what to do with all these *feelings,* and there was only one person I trusted implicitly with advice about feelings.

"So is this a get-in-her-pants situation or what?" My sister Avery was clearly annoyed that I was interrupting her at her work in the bank on a busy weekday morning. She drummed a pen impatiently at her desk.

"Uh, well . . . no. And yes?"

"Well I can't help you if you're going to be vague as hell." Irritation had Avery blowing her curls out of her face in a huff.

I breathed out a heavy sigh. "Okay, so we technically already had sex a couple of months back . . . and a heavy make-out session a few days ago. But . . ." I felt ridiculous admitting this to my sister, but I needed the advice. "I think I actually like this one. Like, *really* like her."

Avery's eyes, the same greenish brown as mine, grew wide. "Oh, shit . . . that's a first."

"Yeah."

Avery cleared her throat gently and started nervously rearranging random office supplies on her desk as if the state of her desk would somehow rearrange my love life. "Okay.

We've got this." I could see the wheels turning in her mind as she thought about the options. She suddenly stopped drumming a rhythm with her pen and looked directly at me. "Got it . . . Woo her."

"What?"

"Woo her, idiot." Avery rolled her eyes as if I was the dumbest fuck she had ever seen. "*Woo* her. Every woman—I don't care who she is—wants to be wooed. Trust me."

"Like flowers and hearts and rainbows and shit?"

"Well, sure, if that's what she's into. Look, you can't just stroll through the door after a two-week business trip, order Chinese takeout, sit in front of the television and expect her to be throwing herself at you."

I furrowed my brows at her. "That seems oddly specific. Are you okay?"

"I'm fine. Things with Ken are just . . . I don't know. Still not great. But this isn't about me, and I don't want to talk about it."

I hated that Avery was still having issues with her husband, Ken. He was a dipshit, and I thought they got married too young, but until she said otherwise, we were stuck with him.

"You need to figure out how to make her life *better* with you in it," she continued. "Anyone can tell her that they're interested, but you can *show* her. Just don't be creepy about it. Get in, woo, get out. Leave her wanting just a little bit more. Girls eat that shit up." Avery wiggled her eyebrows like she'd just let me in on the ultimate female secret.

"How to make her life better. Woo her," I repeated. On a sigh, I shook my head and dropped my hands to my thighs. "All right, I got this."

"Hell yeah, you do!" Avery went up for a high five and our collective ridiculousness had me laughing and feeling more lighthearted than I did when I had gone in. Avery was always the one who could navigate our messy, emotional landscape.

~

WITH QUICK STRIDES, I left the bank and hustled up the few blocks toward the bar. When I glanced over at the bakery, I saw that Honey had Jo's help. I darted across the street to duck into the coffee shop. I ordered two coffees to go with all of the fixings—I really needed to figure out how she took her coffee if I was going to pull off this wooing shit —and headed back over.

I rapped a knuckle on the doorframe of the open door. "Special delivery," I called over the dance music playing on the radio.

Both Honey and Jo turned at my interruption, but it was Honey's face lighting up that had my chest tightening. Joanna lowered the volume on the speaker.

"Dude . . . is that coffee?" Honey rubbed her palms together and tiptoed around the paint cans and rollers on the floor.

"Look at you," Jo swooned, "aren't you thoughtful." She winked at me and gave me a hip-bump. Joanna and I had become buddies and our easy friendship helped me relax around her sister. At Jo's words, I tried to hide my grin with a swipe across my jaw. Apparently, she knew all about wooing too.

"I heard you two over here working and thought you could use a pick-me-up. I didn't know what you liked, so I got regular coffee. There's cream and sugar in the bag."

"Black coffee for me." Honey scooped up one of the paper cups and rolled it between her palms. When her fingers grazed mine, I felt a surge of heat radiate up my arm. I hated that the contact was so short.

"So this place is coming along." I looked around the open space and felt tongue-tied and awkward, and that was so not my style.

"Right?" Jo chimed in. "Honey has a vision, and it's going to be perfect."

When I glanced at Honey, she was looking away, almost like she was embarrassed.

Fuck. This woman is so complicated. She's normally so confident but seems shy about this. Why is that so sexy?

Honey's straw-blond hair was piled on her head in a messy bun. She wore tight jeans with tears on the thighs and had a smear of paint across her chin. At that moment, I was convinced that they could hear my heartbeat hammer in my chest.

Get in, woo, get out.

Avery's words echoed in my mind, and I cleared my throat.

"Have a great day, ladies." I pulled my sunglasses down off my head but not before sneaking a wink to Honey and turned for the door.

I may have royally fucked up my own life, and my family was a mess, but I could use a distraction from all that drama. I was going to show that little spitfire just how good I could make her feel.

THIRTEEN

HONEY

"Hello?" I peeked around the door, but the soft tinkling of the bells was the only sound I heard. I stepped tentatively into the Chikalu Falls floral shop. "Anyone there?"

"Hello?! Oh thank god! Can you please come help me?" A distant, slightly panicked voice called from the back of the store.

I quickly stepped in, dropping the small white box with a delicate blue ribbon tied in a bow unceremoniously onto the counter and moving toward the voice.

"Back here!" the female voice called again. As I rounded a large, ancient-looking wooden pillar, I saw a pretty brunette on the top rung of a ladder in the back of the room. Her hands held two very large, very unstable vases of flowers. One was slipping down the front of her shirt as she struggled to balance on the precarious ladder.

"Oh shit. Shit!" I lunged forward as the ladder wobbled and braced it with two hands.

A sharp yelp erupted from the woman as the slipping vase came crashing to the floor. Instinctively, I ducked out of the way, under the A-frame of the ladder. Water seeped out between the shards of broken glass and crumpled flower blossoms.

"Well, fuck." The pretty brunette placed the second vase on the high shelf and slapped her hands on her hips.

"Are you okay?" I asked.

"It's what I get for being a stubborn ass." The woman moved down the ladder, and I held it steady for her. "I'm fine. Thank you so much for your help. Talk about good timing. Are you okay?"

I took a deep breath to calm my jittery nerves. "I'm not sure we've met yet, I'm Honey. You're Maggie, right? Hell of an introduction!"

She had a warm, friendly smile, and we both laughed at the adrenaline spike coursing through our veins.

"It sure was. Yes, I'm Maggie. What can I help you with?"

We shook hands and I wiped the water from my palm on the front of my jeans. I couldn't tell if it was from the flowers she held or my sweaty palms.

"You may have heard, but I'm Joanna James's sister, and I'm opening up a bakery down the street. I just wanted to stop by with a few treats and say hello."

Maggie's eyes lit up as she noticed the white box of treats over my shoulder. "That's so thoughtful of you! My daughter, Charlotte, will be thrilled."

I looked around the lush shop. The storefront was narrow, but each side was lined with stems and flowers in an array of shades. Maggie had creatively displayed her floral arrangements in buckets and bowls, crates and antique vases. From simple arrangements to ornate center-pieces, she had an impeccable eye for color and design. Every single bouquet was unique and meticulous.

"Wow," I turned slowly, taking in the heady smells of the shop. "This is incredible."

When I met Maggie's eyes, she was smiling, hands on her hips. "Thank you, I've got to clean up this mess but please, look around."

I softly touched a fingertip against the petals of a deep crimson flower. The vase was full of riotous color and had twisting branches reaching up in all directions. "These arrangements are so unique. I've never seen anything like it."

"Thank you! That's the wonderful, but sometimes frustrating, part about design. I try to write it down, especially when something works and I'm happy with it, but I can never seem to recreate it. Whether it's the way the blooms are laying or a shade is slightly off, it's never quite the same." Maggie shrugged and after dumping the broken glass into a metal trash container, found a new vase and began snipping the ends off of the flowers in front of her.

"So every piece is truly unique. I just love that," I breathed in the delicate scent of a pale pink peony—my favorite. "Where do you source your flowers?"

"Well, I grow them on my farm, mostly. Anything I can't grow I can place a bulk order, but since we're way out here, that takes *forever*. I like having control over what comes in and the quality."

"Smart businesswoman," I beamed at her. "I love that too."

At a small side table near the back was an arrangement of potted succulents. Among them was a group of cacti that looked strikingly similar to the male anatomy. Some were standing tall and firm, others short and squatty, some hung over limply out of their small pots. I turned toward Maggie and pointed at them. "That's a cock-tus."

"*Echinopsis lageniformis monstrose,*" Maggie wrinkled her nose. "But now I'm officially calling it a cock-tus." Her bright smile grew, and we shared another laugh. Maggie wiped her hands dry on a towel. "Mostly the college girls buy them, or they're a fun bachelorette party gift. I think they're hilarious, so I keep a small collection tucked away for any customers with a good sense of humor." She winked at me and continued arranging flowers into the vase.

"Can I get you something to drink?" Maggie continued. "If you have a few minutes. I'd love to chat with a fellow female entrepreneur. Plus, I can get you up to speed on all the small-town gossip." She dipped below the counter. When she came up with a bottle of water, I grabbed it and found a stool.

"We used to visit in the summertime, Jo and I, when we were kids. Sometimes it feels like nothing's changed."

"Jo has been such a breath of fresh air in this town. And I totally get that Chikalu can feel old-fashioned. The local paper runs pretty much like a gossip column with very little actual news, but it's fairly harmless, as long as no one takes it too seriously." Maggie was so warm and friendly. I couldn't help but feel completely comfortable around her.

Oh, shit. This is like a girlfriend date. Okay, be cool.

I felt a little silly when the thought of finding a new friend made me nervous. I hadn't realized how much I missed a genuine, female friendship, but Maggie was so easy to talk to. She had a great vibe—confident, open, and *real.* I didn't feel like she expected me to be anyone other than myself and that was refreshing.

"Have you always lived in Chikalu Falls?" I asked between sips.

"Oh yeah. I'm a lifer." Maggie laughed. "Lottie swears she's on the first plane out of here when she's eighteen, and

I just have to remind myself that I said the same thing when I was thirteen."

Maggie's daughter was thirteen, but Maggie herself seemed really young. She must have been barely twenty when she had Charlotte. I didn't want to pry so I let that thought drift, but I did glance briefly at her hands to see if she wore a ring—she didn't.

"Thirteen. Wow. How are those teen years treating you?" I joked, knowing full well that I was a hormonal, raging bitch at thirteen. My heart truly went out to her.

"Shit," Maggie said with a laugh. "You have no idea. I was seventeen when I had her, and she forgets that I was the master of the eye roll. But, damn, if she isn't giving me a run for my money . . ."

My heart ached for this incredible, open woman who was a child who raised a child. That couldn't have been easy.

A light silence fell over us as we each took another sip of water. I didn't know how much Maggie wanted to share with me, and while I was eager to get to know her, I didn't want to come off as weird or clingy.

"So let's see," Maggie spun the plastic bottle between her fingers, "what do you *really* need to know about this town?" She tapped the bottle against her bottom lip, thinking hard about her own question.

"Well, I know that Mr. Stevens has a sweet tooth that worked in my favor. Oh, and Trina at the Blush Boutique informed me that the bakery will be good for business— according to her, thick thighs are very sexy right now."

"She did *not* say that! That woman, I swear." Maggie laughed and shook her head. "She's a meddler but, I have to say, this town has seen her lingerie work some magic."

"Oh yeah?" I asked, hoping to learn more about my new friend.

"Well, unfortunately not for me personally, but . . . a girl can hope."

"So no Mr. Flower Shop?"

Maggie's cheeks blushed slightly as she swept a stray piece of hair away from her face. "Maybe once upon a time there was someone who I hoped would be, but that's just not how my life worked out."

The gentle sadness in her voice caused an ache in my stomach, and I placed my hand on hers and squeezed. Our eyes met and I knew, right then and there, I'd made my first friend in Chikalu Falls.

"Okay, well, I'm just having a moment." She laughed nervously. "Enough about me, I'd love to know about you. Is there a Mr. Bakery? I have to be honest, word around town is you've caught Colin McCoy's eye."

A quick laugh escaped through my nose as a flutter of butterflies rippled through my stomach. I tried to hide my reaction at the mere mention of his name.

"I'm not sure about that. Seems like there's a lot of women who might catch the eye of someone like Colin." I tried to sound flippant and stopped myself from nervously chewing the inside of my lip.

Maggie's eyes danced as her smile widened. "No, you're wrong there. He might look like he fits the rock star playboy bill, but he's a good guy."

Oh, thank fucking sweet baby Yoda!

I couldn't place why hearing that Colin was well-respected and a good guy caused a sharp sting beneath my ribs.

"You've known him a long time?" I asked, feeling a little braver.

"Only my whole life. Him and Lincoln and Cole have been running around causing trouble our whole lives."

Maggie's blush returned and deepened at the mention of Cole Decker's name, but in the blink of an eye she bristled, and a strange expression flitted across her face . . . *Interesting*. I tipped up an eyebrow, and Maggie quickly cleared her throat.

"You really should give Colin a fair shake, if you're interested. He's one of the good ones," she offered with a shrug of one shoulder.

"I appreciate that, but right now I need to focus on getting the bakery up and running. There's not much room there for a relationship, and that man screams *complicated and intense.*"

Maggie's laughter bubbled out of her. "Yeah, you pegged him there. Colin can be intense. He was a monster on the football field in high school, and I'm sure you've seen him on stage. It seems like when he sets his mind to something there is *nothing* that's going to get in his way. I always kind of admired that about him."

"Girl, I heard him sing the other night, and I couldn't believe it. He should be on the radio. There was not a single pair of dry panties in that place. I shit you not." I thought back to the deep, warm sound of Colin's voice. It was like honey sliding off a biscuit. When we swayed on the dance floor and he hummed the melody in my ear, I could feel the buzz of electricity run through me.

Maggie placed her slim hand across her heart. "It *is* tragic. Colin would have made it big, I think. But he left that all behind after his brother died."

My eyes went wide, my voice soft. "Oh, shit. I didn't know that."

"Yep," she nodded solemnly. "I mean, it's his story to tell

but it was bad. His mama completely fell apart, and he's been trying to put the pieces back together ever since. When he came back from the tour after Nate died, he never went back."

My breath caught at this new information, and I felt the familiar sting of tears pierce the sides of my eyes. I took a slow breath to focus on Maggie as she thankfully steered the conversation back to neutral ground.

She and I chatted for another twenty minutes about life in a wonderfully quirky town before we hugged and said our goodbyes. She asked if I could leave some business cards to share with her customers, and I was thrilled to have a little cross promotion for my fledgling bakery.

Leaving Maggie's flower shop, I felt a spark of brightness in my heart. I was sticking to my rules—no fake friendships. Connecting with her was a start.

But I couldn't shake the cold blanket of dread and sadness that crept just beneath the surface when I thought about what Maggie had told me. Colin seemed so strong and steadfast. Was he always that way or forced to be because of his family circumstances? Maggie was loyal to him, not sharing any more details, which made my girl crush even stronger.

As I walked under the awning of The Dirty Pigeon, I couldn't help but hurt for the man inside. My heart thumped hard against my ribs. I was drawn to him and wanted to peel back the layers of that complicated man, but I had to bury those urges.

If I was going to finally make something of myself, I would have to ignore the fact that Colin McCoy was a slightly torturous glimpse of a life I would have loved to live. And didn't that just suck.

FOURTEEN

CHIKALU CHATTER

IT'S OFFICIAL: HONEY JAMES TO OPEN BAKERY ON MAIN STREET

A NEW BAKERY, *aptly named Biscuits & Honey, is set to open in Chikalu Falls. After several rounds of negotiations and one basket of irresistible confections later, Honey James shook hands with Neville Stevens with a one-year contract to rent the parlor space formerly known as Neville's Dairy Palace.*

Honey also received financing to modernize and improve the shop. "Neville Stevens said her Butte Pasty was even better than his mama's. That's all I needed to know, and I was happy to help her secure financing to update the parlor space," said bank president Brian Dotson.

Biscuits & Honey will feature a variety of baked goods from breakfast pastries to cakes and pies. It will also personally be a welcome improvement from Ms. Rebecca Coulson's dry, overbaked crullers, bless her heart.

FIFTEEN

COLIN

"You REALIZE if this doesn't work out, Lincoln's going to go all jarhead on your ass, right?" Deck's long strides pounded the pavement next to mine, forcing a brutal pace to our run. My breath was coming out in hard pants, and a stitch was just forming at my right side. With his schedule as a cop and my flexibility, we tried to work out together on most days, but fuck, I hated cardio.

"I can't help that she's Jo's sister, man," I ground out, trying to level my breathing around the words.

Cole Decker had been my first friend when my family moved to Chikalu Falls in fourth grade. Back then, he was quiet and wore thick glasses—he was the unassuming nerd. On my second day at school, an older boy tried to pick a fight at recess over a smile I gave his girlfriend, and Deck had squared off with me. A nod of his head as he tucked those glasses into his back pocket was all it took to fuse us together for life. We got our asses handed to us that day— Deck had a black eye, and I had a busted lip—but we agreed it made us look like bad asses.

"All I'm saying is be careful. This is a small town. If it

doesn't work out, you're stuck being around her all the time —hell, you're right next door to the bakery."

That was the problem with knowing someone so well. Deck knew that he, Finn, Lincoln—Jo too—weren't just friends, they were my family. I hated thinking that my attraction to Honey could cause a rift. I especially hated knowing that once she found out about my deal to buy the storefront, she would probably never speak to me again.

I quietly stewed on his words as we made our way around the winding paths. Nestled up to the national forest, there were plenty of running and hiking trails, but this one was the closest to town and the most visited. As we turned the last corner toward the parking lot, relief flooded my aching limbs.

Thank fuck this run is over.

A jolt shot through my system when I saw Honey and her perfectly round ass bent over, tying up her neon running shoes. I recognized her immediately even though her face was obscured by her long ponytail. My eyes trailed up the long miles of her lean legs as she stood upright and my cock stirred. From my left, Deck bumped me with the back of his hand. We slowed, taking the last few feet as a walk toward his truck.

I stopped and glanced over his shoulder. "Hey, man, go on ahead without me."

He followed my stare and turned back to me with a disapproving nod. Without a word, we shook hands, and he climbed into his truck.

I quickened my walk to a slow jog as Honey took off onto the path.

"Hey there, darlin'." My arm brushed hers, and I caught a wicked side-eye before recognition washed over her face. She stopped abruptly on the path, pulling out an earbud.

Her eyes dilated slightly, and I couldn't help but lean in—just a little.

"Are you stalking me, Mr. McCoy?" A playful smile tugged at her full pink lips. I couldn't resist—flirting with Honey was just too much fun.

"Only a little," I smirked. "Deck and I just finished our run when I saw you in the lot. Want some company?"

With a quirk of her eyebrow she looked down her sharp, straight nose at my gray running shorts and sweaty T-shirt. "You sure you're able to keep going, old man?"

"Old man? Pssh. The run with Deck was just a warm-up." To prove my point, I twisted left and right and even bent down in a runner's stretch. My tired thighs ached in protest, and I ground my teeth together to hide my grimace.

"If you think you can keep up, you're welcome to try." She handed over the wireless earbud and started off in a light jog. I popped it in, appreciating the intimate gesture and more so that her taste in music was exceptional. I focused on the path ahead and definitely did *not* use my peripheral vision to set my pace to the jiggle of her firm ass.

Mid-stride, I pulled off my sticky shirt and tucked it into the waistband of my shorts. Honey took a small misstep as she glanced over at me, and I couldn't help but grin at her. "Everything all right?" I asked innocently. Inside I was beating my chest like a caveman at her lusty approval.

When she didn't answer, I asked, "So what's our distance today?" I hoped my already exhausted body could hold out on me.

"Only five miles," she said sweetly and took off like a shot.

Fuuuuuuuuck.

I was officially dying.

By mile four and a half, I had to focus on the trees, the winding path in front of us, literally anything other than the pang in my side and the bricks attached to the bottoms of my legs. This was epically stupid.

Honey's skin was coated in a light sheen of sweat, and every time I thought about licking it off her, I had to remind myself to cut it out. I was already lightheaded and didn't need my blood rushing out of my limbs and down to my cock. If I stayed focused, I might not die a humiliating death in front of her.

In the end I knew this trail well and realized it was only about one hundred yards ahead to the parking lot, but I had to stop.

"Okay, okay. I need a break," I huffed. "I'm spent."

Honey slowed her pace and walked back and forth in front of me as I keeled over at the waist and heaved, sucking in air.

"Okay, big guy. Straighten up. Remember, 'the air's upstairs.' I don't need you passing out on me." She lifted my shoulders and settled a hand on my back. If my sweaty torso bothered her, she didn't show it.

"I'm. Okay. Just. Dying."

Honey's warm laughter washed over me, and I spent the next few seconds focusing on the buzzy feeling it gave me as I leveled out my breathing. Finally I was able to get a few deep, cleansing breaths and scraped together an ounce of dignity.

"I may have to return my Man Card after this but, fuck, cardio sucks."

She laughed again. "That's what you get for running with me *after* your workout!"

"Totally worth it." I gave her my best smolder and wink.

"You," she grabbed my shoulders and looked up at me, "are a fool." She was so cute and warm, and I wanted nothing more than to scoop her up, kiss her softly up against one of those trees, just because she was mine.

"Go on a date with me," I blurted instead.

"Excuse me?" She blinked.

"Please," I tried again. "Okay, I'm fucking this up. Let me start over." I took another deep breath and ran my hands down her arms from shoulders to wrists. "Honey, would you like to go on a date with me?"

Honey's eyes went wide, and I could feel the relentless hammer of her pulse at her wrist. She looked down—right at my dick—then up, back down, then over my shoulder. A chuckle escaped me, and I gently squeezed her hands in mine.

On a huff she said, "I can't think with all your man-ness this close to me!"

I took one step forward, pulling her body into mine. "Honey, please. Let me date you."

She looked up at me, sucking her lower lip into her mouth. "I can't. I've got too much riding on the bakery. Getting mixed up with the local musician hottie will start all kinds of rumors."

"So you admit you think I'm a hottie?" I teased. I was rewarded with a playful roll of her eyes.

It was a weak excuse, and we both knew it. Honey turned me down at every opportunity, and I was already half in love with her. I looked at the path just ahead of us, the tailgate of my truck just barely out of view.

"Race me for it."

A furrow creased her brow. "What?"

"You heard me." I nodded toward the parking lot at the end of the path, convinced my legs could power through.

"Race me for it. You win, I won't ask you for a date again. I win, you go on a date with me."

I half expected her to scoff at the dare—toss the tumbling waves of her ponytail over her shoulder and tell me she would do no such thing. Instead she looked me square in the eyes, and one dimple flashed at the corner of her mouth.

"Fine. But," she held up one finger and poked it into my chest, "play fair. No pushing, shoving, tripping, or any other cheating. No shenanigans. Deal?"

"Yes ma'am. Need a head start?" I asked smugly. Honey rolled her gorgeous cobalt eyes at me again. One hundred yards was all that stood between me and an official date with Honey James. Aching legs and pounding heart be damned.

I had this in the bag.

"All right. First one past the yellow line of the parking lot. On my count," she started. "One . . ." My fingers twitched at my sides, "Two . . ." My left leg shook, ready to push forward. "Three!"

A growl tore from my throat as I launched forward. Honey's muscular arms pumped at her sides as she kept in stride with me. I wanted this date, needed it, and I wasn't going to let my numb feet or raw throat stop me.

Eighty yards—her tight ass popped into view and fanned the flames of my desire.

Fifty yards—my long legs ate up the distance as the dirt and rocks crunched under my feet.

Thirty yards—a sly smile bloomed across my face as I saw her panting hard and fall back slightly.

Ten yards—my vision bore into the solid yellow line, willing my legs to push harder, faster.

Five yards—a battle cry erupted from her, and I caught a terrifying glint in her eye.

No. No. Don't fuck this up Colin. No. NO!

With one long stride, her neon sneaker crossed the threshold, decimating any glimmer of hope I had of redemption.

SIXTEEN

HONEY

I WASN'T PREPARED for the sharp pang of disappointment at winning the race. Unfortunately, my competitive nature kicked into overdrive when I saw the long strides of his thick, muscular legs closing the distance to the parking lot. My thighs burned and I pumped my arms faster, willing my body to carry me over the finish line.

With a long stretch of my leg, I'd crossed the thick yellow line first—just barely.

"Whoo!" I shot both arms above my head but immediately regretted that and dug my hands into my hips, sucking in air. The rush of victory was short-lived when I remembered what had been at stake.

Sure, I could take it back and agree to go on a date with Colin, but that will still go against the rules I had set for myself. The rules that were designed to keep me from making the same stupid mistakes I had been making. I wanted to be taken seriously in my new town. Maggie had confirmed it—Colin was intense and stubborn but so was I.

"Damn it!" Colin swore as he kicked a rock and continued pacing around me to catch his breath. He was sweaty and pouty and absolutely adorable. I couldn't help but tease him, just a little bit.

"Aw, you okay over there? Nothing's hurt, is it?"

"Just my ego," he grumbled.

A laugh erupted from me, and I gripped my aching side harder.

"I almost had it." Colin arched his back and looked up to the sky as his breath leveled. With his eyes closed in the sunlight, I got a nice, long peek at the bulge in the front of his shorts.

Well lick my clit and call—no. No. There will be no clit licking.

If we were going to manage to stay friends, I needed to cut that shit out, but being around Colin stirred up all kinds of dirty thoughts. A cool tingle ran down my back, and I suddenly felt several degrees hotter.

"Well, come on then," I called over my shoulder. "I keep some cold drinks in my car when I go for a run."

Not waiting for him to follow me, I sauntered toward my car.

"If that smug, ass-swaying walk is your victory lap, I'll lose to you every day of the week." Colin's mouth was turned up in a wickedly sexy grin as he eyed my backside.

I quirked a brow over my shoulder at him, but I kept walking and added a little more sass, just to torture him.

When we got to my car, I popped the trunk and dug out two ice-cold water bottles from the small cooler. I handed one to him and pressed the wet bottle to my throat. The icy trickle down my neck did nothing to extinguish the fire building in my belly. Just being close to Colin set off all kinds of little sparks underneath my skin.

I watched him take a deep, long pull at the bottle. His throat bobbed and I nearly groaned out loud. Colin finished the bottle in a few quick chugs and crushed it in his hands. I pulled out a small grocery bag and tossed in my empty bottle, opening it for him.

"So that's it then." He shifted his massive body toward me and placed both hands on the car beside me, locking me in place. "I lost fair and square . . . which means I won't ask you for a date again."

I tried to ignore the annoying way my heart tumbled at his words. Colin leaned down slightly, and when I hitched in a breath, my breasts grazed his chest.

"We can be friends," I breathed. When I licked my lip, his gaze lowered to my mouth.

Kiss me. Please. Break the rules and kiss me.

"I'll always be your friend, Honey." Mere inches away from me, I could enjoy how deeply *manly* he smelled, and it was intoxicating—like soap and leather and sex and all kinds of naughty things that respectable girls shouldn't know anything about.

"But," his voice dipped low and gravelly, "when you ask *me* for a date . . . I'll say yes."

"THE ROW of computers is just that way." The frail librarian pointed a crooked finger, her skin so thin it looked like crinkled parchment paper. "If you need to print anything, it gets posted to your account. Have a lovely day, dear."

I thanked her and moved to the very end, tucking myself into the quiet corner. The new laptop I had ordered was held up somewhere in Omaha, and I desperately needed to get caught up with emails. Baking had always been easy, but I learned quickly that the business side of running your own bakery required a stupid amount of paperwork.

After emailing final signatures to my lawyers, printing additional copies of my building permits, and placing a ridiculously large bulk order for baking supplies, I massaged a knot that had formed behind one shoulder blade. The ache in my legs from pushing too hard to win the race with Colin was setting in. It paired nicely with the ache that formed in my chest when I thought too hard about turning him down.

The small library had grown quiet, and the afternoon light slanted through the large windows as the sun dipped low behind the mountain. I stretched in my seat and took in the aging building. I loved the smell of books and furniture polish, and appreciated how neatly each stack of books looked tucked into the bookshelves. Despite its age, the building was well-loved and saw a steady stream of Chikalu residents and a lot of college students. Several librarians, some with tidy buns, assisted students hunched over piles of books or instructed their elderly patrons on how to use computers and fax machines. I smiled to myself, taking in the small-town charm of it all.

As I sat quietly, a soft, muffled noise caught my attention. I couldn't quite place it, but it sounded a lot like a small animal. Intrigued, I looked around but didn't see anyone. I tiptoed toward the sound, looking down the long aisles of books. The small noise was getting closer as I moved toward the far back corner of the library.

In the very last row, hunched over and shaking, was a woman.

I looked around, finding myself in the loss and grief nonfiction section. I was still getting to know the people of Chikalu, but I didn't recognize her. Her auburn hair was cropped short, and her delicate hands covered her face as she sobbed. She was in the throes of an emotional breakdown. I moved forward quietly—I didn't want to startle her, but I couldn't leave this woman if she needed my help.

I crouched down next to her as she shook with long, wracking sobs, and I gently placed a hand between her shaking shoulder blades. She startled with a quick intake of her breath as her head whipped toward me. Her stormy caramel eyes searched mine before pinching tightly closed. I had no words, but she didn't move away from me. I sat next to her and wrapped an arm around her shoulder.

"I'm sorry for the pain you're feeling right now," I whispered to her.

The woman pulled me in tightly and continued her soft, hollow crying. I examined the books littered at her feet —books of loss, grief, surviving the loss of a child.

After quietly hugging each other long enough for my arm to start tingling asleep, her sobs gave way to whimpers. Eventually, she lifted her head and began wiping aggressively underneath her red, puffy eyes.

"Oh my," she sniffed. "I am terribly embarrassed. I'm such a mess."

I smiled gently at the woman. She looked to be in her fifties, and her pixie cut was flecked with gray. She had lines on her face that told me she normally smiled a lot.

"Is there anything I can do?" I asked quietly. She only shook her head.

I pointed toward the books at our feet and gave her shoulder another gentle squeeze. "I'm sorry for your loss."

"Thank you. You're very kind. My son . . ." she trailed off as her eyes filled again with tears.

My heart broke for this woman who had lost a child. That was a pain that I couldn't even imagine. I had never really imagined myself with children—I loved kids and could see myself being a mother, but it always seemed distant, like a fuzzy daydream that didn't fully come into focus. Maybe it was just that motherhood was meant for women who were characteristically more maternal than I was. If Jo and Lincoln ever had children I would revel in being the *Fun Auntie*. But to lose a child must be a punishment worse than death.

After several minutes of comforting her in silence, I pulled away from our embrace to look at her sad, hazel eyes.

"Do you have plans?" I asked. "Can I buy you a coffee?"

Her eyebrows lifted and she squeezed my hand. "I would love that."

And just like that, I had made another, albeit unlikely, friend in Chikalu Falls.

SEVENTEEN

COLIN

IF YOU WOULD HAVE TOLD me that wooing a woman wouldn't be a chore but would actually be *fun*, I would have called you a fucking liar.

The truth is, finding small ways to impress Honey or make her smile had become the highlight of the past two weeks. Coffee delivery, random lunches sent over, movie recommendations, and watching her eyes light up when we talked about the epic twist ending over a drink at the bar. The longer it went on, the more creative I tried to become. Surprising Honey James and making her eyes go wide and her lush mouth pop open in an O became my life's mission.

I may have lost our bet, but I had decided that maybe I could find a way to date Honey without her ever knowing it.

"WELL IT's a surprise to see you in here!" Maggie popped up from underneath the counter of the flower shop and nearly gave me a fucking heart attack.

"Jesus!" I clamped a hand over my heart and laughed at the spike in adrenaline.

"Sorry, I was just cleaning up when you came in," she laughed. "So," her eyebrows crept up her forehead, "what brings you by?"

"I figured I could visit another local entrepreneur," I shrugged. "Support a local business."

Her eyes narrowed but she didn't call me out on my bullshit. Maggie had a built-in bullshit detector, but I wasn't ready to let anyone in on my plans for Honey just yet.

"I thought I could pick up something simple for Mom," I decided on the spot. "Any recommendations?"

"Hmm . . ." she added, still not quite believing me. "Why don't you look around? She loves dahlias so I'll see what I've got in the back cooler."

Maggie rounded the large oak counter and disappeared into the back. I had only been in her store once or twice despite the shop being just down the block and across the street from the bar. My knowledge of flowers stopped at the basics but there were plenty of arrangements that seemed pretty enough. Today I didn't need anything extravagant—just something to let Honey know I was thinking of her.

I meandered around the little shop and stopped in my tracks. On one small table, there were tiny ceramic planters, each with a little cactus that looked like a dick. The small card had "cock-tus" written in cursive. Laughing, I picked one up to examine the spiky phallus more carefully. When Maggie walked back up front, I slowly turned, raising one eyebrow in her direction.

"Hilarious, right?!" Maggie carried three small bundles in her arms.

"It's . . . something all right." I placed the tiny pecker down, chuckling to myself.

"Okay, so no dahlias but I do have some ranunculus and peonies . . . maybe some eucalyptus to round it out."

"Uh . . . sure?" I lifted my shoulders to my ears.

Maggie playfully rolled her eyes in my direction and started trimming stems. Her hands moved with quick efficiency as she pared the stem ends with a sharp knife that had a hooked blade. Maggie arranged the blooms in a tall glass vase.

"I'll wrap this up for you, but I like to see how it looks in a vase," she said.

I nodded, feeling guilty as hell as the beautiful arrangement started taking shape.

Real nice—lie about getting your mother flowers. What if Maggie asks her about them? Fucking small towns.

"Hey, uh," I hesitated and cleared my throat, "any chance you can make two of those?"

A sly smile pulled across her face. "Sure thing."

Maggie split the bouquet into two smaller bundles, filled them each with more flowers, and wrapped the bouquets in brown paper and twine. She rang me up, and I tipped her generously, despite her insisting it wasn't necessary.

Hopefully she knows hush money when she's sees it . . .

Walking back toward the bar, I noticed Honey's vintage car was parked out front, but I hadn't seen her for over an hour. Not wanting to be caught, I had to think about how I could deliver the flowers.

"Would you like some cookies, Mr. McCoy?" A little redhead with a missing front tooth called to me from the sidewalk.

I looked over to see Ellie Wilcox with a wide smile and dirty knees.

"Well I'd love nothing more, Ms. Ellie." I smiled up at

her mom who was helping her and a friend sell Girl Scout cookies from behind the rickety table. "How about a box of the peanut butter ones?"

Ellie told me my total, and her mom helped her get my change. I waited while she painfully counted out the coins and bills and a thought sparked. I couldn't help the trill of excitement that bounced through me.

"Hey, Ms. Ellie. Do you think you could do me a favor? I have these flowers here, but need a delivery girl."

Her eyes went wide as she nodded in excitement.

"Okay." I crouched down to her level. "Her name is Ms. Honey, and she'll be at the new bakery soon."

I pointed to the entryway two doors down. "I'd appreciate it if you could make sure they get to her. It's *very* important."

I leveled my eyes to hers to emphasize the importance of her mission.

Ellie held up three fingers in what I assumed was a sacred salute and said, "I won't let you down, Mr. McCoy."

That kid was so damn cute, I couldn't help but smile. On a scrap piece of paper, I scrawled a note to Honey and tucked it into the bouquet. "You're the best Ellie!" I called out as I ducked into the bar before Honey could see me.

EIGHTEEN

HONEY

Honey,
This is not a romantic gesture.
Love,
Your favorite neighbor

I LOOKED DOWN at the note I had found tucked into the rustic and gorgeous bundle of flowers. When I'd returned to the bakery from the grocery store, a cute little girl with red waves and a mountain of freckles came running up to me.

"You're Ms. Honey, aren't you?" She was breathless with excitement.

"That's me!"

"These are for you, but I'm not supposed to tell you who they're from." A giggle bubbled up from her belly, and her sweet laughter was infectious.

"Well thank you. That *is* mysterious. I wonder how I'll ever figure it out." I winked at her, and it threw her into another fit of giggles. She looked over at the large wooden door to the bar with wide, knowing eyes.

Attagirl. You already know the girl code.

The little girl bounced away back toward the woman I assumed was her mother. I waved to her and called, "Thanks again!"

The note was scribbled in Colin's masculine handwriting on a torn piece of white paper.

I sighed when I thought about the rules I had put into place.

Honey's Rules for a Better Life:

No fake, shallow friends

No hookups {no matter how hot}

~~No swooning~~ *Damn him.*

<u>Definitely</u> no falling in love

No deviating from the plan

Not a romantic gesture, my ass.

I buried my nose in the soft petals and smiled. In all my twenty-seven years, I'd never loved a bundle of flowers more.

"Sorry I'm late!" I huffed as I dropped my shoulder bag into the booth and scooted across the cheap red pleather seat. "I was pulling down the last of that god-awful wallpaper and lost track of time."

"Okay, Artie, I have to go. Bye, hun." Jean spoke into her phone.

"Sorry," I whispered as she hung up and placed her phone in her purse.

"Oh, enough of that," Jean waved her hand in dismissal in my direction. "Just hanging up with my son."

In the weeks since we'd had our unlikely meeting in the library, Jean and I had spent a few friendly afternoons together, and she'd never mentioned her children. Given the books on loss and grieving, I didn't want to bring it up.

"Besides," she continued, "it also gave me plenty of time for people watching." A delicate smile crept across her face, and the lines around her eyes deepened. Jean was older than me, old enough to be my mother really, but somehow we both felt comfortable and connected in a way I never had with my own mother.

"Don't you already know every single person in town?" I asked before giving my order of black coffee and an apple fritter to our waitress.

"You'd be surprised. Chikalu isn't *that* small and families come and go. Every year it feels like it gets a little bigger." Jean sighed lightly as if she was thinking back on a time when life felt smaller, simpler. To me, Chikalu Falls felt tiny compared to Butte, but with the big news of an interstate bypass, it was hard to deny that growth was inevitable.

"I can see that," I conceded. "So what's new with the Women's Club?"

Jean and I chatted and together we watched the other patrons of the small diner. She told me all about her work with the Chikalu Women's Club, the local group of women that organized food drives, letters to soldiers, and other community events.

"That actually brings me to why I asked you to meet me today." Jean's coffee mug rapped against the dingy beige laminate tabletop.

"You mean it wasn't the pleasure of my company?" I clutched my invisible pearls and feigned shock.

Jean laughed and it was a melodic, tinkling kind of

sound. It made me wonder if she ever sang in the church choir—she seemed like the type. Hearing her laughter was a nice change from the mist of sadness that sometimes crept into her eyes. Jean wasn't broken, she was just a little fragile.

"Honey, you are the sweetest thing to happen to me in a while. That and Artie acting all gobsmacked lately, but that's a story for another time. I have *big* news!" Her voice rose an octave with excitement.

"The Women's Club is putting on our annual Sagebrush Festival," she continued.

"Sagebrush Festival?"

"Well, we are in Montana, and the *Dirt Festival* just didn't have quite the same ring to it." Jean pinned me with a stare and lifted an eyebrow.

Together we dissolved into a fit of laughter. This adorable, complicated woman pulled at my heartstrings. She was generous and kind and funny, and I couldn't believe that I met her because she was bawling her eyes out in a dark corner of the library. Whatever the circumstances, I was glad our paths had crossed.

"Okay, so this Sagebrush Festival . . . *please* tell me that it's as incredible as the small-town festivals in movies."

Jean leaned forward and covered my hand with hers. "Darling, it's better. There's music and dancing. Twinkle lights and wine tasting. It's a *ball* and everyone in town makes it down there at least one of the days. You're one of us now, you have to come."

Jean gave my hand a pat, and my chest squeezed when I thought about her words.

You're one of us now.

I blinked away the tears threatening to spill over my lashes.

"Well, don't go getting all fussy, not that I can judge."

Jean slid a thin paper napkin toward me. "I'm actually putting you to work."

I dabbed my eyes. "Work?"

"You're a businesswoman now. Most of the local businesses are represented in some way."

I thought about Colin and wondered if he would be playing at the small-town festival. A hot tingle spiraled down to my core as my mind wandered to him and his deep voice. It was primal and raw and forced all kinds of dirty thoughts to run through my mind.

Snapping out of my Colin-induced sex fantasy, I cleared my throat and took a sip of my bitter, lukewarm coffee. "What did you have in mind?"

"With the wine tasting, the Women's Club was hoping you'd be able to provide some treats to offset all the alcohol. Last year, Ms. Gertie got drunk and walked halfway home without her top on. The woman is eighty-one years old!"

I laughed at the thought of the old woman, drunk off her ass, swaying and singing on her walk home—titties in the breeze.

Life goals, right there, man.

I smiled widely at Jean. "This is fantastic! I'd be happy to help and that's such good exposure for the bakery."

"Exactly. I can give you all the details once they're worked out."

A MORNING COFFEE, personally delivered, had become a regular occurrence, and damn it, I had come to look forward to it. It was 10:00 a.m., and there was still no Colin in sight.

I took my annoyance out on a particularly nasty piece of baseboard trim. I was having them replaced professionally, but I was damn sure not letting someone else pry the old wood off when I could take out my pent-up frustration and save money in the process.

For weeks, Colin and I had circled around each other. Dinner at Jo's house had somehow become just the four of us. Playing cards with the house band after their practice. Bumping into each other at the grocery store and winding our way through the aisles together—though I did learn that man had some seriously flawed cereal habits.

Since he lost the race and the bet to go on a date, he was true to his word and didn't ask again. Colin was careful not to touch me much, but when his fingertips idly skated across my arm, I felt a deep pull in my belly.

Every. Fucking. Time.

I wedged the pry bar between the baseboard and the wall, careful to place a piece of wood beneath the pry bar to prevent damage to the wall. I wrenched with all my might to loosen the centuries-old nails and thought about us.

When did this become an "us", and how in the fuck am I going to pull off a grand opening if I can't focus?

I thought about how close I was getting to opening up my very own bakery. I might not have the fancy diploma from culinary school, but I had something better. A long time ago, I had let a man rule my life and left myself vulnerable in the process. I learned from my mistakes and I knew better. I knew myself and what I wanted better too.

With a satisfying *crack*, the nails popped loose, and the board pulled away from the wall. Sweat beaded at my hairline, and I looked around for a rag to wipe it away.

"Fucking gross," I mumbled to myself as I stretched my aching back. I walked back to the kitchen and pulled paper towels from the roll to wipe away the sweat. As I dabbed at my forehead, I saw a small piece of paper, neatly folded on the metal kitchen island.

I immediately knew it was from Colin, and my traitorous heart hammered behind my ribs.

Honey,
I'm sorry I can't bring you coffee tomorrow morning. I'll make it up to you. Pete offered to fix the cracked glass in the back window on Tuesday. Try not to make him fall in love with you.
Love,
Your coffee bitch
P.S. - I was bragging about you at the cafe today. Mrs. Coulson called me your "gentleman caller"—whatever do you think she means?

I rolled my eyes at his comments about Pete and Mrs. Coulson, but pride swelled at the thought that Colin was talking me up around town. The tiny part of me that regretted turning Colin down was an ember, glowing a little brighter every day.

Wait a minute. Wait. A fucking. Minute.

A thought tumbled around in my head while I reflected back on the last few weeks—morning coffee, dinners, flowers, compliments, notes.

That sneaky son of a bitch.

NINETEEN

CHIKALU CHATTER

HAS COLIN MCCOY DEVELOPED A SWEET TOOTH?

ROMANCE IS AFOOT *in Chikalu Falls. Several whispers of a budding romance between local dance hall owner, Colin McCoy, and our newest transplant, Honey James, have been reported. Reports include frequent coffee deliveries, small gifts of affection, and, as one anonymous witness stated, "mutual, longing gazes when the other was none the wiser."*

Long-time resident and Honey's cottage neighbor Mr. Matthew Bailey refused to comment and included several off-color comments that cannot be published but frankly made this reporter blush. Young Ellie Wilcox was seen delivering an impressive bouquet from our very own talented Maggie O'Brien's floral shop. When asked, little Ellie responded, "A good friend doesn't tell."

It seems as though Ms. Honey James may be becoming one of our own, as the residents strive to protect her secrets.

"It's looking good in here," I said, leaning against the open door of Honey's bakery. Soulful country music poured out of the Bluetooth speaker as her pert little ass bopped to the beat. She was high on a ladder, finishing some final paint work on the ceiling.

"Well, hey, you!" She called. Her bright enthusiasm lit me up like a Christmas tree at midnight.

"You know, you can hire someone to do all this dirty work," I teased.

"Maybe you can, Mr. Moneybags, but some of us have to DIY our way through an opening."

I loved how she always had something quippy to fire back at me and that a lull in our conversation was rare.

"Fair enough," I conceded. "You're working late tonight." It was 9:00 p.m. and, while I wasn't working behind the bar tonight, I had checked in with the band before heading toward my house. When I saw the portable construction lights still on next door, they were like a beacon, calling me home.

Honey wiped a bead of sweat from her forehead and

unknowingly smeared a streak of white ceiling paint across her brow. "It's been two months, and I still have so much work to do. If the opening is going to happen in another four months, I have to bust my ass . . ."

I tried to focus on what she was saying and not the ass in question.

"Is the supplier I sent you working out?"

"Oh yeah! I have two kick-ass ovens and a sparkly new display case coming next month thanks to you. Ricardo is a dream!" Honey's face lit up, and I felt a roll deep in my chest. There wasn't much I wouldn't do to keep that look on her gorgeous face.

"It's getting late. Are you finishing up?" I ran a nervous hand across the back of my head. I was testing the waters. Usually, I would drop off food or coffee, leave a business card, or send one of my guys over to do some heavy lifting, but I was hoping to get Honey alone tonight. I had worked nine late nights in a row, booking new gigs and holding band screenings. I couldn't help but miss the lilt of her voice.

Honey sighed deeply. "Five more minutes and I'm quitting. I'm beat," her shoulders slumped slightly as she dipped the paintbrush into the can at the top of the ladder.

"I've got plans for us," I countered. "Finish up and I'm stealing you."

Her eyebrow tipped up, but she didn't argue so I was considering that a fucking victory.

Five minutes later, she was washing her brushes in the utility sink, gathering her purse, and locking the doors behind her.

"So where to?" she asked. Honey hadn't gotten the smudge of paint off, so I leaned into her space, reaching my thumb up to brush the streak from her forehead.

I couldn't help but breathe in her spicy, fruity perfume.

I moved my lips to the outside of her ear, "I'm taking you to the one place that makes the long, hard days worth it."

A slow shudder rolled through her back, and I felt my cock start to thicken at her closeness. A deep part of me had to know if she felt as out of control as I did when we were near each other.

In the darkness of the alley, only a streetlamp illuminated her radiant skin. I let my nose graze up the outer shell of her ear, and I whispered in what I hoped was my deepest, sexiest bedroom voice, "Dairy Palace."

I added a playful tickle to her ribs, just so I could get my hands on her, and was rewarded with a bubble of her laughter. It hit me that her laugh was my new favorite sound.

Honey squealed as I assaulted her sides with more tickles, pulling her into me.

"You dick!" She shouted. "No tickling!" Honey squirmed and I let her go, immediately missing the feel of her against me. I swung an arm around her shoulders, and when she didn't move out from underneath me, a wide grin took over my face.

We walked up the alley, onto the main drag of the road, and Honey carefully stepped out from under my arm before we were bathed in the streetlights of Main Street. My jaw ticked in disappointment. She had convinced herself that being seen with me would be bad for her business. It was a problem I hadn't solved yet, and it was starting to grate on me.

Not wanting to dampen the mood with my hurt feelings, I put my hands in my pockets. I could respect that Honey wasn't interested in public displays of affection, but if I was going to walk this close to her with only the moon and street lamps lighting the way, my hands were safer in my pockets. They itched to brush the tendrils of her hair from her face, and I was sure would be greeted with a swat of her hand.

"So where do you actually live, Colin McCoy? You're *always* at the bar, but surely you have a real home, right?"

A small smile played on my lips. I liked that she was trying to get to know me. "You're not too far off. When I first bought the bar, I slept there. But now I know better."

"Can't always live the rock star life?" she teased.

"Far from it," I bumped my shoulder lightly into hers. "But I do like nice things. Big porches, open concept, fancy double oven and a big kitchen island . . ." I glanced at her to see if she'd take the bait.

"Ooh, now you're just showing off." Honey's cerulean eyes shot me a playful wink as we walked up to the outside counter of the newly erected Dairy Palace. The building was tucked into an alcove of new trees on the west end of downtown. The awnings were playful blue-and-white stripes, and the freshly built picnic tables had yet to endure the sticky spills of summer. As we walked up to the building, I motioned for Honey to step ahead of me.

"No, you go. I still don't know what I want." Her hands were on her hips as she chewed her lower lip. If deciding what flavor of ice cream to have could be sexy, she fucking nailed it.

"Hi Carl, how are you tonight?" I drawled to the skinny high school kid behind the counter. "I'll have an Oreo Peanut Butter Chipper and whatever the lady likes."

I glanced at Honey, still studying the menu as if it were written in a different language. She dropped her hands on her thighs with a slap and confidently strode up to the window. As she leaned in, I placed a hand at the small of her back.

"Can I please get a scoop of mint chocolate chip on the bottom and a scoop of peanut butter chocolate on the top?"

Carl nodded, rang us up, and began dipping our ice cream.

I kept my palm at the base of her spine, gently rubbing a small circle with my thumb. "That is a very intentional ice cream order."

"I'm glad you noticed," she smiled. "I *love* the ribbon of peanut butter but it's really rich. If you put the mint chip at the bottom, you get to end with that. It's like a little palate cleanser."

Honey's self-satisfied grin and ridiculously logical ice cream order had my heart tumbling out of my chest. I couldn't look at her without wanting to know everything about her. I stared at her like a fucking moron because every crazy emotion was bouncing around my brain. I wanted to beg her to tell me everything—her favorite color, her child-hood pet's name, her most intimate secrets.

Rein it in, dude.

In the midst of my near mental breakdown, I smiled, and we walked down the quiet sidewalk toward the bar with our ice cream.

You'll scare her away with that shit. First, she doesn't want a relationship with you, and, second, if you don't get around to telling her about purchasing the store, she'll gut you anyway.

"Can we share?" Honey asked, eyeing my cup and motioning with her plastic spoon.

I happily tipped my cup toward her and watched with envy as the spoon disappeared between her full lips. The small little moan in her throat was like hot liquid down my spine.

I cleared my throat to ease the tension in my chest and said, "Tell me something I don't know about you."

Our strides kept in time with each other, and Honey tilted her gorgeous face up to look at me. Around a spoonful of ice cream, she pondered with a "hmm."

"Well," she started, "I'm a terrible human being." My eyebrows shot up. "Before you say anything, I can explain. Whenever I see someone trip and fall, I can't help it. I laugh. Hard."

She had the decency to actually look guilt-stricken.

The deep rumble of my laughter filled the quiet night air as I thought about my effervescent Honey James laughing at some poor bastard who tripped in front of her.

"That is bad," I teased. "You're an *awful* person. I can't believe I didn't see it before."

We laughed together and I felt the tension of the day evaporate from my shoulders. I could see, with shocking clarity, how spending more time with Honey would drastically improve my life. It was getting late, but I didn't want it to end.

As we walked up to Honey's car, I tossed the remains of my melting ice cream into a nearby trash can. She offered her empty cup to me after one last bite.

When I looked back, I noticed a small blob of mint chocolate chip ice cream on the inside of Honey's left wrist. I reached for her, running my hand from her elbow to wrist. I felt her heartbeat hammering under her delicate skin. Without breaking eye contact, I lifted her wrist to my mouth and licked her pulse point with a mischievous grin.

At the drag of my tongue across her wrist, the playfulness of the evening sizzled and evaporated. I saw need, the same need I had, reflected in her eyes. I stalked forward, pressing her back into the side of her car. Weeks of playful teasing, lingering glances, and intentional grazes came surging through me.

Honey moved her hips forward, pressing into the lengthening bulge of my cock. Through her thin yoga pants, I could practically feel the folds of her pussy. That thought alone caused a hard throb between my legs.

Honey pulled me in closer, hitching a leg along my outer thigh. Our mouths fused together. Her lips were soft and minty from the ice cream, and I wanted to devour every part of her. As her hands skated underneath my shirt and up my sides, I caught her hands.

"Not here. Not like this." I ground out.

After taking two ragged breaths, Honey dug into the purse that was slung across her body. She held her keys out to me like a lifeline. "Take me home, Colin."

In one swift movement, I swiped the keys from her. She got in and scooted across the front, settling into the passenger seat. I cranked the engine, and the vintage beast of a car growled to life. I stomped the accelerator and whipped out of the parking space, barreling toward my house.

Honey wound a hand up my neck and into my hair. She was thrumming with energy, and I had to focus to keep my eyes on the road. I made the mistake of glancing at her and saw her delicate fingers flutter down her thin shirt and over her chest.

"You can't do that," I said. "I need to get us home in one piece."

She laughed playfully. "What, this?" She traced lazy circles, and I imagined it was my tongue around the hard pebble of her nipple.

Fuck. Do not crash this goddamn car.

I stroked one hand up the thin fabric on her inner thigh and was rewarded with the slightest upward push of her hips. I delicately traced the outline of her pussy with my fingertips, keeping my touch featherlight, teasing.

"Colin," she breathed, "you are driving me insane." Honey's lashes brushed her cheeks as she closed her eyes. I moved my touches down her leg and back up to where the heat of her center radiated. My cock strained against the denim of my jeans just thinking about feeling her tighten around my fingers, my mouth, my cock.

She moved her hand away from her full, round tits to palm the thick bulge in my jeans as I drove. I shifted slightly but every stroke of her hand drove me closer to pulling the car over and ravaging her on the side of the road.

I wound the car down my private driveway and skittered to a stop in front of my house. We tore at our seat belts and threw open the car doors. Honey didn't make it three steps toward me before I hauled her over my shoulder. Her laughter floated on the night air as I stomped up the porch steps and landed a smack hard on her ass.

I dug my keys out of my pocket and wrestled with the door, Honey still draped over my shoulder. She squirmed and raked her nails up the muscles in my back. I shifted my weight, pulling her forward and letting the curves of her body drag down the hard planes of mine. Her shirt lifted between us, and as my hands moved up, I felt the creamy smoothness of her skin.

Against the hardwood of the front door, Honey snaked her hand into my hair, dragging her nails against my scalp. A throaty moan escaped me as the pressure in my cock grew. Our tongues tangled, tasting and sucking. I could feel the vibration of her groans pass from her lips to mine, and it drove me insane. I wanted—needed—every part of this woman. My mind unraveled and I was desperate for her.

I moved forward, pushing our bodies toward the stairs. I couldn't get upstairs fast enough so I maneuvered, shifting her body under mine. She sat, leaned back on the stairs as my body covered hers. My arms caged her in, and she pulled my shirt over my head, nipping at my neck with her teeth. As I pushed my hips forward, the hard length of my cock rubbed between her folds.

Her gasp had me seconds from tearing the clothes from her body. "You like that?" I asked as she circled her hips, increasing the pressure where she needed it. My tongue moved up the line of her throat, and I sucked the thin skin that barely contained her frenzied heartbeat.

"I like when you talk to me," she said on a moan. "Tell me what dirty things you want to do to me."

I leaned back, adoring how the arch in her back pushed her tits up and out. My hand moved from her hair, down her neck, to her chest. Over one breast, I found the peak of her nipple, straining against the fabric of her shirt and tugged.

"Baby, there are things that I've wanted to do with you for a long, long time."

I rolled her nipple between two fingers, and when I pulled her nipple down again, her hips jerked into me.

"Tell me," she repeated, sucking my lower lip into her mouth.

I had always been a vocal lover but never given voice to all the deep, dirty thoughts I had when I fucked. I wanted to give her everything, every part of me, and if she needed me to tell her all the ways I could ravage her, then so be it.

"God, I can't wait to taste you, get that pussy soaking wet so I can stretch it open with my cock. I want you to come so good and so hard. When you're dripping wet, I'm going to lick every last drop from your sweet pussy."

Honey hissed in a breath, and her knees squeezed against the outside of my hips. "Colin. Fuck, yes."

Her eyes fluttered closed, and her hips rocked upward. My hand slid back up her neck and traced the sharp edge of her collarbone. When she opened her eyes, a smile laced with wild mischief flickered over her face. She moved up one stair.

"Where do you think you're going?" I growled. She inched up another stair and quirked one eyebrow.

"You better fucking not," I threatened.

She did.

Honey managed to slip from underneath me and scramble up the stairs. I took off after her, my rock-hard dick bobbing up and down as I climbed the stairs two at a time. She didn't know where she was going, and that slowed her down. I was closing the gap, and she squealed and laughed as I chased her.

When she tried to round a corner, I grabbed her around the middle, hugging her body tight to mine. I dragged her across the hall into my bedroom.

Our labored breathing filled the dark bedroom. The tension and heat crackled with energy. Honey's back was pressed against my front—her ass pushed into me as I held on to her trim waist.

"You still want me to eat that pussy, baby?" I nipped at her ear.

"I mean . . . I wouldn't turn you down if you're hungry."

How she could joke right now was beyond me. If I didn't get her naked and on top of me soon, I was going to implode.

"Baby, I'm ravenous."

Guiding her toward my mattress, I wound a hand around her thigh to stroke her pussy. Honey's head dropped back onto my shoulder as a whimpering moan pushed past her lips.

I turned her to face me, cupping her face in my hands. She might have wanted raunchy, playful sex, but I was going to show her what she was doing to me—how she completely upended my life and drove me absolutely mental. I feathered kisses at the corners of her mouth before invading it with my tongue.

When I made my way to her ear, I whispered, "I am so hard for you right now." I stepped back and then removed her shirt. Her breasts filled the delicate lace of her bra, her deep rosy nipples peeking through the fabric.

I towered over her small frame and tugged at the lace cups, just barely freeing the taut buds. Thumbing over one, I took the other with a drag of my tongue. Honey's sharp intake of breath ratcheted up my desire, and I caught her nipple gently between my teeth.

"I'm so fucking wet," she breathed. I worked my mouth down her body—wet, demanding strokes—as I knelt before her. The back of my knuckles teased her as I traced her seam through the yoga pants. Her lower belly clenched in response. I moved forward, pressing my mouth to the outside of her pussy, feeling her soft folds through her pants.

"You're soaked, baby," I growled, "and you smell so fucking good."

I pulled the black fabric down her tanned legs, along with her panties, revealing her smooth, velvet skin. I paused, just a moment, to appreciate the gorgeous woman in front of me—her hair in a messy bun with tendrils framing her face, the nip of her waist that gave way to the swell of her full hips.

I breathed in the heady scent of her arousal as our eyes locked. Her tongue moved across her pouty mouth as she stepped out of the leggings. Grabbing her ass with both hands, I moved forward, running my tongue up her slit.

"Yes," she moaned. "I want your mouth on me."

My cock pulsed at her words. I leaned forward, moving her backward toward the edge of the bed. As I laid her down, I buried my face between her thighs and continued with a slow, torturous drag of my tongue against the delicious warmth between her legs.

Honey clutched at the sheets and gasped, clamping one hand over her mouth.

"Nah, sweetheart," I paused, "No holding back. *Louder.*"

I spread her thighs apart, teasing and sucking. I could feel her body coil and clench as I grunted into her and she listened. Unabashed, she called out my name as I devoured her.

With a swirl of my tongue and a gentle scrape of my teeth against her clit, she came undone. Her hot sex pulsed against my mouth, and my hands squeezed her hips harder.

"Fuck me, Colin. Fill me," she begged on a ragged breath. Her voice was thick and had my skin burning. I had to give her everything she needed.

I shifted my weight, quickly unbuttoning my jeans and gripping my aching dick in my hands. With a hard stroke from base to tip, I squeezed and looked at her warm, pliant body. I grabbed a condom from the nightstand and rolled it down my shaft, loving the way she watched me with hungry eyes.

Lining the tip of my cock against her wet entrance, I teased her with quick, shallow thrusts.

"More," she moaned, lifting her hips in an effort to pull me inside of her.

I needed more of her—all of her. I leaned forward and kissed her hard as I pushed my way into her.

"Oh, *hell*," I ground out. Her walls were wet and tight, and I set a deep and steady rhythm as I pumped in and out of her. Honey wrapped her arms under mine, pulling my chest to hers.

I could feel her hips buck underneath me. I shifted my pelvis, allowing the right angle for her to grind her clit against the base of my cock. Her walls tightened and I could feel that she was close to completely unraveling.

I lifted my torso and laid a hand on the side of her face, brushing a thumb against her plump lower lip.

"I want to watch you come, Honey."

Come with me.

Stay with me.

I rolled my hips into her. I could feel a hot ball of tension creep up my back. I was so fucking close—the edges of my vision going white.

Her wild cobalt blue eyes locked on mine, and a shuddering wave crashed through her. The tight walls of her pussy clenched and gripped my entire length, buried to the hilt as her orgasm tore through her.

I gave in.

With a low groan, I poured myself into her and knew I would never be the same.

TWENTY-ONE

HONEY

WHAT. The actual. Fuck.

Deep, rolling pleasure thrummed through my limbs. The heavy weight of Colin's muscular body on top of me was deliciously uncomfortable. Warmth pooled at my core, and I ran my fingertips up the corded muscles of his back—I was rewarded with a shiver and a pulse of his cock still nestled inside of me.

"Mmm," he hummed and shifted his weight to his elbows. The intensity of his green and amber-flecked eyes had a slight blush tingling beneath my cheeks. "Don't get shy on me now, sweetheart." The pads of his fingers brushed against the warmth under my cheekbones.

"I'm not," I lied. "I'm only trying not to pass out from lack of oxygen."

I had to get this situation under control before my heart leapt out of my chest and danced across the bedroom. Colin was unfazed by my attempt at being aloof—he didn't move off me but shifted his weight backward, giving me more breathing room.

"Thank you," he said quietly as he continued to play with the strands of hair that fell wildly around the pillow.

"That was . . ." I tried to accurately describe the pinch twisting under my breastbone.

Incredible.

Amazing.

Mind-blowing.

Life-altering.

I certainly couldn't say any of *those* traitorous thoughts out loud.

A small smile spread slowly across his handsome face, and a little laugh escaped him. Colin pecked a gentle kiss on the tip of my nose before slipping out of me to take care of the condom. I rolled on his bed, spent and languid, as I stretched.

I surveyed the scene before me and found that Colin's room was masculine. Simple. The only things cluttering the top of his dresser were a dish with a few coins, a watch, and a television remote. It was tidy, which I appreciated, and with him still out of sight in the bathroom, I took a deep inhale of his pillow. It smelled clean and a little bit like his masculine soap. A low, satisfied moan rolled from my chest.

The dim light from the bathroom silhouetted Colin as he stepped back into the dark bedroom. I propped my head on one hand and admired the view. This man was a fucking work of art.

Hard, lean lines. Just enough hair to be masculine but not woolly. Muscles that proved he worked out without being bulky. And that dick . . . This man didn't have a modicum of modesty as he rummaged through a drawer to look for a clean pair of boxer briefs. He stood, thick and long, and I could feel my body waking up to beg for more.

"Enjoying the view?" Colin rubbed his wide palm

across his chest and smiled at me. He adjusted his briefs, and that simple, masculine gesture made my core clench, already missing the way he filled me.

"I forgot how good you look naked."

He smiled and spread his arms wide, "Glad you approve, sugar."

I reached behind me, grabbed a pillow, and threw it at his face. He laughed, catching it midair as he tossed it back and stalked toward me.

"You better watch it." He moved over me, spreading his body over mine. It was like being wrapped in your favorite cozy blanket on a cold day. "Now that I know you're ticklish."

A grin spread over his face, but before I could counter, he dropped a kiss to my neck and shifted off me. I tried to ignore the immediate pang of disappointment. Colin moved back to his drawer and pulled out another T-shirt and a pair of gray sweatpants.

"Here," he said, placing the folded clothes on the mattress. "Go clean up and meet me downstairs when you're ready. You can put these on."

He moved his hand to the side of my face, and before I could stop myself, I closed my eyes and leaned into his palm. His fingers tangled in my hair, and he pulled me closer. His mouth was soft and pliant, his tongue teased the seam of my lips. The demanding fervor was gone and was replaced with tenderness.

I inched my body closer, silently begging to feel the warmth of his body against me again. All too soon he was pulling away and walking out of the bedroom.

Stepping into the hot steam of his shower, I thought about my rules.

Honey's Rules for a Better Life:
No deviating from the plan
No fake, shallow friends
~~No hookups (no matter how hot)~~ *Well, shit.*
~~No swooning~~ *Damn him.*
<u>Definitely</u> no falling in love

❧

After a quick clean up, the smell of bacon wafted up the stairs. I peeked at the clock—11:58 p.m. I pressed the heels of my hands into my tired eyes and followed my nose. I found Colin, still shirtless, and looking more relaxed than I'd ever seen him. His back was to me so I stopped to admire him a second longer. A small speaker played a song I didn't recognize, but Colin sang along—low and intimate. The timbre of his voice was warm and rich with just enough gravel to make a tingle inch up my spine.

He flicked off the burner and started assembling what looked like some kind of sandwich. I was drawn to him and the way he seemed to exist so effortlessly in any space he took up. I walked up and placed my hand at the center of his back, running it down to cop a feel of his firm, round ass.

"There you are." He seemed to perk up at the sight of me.

I realized he had never seen me without my makeup, and I suddenly became self-conscious about the way my typically styled hair hung lifeless in straight curtains and my freckles peeked through without the cover of concealer.

"What do we have here?" I asked, hoping to divert his gaze away from my bare skin.

Colin's lip tipped up, and his sexy, lopsided grin had my core clenching in response.

"Midnight BLTs." He said it like it was the simplest thing in the world, and I felt a warmth spread deep in my belly.

"Are you for real? I *love* a good BLT." My stomach growled at the smell of toast and bacon.

Colin grabbed both plates and tipped his chin toward the high barstools that flanked the impressively large kitchen island. I moved with him, perching on one of the stools as he set both plates down. He smoothed my damp hair with his wide palm and gently squeezed the base of my neck. Colin dropped a kiss on the top of my head, and a hard lump formed in my throat. I had to blink away the tears that burned at the corners of my eyes.

What the hell? Do not cry in front of him. Do. Not.

I'd pulled myself together in time for him to bring us each a glass of cold water. He sat next to me, elbows propped on the table, and took a generous bite of the sandwich.

I smiled and it struck me that midnight BLTs with a kiss on the top of my head was oddly the most romantic thing a man had ever done for me.

Hunger won out against the battle of nerves and the way my heart felt too tight in my chest, and I took a bite. The bread was lightly toasted—just the way I liked it—the bacon crunchy, the tomatoes ripe and juicy, the lettuce crisp. There was also something slightly spicy about it that was *next-level* delicious.

"Oh yeah," I said around the bite. "This hits the spot."

Colin's eyes danced with mischief. "Glad I could do that twice in one night."

I bumped his shoulder with mine on a chuckle. "Seriously, though. What's spicy?"

"Secret ingredient." He popped a rogue piece of bacon

into his mouth. "But," he continued, "if you pinkie promise not to tell, I will tell you."

This ridiculous man held out his large pinkie in a hook. I couldn't help but giggle at how cute he looked. I hooked his finger with mine.

"This is serious, Honey." He pulled our linked hands toward his chest.

I stifled another laugh and leveled my eyes. "I understand."

"It's a little chili garlic paste mixed with the mayo. But you can't tell a soul."

I squeezed my pinkie in his. "pinkie promise."

Smiling, Colin shifted forward and angled his body toward mine. I leaned toward him, and our lips met in a gentle, seeking kiss. Soft at first, our mouths moved together, but a weak moan escaped my throat as he pulled away, leaving me wanting more.

"Mmm. You taste so good," he whispered against my lips.

I am so fucked.

Colin's intensity was laced with tenderness, and I wasn't sure what to do with that. He claimed me in the most delicious and unsettling way.

I leaned my forehead against his. Eating midnight BLTs in the dimly lit kitchen, with the sexiest man I'd ever been with, was breaking down all of the walls I had built to protect myself. My body and my heart didn't give a shit about all of the carefully crafted rules I had tried to put into place.

It had been less than twenty-four hours, and I wanted him to break every rule.

We finished our sandwiches and talked about music,

progress on the bakery, the bar. I stood to clear the plates when Colin placed his hand on my forearm.

"Please stay." His hazel eyes were searching mine. I was sure he was asking me to stay the night, we did leave his truck back at the bar after all, but his request felt heavier. Maybe he wasn't just asking me to stay the night in his bed but rather stay with *him* and carve out a place in each others' lives.

My heart wanted to sing—*yes!*—but my mind stuttered and paused. What would staying with Colin McCoy really mean? Sure, I would have incredible orgasms to come home to, but I also would never know if my bakery was successful because I was capable. What would life be like—how would it *feel*—to do something completely on my own? To not depend on someone else? I couldn't afford an entanglement that felt dangerously close to dependence.

"I will stay. Tonight." Despite the internal war raging inside of me, I couldn't say no to this man.

Colin was fun and considerate and the type of man that doesn't usually stay on the market for long. I'd be a fucking loon to not see that.

We held hands up the stairs, and I nestled against his warm body under the covers. His knees kicked up, tucking my body into the curve of his. He wrapped his arms around me, pulling me so close that I could feel the drum of his heartbeat against my back. I closed my eyes, letting his warmth spread through me, and inhaled his lemon and cedar scent. Being wrapped in his arms felt so damn good.

I drifted to sleep on a singular, comforting thought: *Colin is a good man.*

TWENTY-TWO

COLIN

I AM A PIECE OF SHIT.

I know asking Honey to stay the night was the wrong thing to do, especially considering I hadn't mentioned my business deal with Mr. Stevens, but I pursued her anyway. Hard. She'd said, on multiple occasions, that she wasn't looking to date, be in a relationship, or get involved with anyone—particularly not me. I was a complication she didn't need. Still, I pushed, and there we were.

The early morning sun filtered through my curtains. I had been awake for a while, listening to her deep, relaxed breathing. Honey was warm and soft and tucked right into the nook of my arm.

She belongs here.

I stared at her for longer than I was proud to admit. I never noticed before, but light freckles dotted her nose. Her long lashes swooped low to almost touch her cheeks and without makeup they were so blond that you almost couldn't see them. I had never seen her so undone and I loved it. If she was gorgeous before, she was fifty times prettier without the mask of her makeup.

An ache was spreading in my chest, and I worried that my heart would never find its normal rhythm again. I had never been so aware of my own heartbeat in my life. Honey was changing things for me, and I wasn't sure what to do about that yet.

First, I had to deal with the fact that I was potentially the one person standing in her way to fully owning the bakery. I figured she expected that when it was successful, she would save enough money to purchase it outright. While she thought that she would be buying it from Mr. Stevens, what difference does it make? As an entrepreneur herself, she would understand that I made a business decision.

Lying with her body tangled around mine, the idea sparked inside of me—crackled and burned until it all came into focus. When I owned the shop, she could just rent it from me until she could buy it. I'd help her out, keep rent low, and keep her close.

This is a good thing.

I could ignore the fact that Honey was fiercely independent and that we had definitely moved our friendship to a very personal relationship. Adding a business relationship to that was complicated, sure, but something I knew I could handle.

Mentally patting myself on the back for being a fucking genius, I placed a gentle kiss on the silky strands of her head.

"We got five customers waiting on the rail, a busted keg, the Kalispell Brewing Co. Dunkel is completely out, and a literal frat house just walked in!" My waitress, Isabel, shouted at me across the scarred wooden bar. She was a steadfast, loyal employee, and for the first time, she looked like she was about to burst into tears.

It had been two weeks since Honey and I fell into bed together, and the transition from quasi-dates to spending more evenings together than not, was an easy one. While I still felt a little guilty about tricking her into dating me, it had been transformative for us. Tonight, I was just popping into the bar to snag a bottle of wine. I had plans to take Honey to Canton Springs for an old-fashioned drive-in movie. There, she wouldn't have to worry about anyone from Chikalu assuming we were together.

I ignored the gnawing feeling that grated at the base of my skull when I thought about keeping our relationship on the down-low.

"Fuck. All right." I heaved an irritated sigh in Isabel's direction.

Gonna have to apologize for that one too, asshole.

I tapped out a quick text to Honey, letting her know that there was an emergency at the bar and that I'd need a rain check on our date. Then I texted Russ, one of my bouncers, asking if he wanted to pick up an extra shift. With Chikalu Falls being a college town, frat parties weren't uncommon, but I'd recognized the douche canoe squad when I'd walked in.

It'll be a fucking miracle if we don't have to break up a fight tonight.

I pushed up the sleeves on my Henley shirt. "Isabel, focus on the rail, I'll fix the keg and check the lines. I can sub out the Kalispell for something else."

"On it, boss!" Glasses clattered as she lined up the beers and shots on the dark, splintered oak bar in front of her. Music poured from the stage, making it hard to talk, but

Isabel and I had worked side by side long enough to communicate in nods and shrugs.

In the basement of the bar, the music thumped through the floorboards. It was dim but clean, and I immediately spotted the problem with the busted keg. After a few tweaks and only one spray of beer to the face, we were back in business. I did a quick inventory check and headed back upstairs to update the taps.

Pushing open the door to the main hall, I glanced up and suddenly my boots were filled with lead. Behind the bar, Isabel's raven locks were contrasted by a streak of tumbling blond curls. My heartbeat hammered in my ears.

With a bright, one-dimpled smile, Honey was behind the bar, pouring draft beers like a pro. My mind went blank, and all I could think about was how she electrified any room she entered.

I strode up to her, but before I could make it across the dusty dance hall floor, her head whipped up, and her eyes caught mine. A wide grin, the kind that grew with every footstep toward her, spread across her beautiful face. I dragged a hand across the stubble on my jaw and pushed forward.

"Well, hey, handsome. What brings you here?" Honey's eyes were playful and wild.

"I could ask you the same thing." I had to practically yell at her over the music and the chatter.

"A little bird told me it was really busy here. I figured I could help." With a quick wink, she flicked a bar towel in my direction and turned to take the order of a young couple at the corner of the bar. I stood, dumbstruck, and completely fucking charmed by her.

Isabel bumped into me to reach the sink and wash two

pint glasses. "You gonna stare at her ass all night or help us?"

"Uh. Yeah." I cleared the lump that clogged my throat. "I'm on it."

With an extra bartender—Honey was actually impressively calm for someone who'd never done it—the chaos behind the bar relaxed to a steady rhythm of filling beers, pouring shots, and laughing when someone asked Honey to make a complicated mixed drink. Her go-to reply became, "Awesome! You're the first person to order one! How do you like yours?" Without missing a beat, the customers would rattle off the ingredients, and she'd get to mixing. It was fucking incredible.

Working next to her was like circling the sun—there was an intensity in the room, and I struggled to wrap my brain around why I was so drawn to her. At first I thought our connection was purely mutual attraction fueled by desire, but with every graze of her fingertips across my back, it became harder to deny the feelings taking root.

"I can't believe you dragged me to this shithole." A shrill voice cut above the deep bass of the music and I turned.

Isabel heard it too, and she started toward the far end of the bar when I stopped her. With a curt nod I said, "I got it."

"If she tries starting shit again, just say the word." Isabel's nostrils flared like a bull ready to take charge.

I blew out a heavy sigh, poured myself a Whiskey Ditch, and downed it in one painful gulp. Honey's eyes were on me—I could feel them roving over my face—but I couldn't look her in the eye.

Jackie sat with her back to me, but I could feel the disgust rolling off her in waves. Her short hair was still bleached past the point of looking brittle. When she turned I saw she still wore black eyeliner so thick and smudged you could never tell if she was going out on a bender or coming back from one. Her eyes took one long slow rake down my body and back up, her lip curled in a sneer that was aimed in my direction.

"There's nothing here except liars and has-beens." Her lips pursed at me. "Sometimes both."

I clenched my teeth and willed myself to take a breath before I spoke. "Hey, Jackie. Can I get something for you and your friends?"

When I spoke, I saw her façade crack—just a little— before crumbling altogether. Tears welled in her eyes, and when one spilled, it dragged a streak of black down her cheek. "I can't fucking do this." She turned to her friend. "I'm leaving. He makes me sick." Her bitterness was so thick I could taste it. She grabbed her purse and stormed away from the bar, shouldering her way past the crowd near the dance floor.

A sharp pain bloomed behind my right eye, and I tried to rub it away. As I turned my attention to another patron, I heard, " . . .yeah it's him. Nate needed help and he left him to die." The other women hurried after Jackie but had no intentions of keeping their conversation private. A few curious eyes slanted in my direction, and I moved to busy my hands.

I stood with my back to the bar, both hands over the back sink and my head held low. I blew out a hard breath to release some of the tension that had knotted between my shoulder blades. Her warm apricot and spice perfume reached me only seconds before her hand smoothed up my back. At her touch, heat spread and dissolved the pressure that lived there.

Her soft voice tingled in my ear as she whispered. "You doing okay, cowboy?"

I cleared my throat to keep from dropping to my knees and throwing myself at her mercy. "Right as rain, darlin'." My hand found the small of her back, and my thumb grazed the sliver of skin above the waistband of her jeans. Honey chewed her lower lip and acted like she wanted to ask questions about who I spoke to at the bar and why the conversation had me so rattled but she didn't press.

A whistle caught my attention, and I looked up to see my bouncer, Russ, standing in between two college guys ready to brawl.

"Fuck this." I reached under the bar and grabbed my baseball bat before vaulting the bar and rushing toward them. Mostly the bat was for show, and it worked pretty well at scaring the shit out of little boys who thought they were tough guys. My fist was clenched at my side, and it ached for the wrong person to shove me so it could connect to a face.

Between the two of us, Russ and I were able to shove the guys apart and defuse the situation. They were ready to throw down over a rum and Coke that was elbowed and spilled on a new pair of overpriced Tony Lama boots. They liked to talk a lot of shit, but we walked them outside and made sure they left without causing more trouble.

As we watched the trucks pull away, Russ dropped a hand on my shoulder. "I'm too old for this shit, man."

"Ha. You and me both." I rolled my shoulders and tried to loosen the kink I felt.

"You're still scary as hell when you jump over that bar though." Russ pushed his fist against my arm.

I grinned. "I still got it."

The crowd inside was unfazed by the scuffle, and they were back to drinking, dancing, and laughing. I shook Russ's hand and walked toward the bar. It had slowed significantly, and I was confident that Isabel could handle the customers on her own. I caught Honey's eye and tipped my head toward my office.

Once the door clicked shut, I pulled Honey in close and pressed my forehead to hers.

"Tonight wasn't so bad." Her voice was soft and low. Her arms wound around my neck, and I breathed her in.

"Compared to what I had planned, tonight was a kick in the balls."

Honey's hands came to the side of my face, and her eyes searched mine. "Who was that woman who came in tonight?"

I sighed. I really didn't want to get into it with her. It was a lot to unpack and I was drained. "Jackie was my brother Nate's on-again-off-again girlfriend. They were on-again when he died."

"Oh . . ."

"Yeah." I wasn't ready to let Honey see the dark side of me—the side that knew, deep down, Jackie thought I was responsible for Nate's death. The worst part was, I agreed with her.

∿

DATING HONEY WAS as easy as breathing. The woman wove herself in my brain, her presence at the edge of every thought. What was she up to? What was she wearing? Were things going okay over at the bakery? Did she notice that I walked past her window? It felt like being eighteen again. It was fun, exciting, and surprisingly easy. The summer weeks tumbled by, and we each kept secrets and pretended they didn't exist. I let my potential ownership of the bakery space get buried in the back of my mind, and Honey continued keeping our relationship a closely guarded secret. We ignored them altogether and hoped they would fade away on their own.

We shared dinner with Joanna and Lincoln. Bowling and beers with Deck. Group outings that from the outside looked like nothing more than a group of friends hanging out and shooting the shit. We both ignored the sideways, knowing glances our friends would shoot us and pretended that we'd settled into an easy friendship.

Every night, Honey would pull her Chevelle into my garage under the cloak of darkness, and we'd live our delightfully sordid fantasies. In public, we had mastered the art of playing it cool.

Except for the time Isa caught us making out in the stockroom. Honey whipped around and pretended to look for some unknown item. "Well, no. Sorry. I can't seem to find it," she said on a breathless huff. I hid my rock-hard dick with an oversized can of baked beans, and Honey dissolved into a fit of giggles as Isabel rolled her dark brown eyes and quickly closed the door behind her.

Or the time I was licking a dollop of cinnamon bun icing from her inner thigh. Honey was perched on the kitchen island with my head nestled dangerously between her thighs when her supplier, Ricardo, pushed through the kitchen door. She nearly flipped backward off the island before I caught her. Ricardo was so secondhand-embarrassed that he couldn't look Honey in the eye for a month.

Maybe even that once when Ms. Trina was closing the ladies' boutique and might have seen us holding hands in the darkness. Her eyes flicked down as Honey released my hand, and Ms. Trina gave us both a not-so-subtle wink as she hummed and walked to her car.

A small part of me fucking hated that I couldn't walk

around town with my arms wrapped around her or tell everyone that something I did was the reason she wore that one-dimpled smile. It was childish and I knew it, but I couldn't help but feel a little hurt that I was her dirty little secret. The fact that it was even a secret around here was a goddamn miracle. For the time being, I had to bury my feelings and put on a good show if I had any chance of truly winning her over.

"Dude, are we even on the same planet?" Deck placed a beer in front of me.

I had been lost in my thoughts of Honey and didn't notice him walk into my house for our poker night.

"Sorry, man," I started. "There's just a lot going on right now."

Deck eyed me warily, deciding whether or not to push for more information. Thankfully he let it drop—for now.

"Finn and Linc are coming together tonight. They should be here any minute, but I wanted to tell you . . ." Deck trailed off.

He cleared his throat and continued, "One of my patrolmen drove your mom home today."

I felt a heavy weight press down on my shoulders, and a deep sigh left my body. "Shit. From where?"

"Her car was on the side of the road. I think she left the cemetery and didn't quite make it home."

"Fuck."

"Sorry, man. I just know you'd want to hear it from me. They drove her home, and we made sure her car made it back to the house. Keith asked if we should call you or Avery, but your dad said not to bother you."

"Thanks, brother. Thanks for taking care of her."

I felt my jaw tighten. Nate's death had been hard on all of us, but losing a sibling was nothing compared to the grief my mother felt at losing her youngest child. It ebbed and flowed, but she was still drowning in grief, and I was helpless—nothing I could do would take away the pain that I had caused her. While she fell apart, my father used all his energy to support her. It left very little leftover comfort for Avery or me, so we used each other to shoulder the burden.

One selfish mistake and I was stuck living my life in the shadow of Nate's choices. Most days I buried that resentment, but ever since seeing Jackie at the bar, it had been flaring. I wanted to stop feeling the hot, searing stab of guilt over not answering the phone that night. I wanted to bring Honey home and have a normal dinner with my parents without my mother's tears spilling into the lasagna. I wanted to be able to think back to what should have been the best parts of my life and not think about how I fucked it all up.

"So what's the deal with you and Honey?" Deck asked. I was glad he changed the subject away from my family drama, but turning the spotlight on my relationship with Honey was almost as bad.

"Not sure what you mean," I mumbled as I shuffled the cards with more concentration than was necessary.

"You're a terrible fucking liar," he laughed. "Everyone can see that you're completely out of your gourd for her."

"Whatever, dude." Deck could fuck off. I'd been playing it pretty cool.

"All I'm saying is that if you have a shot, take it." Deck tipped his beer back and took a long gulp.

"Now you're dishing out relationship advice? Kind of like the blind leading the blind, don't you think?" I clanked my beer against the neck of his bottle, and his eyes snapped to mine.

"Think about it. If you miss your chance—if you don't

take it because you're acting like a chump—you'll spend a long time regretting it."

"Spoken like a true romantic. Did that waitress from Canton Springs dump you already?"

Deck shook his head and shrugged off the hand I'd clamped on his shoulder.

He wasn't talking about the easy lay he sometimes hooked up with in the next town over, and we both knew it.

"Who's ready to lose their ass?" Finn's voice boomed from the front porch, breaking the tension between my best friend and me.

Standing, I moved to the door to welcome Lincoln, Finn, and Finn's new boyfriend.

"We brought Chinese," Lincoln said sternly, lifting the heavy bags filled with paper cartons.

The awkwardness I'd felt when Decker and I were talking dissolved, and we fell into an easy rhythm. Bellies full of shitty takeout, we played several rounds of poker, and Finn was right—we lost our asses.

Deck's advice rolled around my head the rest of the night. I knew he was right. Honey and I were great together, and I was done hiding my feelings for her.

TWENTY-THREE
HONEY

"Who says they'd gossip?" Colin shrugged at me, popping a french fry into his mouth.

"Are you kidding me right now?" I pinned him with a stare that I hoped made him pause and think about the stupid shit that tumbled out of his mouth. "Every woman you're seen talking to at the bar is the main topic of conversation at the cafe. Trust me. I get to hear about it! It's hard enough to open a successful business as an *outsider* in a small town. But one who's banging the local golden boy? I'd never be taken seriously."

"Honey, people will take you seriously because you're an amazing baker and businesswoman."

I wanted to believe him. So fucking badly but I couldn't help the gnawing feeling of inadequacy. In the low light of the bakery kitchen, we sat shoulder to shoulder on top of the large metal island, sharing a dinner of diner burgers and fries.

"Look, I don't have any other options." I spoke deliberately, hoping he'd finally see what I had been trying to tell him. "This has to work."

"And it will." He pressed his shoulder into mine. "I just can't walk around this town hiding the way I feel about you anymore. Yesterday, you wore my T-shirt, for fuck's sake."

He was teasing me but it was true. I had stolen his shirt after a round of hot, sweaty sex and the next day had worn it knotted and off one shoulder. The steamy, possessive look I got the next morning when he saw me in his shirt shot a bullet of tingles between my thighs any time I thought about it. I figured if he was going to torture me with winks and dreamy gazes, I was going to torture him too.

"Look, if I want to hold your hand or kiss you or slap your ass in public, I don't want to worry about you going nuclear." He dragged the last fry though ketchup, ate it, and brushed his hands on a napkin.

The warmth that spread at the thought of the freedom we'd have by no longer hiding our relationship was squelched by his meaning.

Nuclear? Is that really what he thinks?

I thought back to all the times he'd reached for my hand, and I picked at an invisible piece of lint, moved from under his arm when someone walked in, or purposely stepped back when he stepped closer. I considered how that must have felt for him and fresh shame washed over me.

On a huff, I smoothed my hands down the length of my flowy skirt and made up my mind.

"You said that when I ask you for a date, you would say yes." I hopped off the island to stand in front of him. I slid a leg between his and placed my hands on the corded muscles of his forearms. "So I'm asking."

I took another deep breath and looked up into his eyes. "Colin McCoy, will you go on a date with me?"

"Nah." He said flatly, lifting one shoulder in dismissal.

My mind stalled and sputtered. I blinked once. Twice. I

couldn't keep up as embarrassment heated my cheeks. I was too late. I had pushed him away, and he was sick of my shit. I nodded curtly and shifted away.

Colin turned his hands to grip my arms. He pulled me closer, and I could feel the heat rolling off of him.

"No," he drawled, "because I am asking *you*. Honey James, will you please be my date to the Sagebrush Festival?"

A lopsided grin spread across his handsome face, and relief washed over me.

At that moment, I let myself listen to what I had known for a while—I wasn't the same girl that blindly followed a man and disregarded her own dreams. I wasn't even the same woman who had left Butte. It was time to stop putting up walls, stop chasing the detached executives with stony exteriors and fabulous cocks, and open my eyes to what was right in front of me.

I had managed to find a man that believed in me, made me laugh, could melt my panties with a charged look, *and* had a fabulous cock.

Colin moved forward, holding me tightly as he moved off the island. I traced the line of his swollen cock through his jeans. He spun me and my ass pressed into the cold metal. Disregarding our lackluster dinner, Colin touched his lips to mine. He tasted like salt and promises and hope.

His tongue slid over the seam of my lips, and I opened for him, deepening the kiss on a soft moan. My arms looped around his neck and pulled him closer as I arched my back. I had an overwhelming need to show him just how my body reacted to him. How my heart caught in my throat whenever he walked into the room.

My legs turned to jelly as hot pulses rolled down to my core. My hands swept the paper next to us, clattering the remnants of our dinner to the floor as I braced my arms behind me. Colin moved one knee between my legs, and I pushed my hips forward, seeking the pressure of his cock against me. My hands tangled in his hair, and I pressed my clit harder into his firm, muscled thigh. Colin wrapped his arms around my middle, crushing my chest to his, and his tongue slid across mine. A moan rumbled out of him, and my nipples pebbled.

Colin's rough hand slid down my hip and lower, to the hem of my skirt. Hot sparks of electricity shot through my veins as his fingers dragged up the sensitive skin of my inner thigh. His fingertips moved achingly slowly as he teased my sensitive flesh and traced the outer edge of my panties. My pussy throbbed in anticipation.

"I can feel how wet you are." Colin growled deep in his throat. "I want to lick your pussy, baby. I want to feel you come on my tongue."

I shuddered at his words—I loved that dirty fucking mouth. "The front door is unlocked. Anyone could walk in on us."

"Do you want me to stop?" Colin kissed my neck.

"Fuck, no. I want to feel you." I panted the words as my heartbeat ticked upward.

I reached for the hard lines of his abs, tracing them down to the buckle of his belt. His hands covered mine, stopping me from unfastening his belt. His heated gaze held me like a wolf eyeing his prey. Slowly, his fingers undid the buckle. In one swift movement, he pulled his belt, and the *zing* as it whipped through the belt loops had gooseflesh erupting on my skin.

Colin lowered the zipper and reached into his jeans, pulling his thick erection over the top of his boxer briefs. I watched as he pulled once, and a drop of wetness coated the head of his cock. I wanted to lick that bead of salty sweetness, and I moved toward him, but instead he hoisted me up onto the island. The cold metal felt glorious against the heat radiating from my center.

Colin pressed his hands to the inside of my legs, spreading me wide open for him. He teased the outside of my panties before sliding one finger back into my wet folds. My head dropped back at the way he moved that finger inside me and used his thumb to tease my clit. He dropped his head forward, licking my seam with a drag of his tongue. One hand tangled in his hair while the other struggled to keep my balance.

"Oh, god," I whispered.

Colin dragged my panties down my legs, gaining more access to my center. His tongue felt warm and thick as it moved up my velvet skin from back to clit. His two-day stubble dragged across my sensitive skin, and my legs jerked in response. He grunted into me like I was the best thing he had ever eaten as he devoured my pussy.

A million thoughts swirled through my mind as every nerve ending crackled to life. I could feel my orgasm build as he licked and swirled and nipped at my clit.

"You taste so fucking good."

Oh, fuck.

My vision went blurry, and my arms began to tremble as I felt my inner muscles tighten around Colin's expert tongue. I couldn't help but pull his hair, just a little, and grind my pussy into his face. I came so hard I was consumed by it. Every wonder, every doubt about who I was evaporated as I shuddered and let go. Through my orgasm, Colin was relentless, continuing to pleasure me like it was his fucking job.

My throat was raw from panting, but I managed to

steady myself with shaking arms. When his eyes shot forward, a wicked gleam showed me just how much he'd enjoyed it too. With adrenaline and endorphins pulsing through my system, I had a renewed sense of vigor.

I lowered my legs onto solid ground. Colin's cock was still rock-hard and straining against the fabric of his boxer briefs. I grabbed him by the hips and turned him so he leaned against the island. I raised an eyebrow and slowly sank to my knees, dragging my nails along the sensitive skin of his lower belly.

"Honey." He grunted and I loved that he was breathing hard.

I eased his boxers and pants down and took his solid flesh into my hands. I licked a slow line up one long, hard side and down the other and swirled my tongue around the tip. A thick vein twitched against the flat of my tongue when I dragged it along the bottom from the base of his cock to the hard, pulsing tip.

"Baby, you're fucking killing me." Colin's hands gripped the steel island behind him, and I loved that he was aching for me. I licked my lips, just to torture him a little before pressing him against my mouth. I opened just enough to allow the first couple inches slip past. I swirled my tongue gently as I gripped the base with a free hand.

I moaned and slid another inch into my mouth. I glanced up and saw his eyes going darker, the tension coiling in his tight abs. I bobbed my head and with each thrust, pulled him deeper until he hit the back of my throat. Keeping one hand on the base of his cock, I could control the speed and pressure, teasing him and sucking him hungrily.

Colin brushed a strand of hair from my face and

threaded a hand through my hair. I paused and a prickle of panic swept through me, but I kept my agonizing pace.

"Is this okay?" His voice was strained, and I knew he was close. I was into some kinky shit and all about rough, dirty sex, but there was something about having a man hold your head while he pumped his cock into you that had my nerves simmering just underneath my skin. He was in total control, but I knew him, trusted him.

I pulled him out of my mouth and licked my lower lip. "I trust you."

Easing him back into my mouth, I allowed him to keep his hand tangled in my hair. He didn't move at first, but as I took him deep again and again, his hips started moving—gentle thrusts forward as he lost himself to how I could make him feel. I moaned to let him know I liked what he was doing, and a stream of *fucks* and *holy shits* sprang from his lips. I could feel his cock pulse in my mouth, he was so close.

"Baby, I'm . . . I'm close. Where . . ."

The sweet, simple fact that he wanted me to choose where he came had me grabbing his ass and pulling him as far down my throat as I could manage. I wanted to feel him, taste him, and watch him let everything go. Hot pulses coated my throat as he released himself into me. My ears were ringing with triumph and the heady rush of great sex. When he stilled, I eased myself back, stopping just at the tip to swallow and swipe the back of my hand across my lower lip.

I looked up at him and smiled a mischievous, self-satisfied grin as he struggled to regulate his breathing. Colin reached down, pulling me up by the arms and crushing me against his hard, linear body. His cock was trapped between us, my panties were crumpled in a sad pile on the floor, and I couldn't think with the deafening thump of his heartbeat.

"I have never needed anyone the way I need you." Colin brushed a tendril of hair from my face, and my stomach cartwheeled at his words.

His fingers moved down the line of my neck, lingering and burning a path down my skin. I tipped my head back, exposing the pulse that beat uncontrollably inside me. Colin's mouth moved over me, and the pressure between my legs built. I needed to feel my pussy, hot and tight, around his thick cock.

"Show me." I exhaled on a shudder, desire coursing through me.

Colin's hands unbuttoned my top at a devastatingly slow pace. When he spread my shirt open, the cool air hit my breasts, and my nipples hardened through the flimsy lace. He dipped his head low to tease my rosy bud through the fabric. He grunted and a rush of wetness had my center clenching. Colin turned my body and thrust his hips into mine. My arms splayed over the island. I was bent at the hips, ass in the air as the cold steel felt torturously divine on my nipples. He hiked my skirt up, exposing my bare ass as he lined himself up at my entrance.

"Round two already?" I shot him a wicked smile over my shoulder.

"Once is never enough with you," he said. He dragged the tip of his cock through my wet slit.

"Do you have something?" I could hardly get the words out. I was so ready for him to fill me.

Colin pulled a condom from his jean pocket and sheathed himself. "I got you, baby." He grabbed my hip and slid inside me in one long, smooth stroke. I felt every thick, hard inch of him, and my body rocked in response. He set a demanding rhythm—pushing in and out of me as my hips slammed the hard metal island. I would probably have bruises on my hipbones, but I didn't give a *fuck*. My body was humming with pleasure. Colin ran one hand delicately up my back, and his fingertips left a trail of tingles in their wake.

"Jesus, baby." Colin's voice was deep and strained. "I love watching your pussy suck my cock. You feel so fucking good."

I lifted to my toes to adjust the angle and allow him to go deeper. We were straddling the line between pleasure and pain, and I couldn't get enough. He loved it too. His thrusts became erratic, like he was about to lose control. Needles prickled at the base of my neck and down my spine. I was chasing my orgasm, and as if he knew it too, his hand found my clit and gently pinched. My body tightened once and released wave after wave of pleasure. Colin's hand found my shoulder, and in one final, forceful thrust, he was coming right behind me.

Our breathing slowed but my heartbeat ticked upward. I closed my eyes and gave myself a moment to enjoy how *real* this all felt. Still, in the dark corners of my mind, there was fear. *Will I break my rules for him, and he will leave me anyway? Will I be able to pull off the bakery opening and have room for him in my life? If I am with him, will I still be taken seriously?* The doubts tumbled through my mind—building and expanding on each other. I rested my forehead on the cool island surface.

"Hey, are you okay?" Concern was laced in Colin's voice. "I didn't hurt you, did I?"

"No. No," I breathed. "Just getting my bearings, that's all. It was intense." It really was and I forced myself to ignore the doubt that tried to clutter my mind and dampen my mood. I had just had spontaneous, electrifying sex with Colin, and I was determined to enjoy the warm afterglow.

One thing was for certain, I would never walk into this kitchen again and not think of Colin McCoy.

BACK AT HIS HOUSE, Colin sat on the floor of his living room with an acoustic guitar across his muscular legs. I sat behind him, one leg draped over his and my head resting on the center of his back. As he sang a song I didn't recognize, I could feel the low rumble of his voice vibrate through his back and into me. I closed my eyes and slowly breathed in his scent of fresh laundry and good-smelling-man, pulling it to the bottom of my lungs and let it linger there.

He feels so good.

My hands stroked down his sides as I listened to the soulful music roll out of him. Colin's corded forearms flexed and rippled as his fingers moved over the guitar strings. I tried like hell to ignore the tiny hiccup beneath my breastbone. The gravel in his voice filled me with heat but it was more. Colin had always worn his heart on his sleeve, and I didn't know how to do that.

This man was an experience, and he checked all my boxes:

Playful: check.

Kind: check.

Successful: check.

Sexy as *fuck*: double check.

Over his shoulder I saw a framed picture of him, Decker, and Linc as teenagers, dressed in football uniforms with the joy of a victory painted on their youthful faces. Colin was in the center, his hair was longer, flopped over one eye in the front, but his lopsided grin was just as endearing then as it was now. His arms stretched open to pull his best friends into a hug. Linc looked serious as ever, and Decker's warmth was apparent, even then. My heart tumbled a little harder for the man I was wrapped around, and the rest of the guys.

Colin hummed his way through the bridge of the song he was playing.

"Forget the words, big shot?" I teased, keeping my voice just above a whisper.

Colin harrumphed. "Haven't written them yet."

"You wrote that?" I paused and blinked once, emotion thick in my throat. "Colin. It's beautiful."

He turned his body to angle it toward me. "Thanks, darlin'." His lips met mine in a soft, sensuous kiss. "It's special and I'm glad you like it."

"There's not much you do that I don't like," I countered, kissing him again and squeezing him with my arms and legs in a bear hug.

A heavy sigh I didn't know I was holding left my lungs in a whoosh. "So we're really doing this?" I toyed with my bottom lip, unable to look him in the eye.

Colin tipped my chin with his finger, gently forcing my eyes to meet his. "Baby, I have never been so sure of anything in my entire life."

His hand spread to the side of my face, and I leaned into him, allowing him to cradle it as I closed my eyes and soaked in the moment.

"Honey, you aren't just some girl. When you're here, in my home, I can feel it. Every part of me knows it. I'm just waiting for you to catch up."

The knocking behind my ribs was deafening—it was a wonder Colin couldn't hear it too. Unable to find the words to tell him what I was feeling, I brushed my nose along his before trailing soft, wet kisses down the hard line of his neck. I dipped my tongue into the hollow of his throat and worked my way back up to the tender spot behind his ear that made him moan. Kissing him in the dim lights of early evening felt familiar and comforting. I felt something shift and click deep inside of me.

My eyes shifted to another framed photograph on the small table. It was old and faded, two little boys with tube socks pulled up to their dirty little knees, holding small wooden swords. A little laugh escaped me, and it drew Colin's attention. He looked over and smiled. "That's Nate and me."

"So you've always been adorable," I said and leaned my ear against his back and listened to his heartbeat. "Were you slaying dragons?"

"Sort of," he laughed. "Knights. Nate *loved* to play knights. Arthur and Lancelot, damsels in distress, that kind of thing."

"Mmm," was all I said. Colin was opening up about his brother, and I didn't want to ruin the moment by saying the wrong thing.

"Nate was funny—really creative too. *Always* getting into shit." Colin shook his head lightly as he continued to pick soft, random notes on the guitar.

"I think I would have loved Nate. He sounds like a fun guy." I said gently.

"You're both trouble." He laughed lightly. "He would have loved you too." The thickness that crept into his voice had tears stinging at the corners of my eyes, and I held him closer. I had never felt more special.

"Honey? After Sagebrush, will you come home with me and meet my parents?"

TWENTY-FOUR

COLIN

ASKING Honey to meet my parents was a spur of the moment decision, but after the intimate moment we shared —her wrapped around me while I sang along with the guitar —and the warm ache that spread across my chest, I just went with it.

"I'd love to," she answered without hesitation.

"I was expecting at least an arched eyebrow but I'll take it." I lifted her hand to my lips and gently kissed across her knuckles.

Things were moving fast with Honey. I could see, with stunning clarity, how she could be the woman I loved forever. I knew I had to come clean about my underhanded deal to own the shop. I also needed to tell her about the choices I made that resulted in Nate taking his own life.

Fear bubbled to the surface—once she knew the truth, would she look at me the same way? Would she realize deep down I'm still trying, and failing, to make up for it? I wanted her to meet Avery and my parents. I resigned myself to the fact that the truth would come out and I would have to make peace with my choices. Those choices brought me here and her into my life. But in moments like that, with Honey draped over me in the darkening evening light of my living room, I just couldn't give it up yet.

THE ANNUAL SAGEBRUSH festival was a master class in small-town living. For three days, tourists from across the county and farther came together for music, home-cooked food, dancing, and a 5K run that ended with a signature Sagebrush cocktail, compliments of The Dirty Pigeon.

The whole town took the three-day festival *very* seriously, but the Women's Club was next-level organized. Every year, the community voted for an organization to donate the proceeds and donations collected. This year, the vote was between a nonprofit that provided mental health care to veterans and, of course, Mr. Bailey's bid to block the entryways into Chikalu Falls in order to keep our small town small. Every year he submitted a new idea. His big idea this time around was to erect a dilapidated sign which included the phrase "Town's closed. Go Home." Last year's idea included armored tanks, so the sign was actually an improvement.

Across Main Street, the businesses hung string lights in a zigzag, and I had to admit when they were all lit up at night it was pretty magical. The bar would see a steady stream of customers, and we also set up a large stage on the far end of town. I helped to book bands and scheduled local musicians to spread across the three-day festival.

From the top of my ladder, I attached the last cord of lights, climbed down, and wiped my hands across the thighs of my jeans. I could see Honey pulling out a step stool to hang a banner in front of the shop. From this angle, I could see her tight little ass, and her top rode up the side just a little as she stretched. A tingle ran down my spine and settled in my groin. We agreed that we wouldn't keep our relationship a secret, and this was the first opportunity I would have to interact with her in public, right out in the open. I jogged across the street and stepped onto the stool behind her. I grabbed the banner and hooked the loop in a nail.

"Thanks!" She huffed out a breath. "I couldn't quite reach."

The smile that she gave me had my heart falling to my boots. I was about to stifle the urge to run my hands up her trim waist when I reminded myself I was allowed to do that now. Sharing the small space on the ladder, I leaned in and wrapped my fingers around her hips. "Get over here," I growled.

Our kiss was tentative, I only teased the corner of her mouth with a soft peck until she moaned quietly into my mouth. My hands instinctively pulled her closer, and my thumbs slipped through her belt loops. I changed the angle of my head, deepening the kiss and not giving a *fuck* who could see us. Honey wound her arms around my neck, and her heartbeat hammered in rhythm with mine.

When we stood apart, we were both a little breathless. I stepped off the ladder, back onto solid ground, but I kept my hands on her hips.

"That was a pleasant surprise," she said.

"I can do that now. I don't care who sees it—in fact, I want them to see it."

Honey popped on hand on her hip. "Staking your claim?" she teased.

"Damn right." I winked at her, turned, and strolled into The Pidge. A flurry of blue-haired old ladies scurried away from the window of the beauty parlor, and I couldn't help but laugh. Well, word was bound to be out now—Honey and I were officially dating.

TWENTY-FIVE

HONEY

AFTER COLIN SNUCK up behind me to help with the banner, his kiss left me a little dizzy and feeling weightless. Warmth pooled in my cheeks, and the flap and flutter of butterflies wouldn't leave my stomach. I stood back to look at the banner and fanned myself. I tried not to think about the way his backward ball cap and swagger had heat spreading throughout my body.

I couldn't help but look around, curious about who may have seen us—old habits die hard, apparently. I saw the ladies in the beauty parlor trying to act like they didn't just see Colin and I locked in an embrace. Instead of the normal feeling of dread at being caught, I was content—happy even.

Looking at the banner with my newly designed logo for the shop, Biscuits & Honey, I couldn't believe I was actually opening a bakery. Joanna walked out from inside of the shop as I continued to stare at the banner.

"It's really happening!" Her voice was laced with playful excitement and happiness. If she squealed, I wouldn't have been surprised.

I blew out a shaky breath. "I am ninety-nine percent

sure I can do this . . . but that one percent really fucking sucks."

Jo's arms wrapped around me from behind and I hugged her. "I can't believe I'm going to say this, but I don't think I ever want to leave. This bakery? This town? It all feels so good."

"That's because you're finally home."

Jo's words had me squeezing her tightly, willing my tears not to fall.

~

FRIDAY NIGHT of the Sagebrush Festival was a success. Everyone seemed to love my spiced apple butter cake, and Ms. Gertie did not have a repeat performance of her drunken striptease. In fact, I baked even more treats for Saturday night. All day, people had stopped by to ask about the bakery and sample the different recipes I had prepared. A buzzy energy had my knee bouncing as I watched the hours tick by.

Colin and I had agreed to meet up at Sagebrush. He was playing with the band, and I could refill baked goods for the Women's Club. Then, we planned to meander around and enjoy the festival as a couple before heading home.

Home.

His home, specifically. Lately, I had been spending more time at Colin's house than at the tiny cottage on Jo's property. What started out as a change of clothes or an extra toothbrush had turned into him making room in his closet and drawers for some of my things. While I was quite sure we were not ready for a *move-in* level commitment, it felt easy—natural—to be a part of Colin's life. It fit.

The sun had set over the mountains, and the twinkle

lights across Main Street winked to life. I wished I had more than just my phone to take a picture. The town was quaint and quirky and the kind of place that didn't give up on one of their own. I couldn't imagine being this happy anywhere else.

As I walked down the middle of Main Street, I stopped to wave at the neighbors and business owners that dotted the sidewalk. I smiled at Trina in front of the Blush Boutique, her bright blue eyeliner twinkled in the lights, and she gave me a knowing smile. Yesterday, I had stopped by and picked up a very special set of lingerie. It was for Colin, but also for me because I felt like a fucking badass in it. Her wink as I walked by had me laughing and rolling my eyes. That woman was a hoot.

Under the large tent at the far end of the street, I saw Lincoln's large frame on the outskirts of the crowd and headed in that direction. Peeking around him, I searched for Jo. She was all smiles, laughing as she chatted with a small group of people waiting in line to grab a beer.

As I approached the main tent, I patted Cole Decker on the shoulder as he stood, feet planted, thumbs hooked into his utility belt. "Hey, Deck. Quiet night?"

His eyes continued scanning the crowd, but a small smile tipped up the corner of his mouth. "So far, so good."

"You still looking for the Dick Bandits?" I teased.

A low, throaty growl was his only response. Laughing, I continued on my walk. I couldn't help but follow his gaze as it raked over Maggie across the street. His scowl deepened and I watched Maggie laugh and toss her hair over one shoulder as she wrapped a bundle of flowers for a customer. Something fucking weird was going on with those two, I was sure of it. I reminded myself to try to carry a basket of scones over and bring it up with some of the beauty parlor ladies to see if I could get a little dirt.

I came up behind Lincoln, but his military training was so ingrained that he turned when I approached. His steely features softened, only slightly, when he recognized me.

"Hey, Linc, what do you know?"

He leaned in for an awkward hug and returned his eyes to Jo. "I know I hate crowds," he grumbled. "But she'll be excited to see you."

"I'm sure she'll let you off the hook after a dance or two. In the meantime, let's get a drink."

"Copy that." Lincoln let out a sigh of relief and walked with me to get a beer.

The music from the stage shifted as the first band left and the house band from The Pidge took center stage. Cradling my cold beer in all its plastic cup glory, I watched Colin move with precision on the stage. He was at home there, relaxed and comfortable. I saw him scan the crowd, and when we caught eyes, a lopsided grin spread across his face. Desire swirled through me, and I had to clear my throat to keep from moaning out loud. Lincoln glanced at me with a mixture of concern and skepticism.

Easy, girl. Let's not get ahead of ourselves.

The band started with some well-loved country classics, and after catching up with Jo, I wandered closer to the stage to get us a table while she finished her conversations. I wanted to get good seats and enjoy Colin's set up close. The makeshift dance floor was filling up with couples two-stepping and a crowd of people line dancing. As I skirted around the edge, I heard a familiar voice call my name.

"Honey!"

I turned and saw Jean moving from behind the table for

the Chikalu Women's Club. It had been a while since we had coffee and I missed her. It was a good day for her—you could see it in the way her eyes sparkled, and her skin had a warm glow to it. I moved toward her and held her in a tight hug.

"Jean, how have you been? It's been too long since we've been able to catch up."

"Oh, dear, it's been really good. I'm keeping myself busy. More good days than not lately." Jean shrugged. "Oh! Artie has himself a girl. He's in *love* with her, and I could just burst."

"It's good to see you so happy, Jean. What do you think about coffee on Monday morning? You can tell me all about it."

"It's a date!" Jean hummed along with the band as she walked back behind her table.

I found a small wooden table on the outside edge of the dance floor and borrowed a few chairs from the table beside me. From there, I had a great view of Colin, and it was a short trip to the bar. I sipped my beer and scanned the crowd to see women of all ages swoon over my man. His voice was smooth like syrup but with just enough gravel in it to make a tingle race from toes to titties.

Go on and look ladies, because I know what that voice sounds when it whispers dirty things in the dark.

"I bet I can guess what's got you smiling like that." Maggie wandered up to the table with a large smile spread across her pretty face. She wore tight jeans that hugged her in *all* the right places. Her lacy top was flowy and had a bohemian vibe to it—Maggie was stunning in the best way. She didn't try too hard or attempt to be something she wasn't. Maggie was confident and that quiet confidence gave her a warm glow that followed her around. Everyone seemed to love her—well, everyone except Cole Decker, who was scowling in her direction. When he caught my eye over her right shoulder, he adjusted the vest on his broad chest and looked away.

Fucking weird.

I twisted my face as I considered what the hell was going on with those two.

Maggie glanced over her shoulder. "What?"

"Oh," I laughed, "nothing. Something caught my eye but it's gone now. Sorry." I smiled at Maggie and fluffed my hair. "Want to sit down? I think Jo and Linc will be by in a few."

"I wish I could, but I need to check up on Lottie and close up the flower shop. Catch up with you later?"

"Definitely." I hugged Maggie tightly and watched her walk away, noticing how Deck's dark eyes followed her as she wove through the crowd. What I thought was a grimace transformed into something sadder.

Very curious.

When Jo and Lincoln found me at my little table with the fake candle flickering its heart out, Linc put a fresh beer in front of me. He folded his enormous frame into the rickety chair and tucked Joanna under his arm. He whispered to Jo, and the blush on her cheeks deepened. The twinkle lights overhead illuminated the dance floor, and part of me wished Colin was pulling me close and spinning me around that floor. I closed my eyes and swayed gently to the music, tapping my foot to the beat and letting the warm tones of his voice through the speakers wash over me.

Joanna kissed Lincoln's neck and he stood, pulling her out to the dance floor. I watched my older sister move and glide with her fiancé. Happiness bubbled inside me for them. Through it all, they had found each other. My eyes swept to Colin, sitting with his knees wide, guitar balanced across his muscular thighs.

As the band transitioned to a new song, he strummed chords that felt vaguely familiar. "This next song is an original. I started writing this song about six months ago about a girl who got away." Colin's eyes swept over me, and I felt the crowd evaporate as his heated stare melted my insides. "Turns out, she didn't get too far because she's here tonight, and, uh," Colin cleared his throat gently, "I hope she likes it." He shifted on the stool like he was nervous. "It's called Wildfire and Honey."

Heat swept over me, and I felt a thousand pairs of eyes move in my direction, but I couldn't look away. He broke eye contact only to look at his guitar and play the chords. The house band joined in right as I recognized the song he had played when we sat on the floor of his living room. His words buzzed in my ears as my heart pumped harder and louder. Colin closed his eyes and poured himself into the song. The thick cords of his neck stretched and moved as he belted the lyrics.

"Next to you I feel like I'm dyin'...

...wanna hold you close to me ...

... Baby, I'm tired of trying to act like you don't unravel me ...

... I know what you need, and you know what I want..."

His deep, scratchy voice raked over me. A thousand sensations moved through my veins—surprise, desire, giddiness, embarrassment, longing, *love.*

Holy shit. I am in love with Colin McCoy.

TWENTY-SIX
COLIN

My heart thumped in my chest as I tried to get through the song without coming completely undone. I had played bits and pieces of the song in front of Honey before but never all at once and never with her knowing I had written it specifically for her. I felt raw and open, but I couldn't hide the fact that I was completely enamored with that confident, wildfire of a woman. Looking at her over the crowd, nothing mattered but her. It seemed like forever since I had been this sure about anything, and it was infused in the music that I was singing as she swayed and locked her gorgeous sea blue eyes on mine.

As the last chords faded, the crowd roared with applause. I cleared my throat and spoke into the mic. "Thank you."

Honey stood and I tipped my head toward the edge of the stage. She smoothed a hand over her curled blond hair, and my heart dropped to my knees when she moved through the crowd toward the stage. I handed my guitar to Jose backstage, hopped off the platform stage, and landed at her feet. Without a word, she crushed her lips to mine.

I wound my arms around her small waist, pulling Honey into me. I could smell the warm citrusy scent of her and I was drowning. A catcall from someone in the crowd was the only thing that stopped me from completely devouring her.

"You sure know how to sweep a girl off her feet." Honey smiled into our kiss, and I held her breathless body hard against mine.

I laid a kiss against the thin skin just below her ear, and her throaty laugh was a shot of desire that settled straight between my thighs. "Let's get outta here."

"No way, rock star. You just outed us in front of *everyone*. The least I get to do is show you off a little."

I pulled back to look at her gorgeous face and try to see if she was really upset about my very public declaration. Her eyes sparkled with mischief, and I sighed in relief. I knew that Honey was still a little hung up on keeping us a secret but on that stage I said *fuck it* and followed my gut.

Thank fuck that worked out.

Honey wound her arm in mine and leaned her pretty blond head against my bicep. I leaned over, took a deep pull of the warm scent on her hair, and kissed the top of her head. For the first time in my entire adult life, she made me feel like I could say goodbye to all the horrible things that I had done before her.

～

"You aren't going to let me win, are you?" Honey glared at me through her thick, long lashes.

I grinned at her and squeezed the baseball in my hands. Six milk bottles were all that stood between me and winning our bet. I knew these games were rigged and the money went to charity anyway, but the athlete in me couldn't walk away without giving it my best shot. I traced the red laces of the baseball with the tips of my fingers. One swirl of the ball in my hand and I wound back and pitched, releasing the ball toward the stack of aluminum milk jugs at the opposite end.

"All but one!" I whooped, pumping one fist in the air with a smile.

"Show off," she said and moved closer, bumping my hip with hers. I pulled her close to me and tried to ignore the proximity of her ass to my dick.

Fuck, man. This girl is something else.

Honey was so effortlessly sexy that I couldn't help but feel the pulse of my cock at her nearness. She bumped that firm, round ass backward, moving me out of her space.

She tossed the small baseball from one hand to the other, and determination creased a hard line in her forehead. With the ball in her left hand, she pulled back and let it fly. All six milk jugs exploded and came tumbling down.

"We have a winner!" called Mr. Richardson, who was working the game. "One twenty-five dollar gift certificate to the grocery store, ma'am." He dramatically placed the paper voucher in Honey's hands with a bow. She clutched it to her chest and jumped with excitement. My chest pinched at how fucking cute she was.

"You cheated," I teased, plucking the voucher from her hand and pretending to look at it carefully.

Honey jumped to try to grab it as I held it out of her reach.

"I did not! That was four years of high school softball, thank you very much. Hand it over!" She giggled and squealed as I handed her the prize but wound my arms around her midsection.

"You smell so good. I think I dream about how good you smell," I whispered in her ear. A low *"mmmm"* rumbled in her throat. "You finally gonna let me twirl you around that dance floor?" I nipped at her neck and was rewarded with a hitch in her breath as she pulled me through the crowd toward the wooden dance floor.

Once we got there, Lincoln had Joanna wrapped in his arms as they swayed to the music of the band. He reached a hand to me and shook it once, hitting me with the intensity of his stare. "'Bout time, brother," he said with a hard pat to my back.

I nodded at him and squeezed his hand in return. I placed my hand in Honey's and twirled her once as we walked toward the center of the dance floor. Her eyes were on fire, and laughter bubbled out of her. I couldn't imagine a better feeling than holding Honey in my arms while we were surrounded by our family and friends, all having a great night at the Sagebrush Festival.

I scanned the crowd, looking to see if my parents were still around. I planned to introduce Honey to them as soon as I could, but there was no sign of them. Last I'd seen my dad, he was shooting the shit with the old ranchers who swapped bull riding stories or tall tales about the land—most of which were total bullshit. Mom wasn't near the ladies of the Women's Club so I assumed they must have gone home. As my eyes swept past the crowd, I did see Jackie—her frizzy, bleached hair and dark eyes pinned me in place. She shook her head once in disgust and rolled her eyes before turning her back to me.

Acrid bile rose in my throat, and I tried to clear it. I hated that the return of Nate's girlfriend, the mere sight of her, caused needles to prick at my scalp and a cold tingle to run down my spine.

She knows the truth. She knows you really aren't the good guy you pretend to be.

"Hey, where'd you go?" Honey's eyebrows furrowed and she brushed a stray tendril of hair off my forehead.

I looked into her deep blue eyes, admiring the small ring of emerald green that wound around the irises. "I'm right here with you, baby."

She eyed me warily, but as the song wound down, she brushed her lips against my ear. "How about we go to your place and you can sing me that song again?"

"One condition," I growled. "You get naked and let me worship your body while I do it."

IN THE DIM light of my bedroom, I leaned against the headboard and felt supremely self-conscious. I plucked a few chords but didn't start a song. Honey walked out of the bathroom, her curled blond hair tumbling over one shoulder and I couldn't breathe.

She wore a red lace lingerie set—her tits were pushed high, and the thin red lace barely covered her hard, tight nipples. A second strip of fabric traced over the curves of her breasts. My eyes roved over her tight little body, and heat wound around my back as I took in the thin swatch of red lace that dipped in a V from her hips to between her thighs. A matching garter belt showed off her trim waist and the swell of her hips, and I ground my teeth together to keep from coming on sight.

Where the fuck she found something like that in Chikalu Falls was a mystery but I didn't care. She stopped at the door to the bathroom. Her eyes raked over me as she bit her lip. Sitting, with my guitar across my lap, I covered the growing swell of my cock through my boxer briefs.

One hand brushed across her midsection as she bit her lower lip and looked at me under heavy-lidded lashes. "Sing my song," she said warmly as her eyes darkened. Her voice was quiet but thick with desire.

I obeyed, starting slowly and plucking the chords to the opening lines. I cleared my throat, suddenly feeling more and more nervous to sing Honey her song in the intimate confines of my bedroom.

As I sang, I watched her start to move her body with the music. She swayed and twirled as the light from a candle on my dresser flickered across her golden skin, and my nerves were replaced by a heady determination. I had to close my eyes to concentrate on the song and not on the hard throb of my cock as I watched her.

I could feel Honey move toward me, sliding her body against mine as the last notes of her song rattled out of my chest. Honey arched her back, and I moved the guitar to the floor so I could cover her warm, languid body with mine. My cock ached to be inside of her. I pressed my body against her skin to feel every part of me against her softness. The hard length of my dick pressed against her thigh, and I felt my insides hollow out.

Honey had never been a quick fuck, but somewhere between a fun roll in the hay and her moving to town and upending my life, she had become my everything.

I dragged my fingertips from her knee, up the inside of her soft thighs, and teased the seam of her lacy panties that were pulsing with heat. Tension shot straight between my legs as my cock begged to be inside of her. Being this close to her was the closest I'd ever let myself come to pure, blissed-out happiness.

I moved my body over hers, placing a searing kiss across her full lips. "I love you like this."

My heart stuttered. An *I love you* definitely slipped its way in there, and I didn't let my mind travel to what exactly that meant or that I almost stopped that phrase with a period. I was completely in the moment and decided to just ride out the feeling of hope mixed with fear.

My palm paused at the junction of her thighs as my middle finger traced her thong from her soft ass cheeks up her center and to her clit. I pressed and teased circles around that tight bundle of nerves.

Honey's hands fisted at her sides, clutching the sheets beneath her. I licked and sucked a burning path down the muscles that ran up the sides of her slender neck. A low moan escaped her full lips.

She moved her hands between my legs and traced the ridge of my cock through my boxer briefs before pulling them down. I helped and tossed them on the floor.

"Why do you feel so good?" she asked.

"I think I was made for you, baby." My breaths were coming out hard and fast as she palmed my cock. My hands moved up toward the thin fabric of her bra. I thumbed over the hard peaks of her nipples before tugging at the edge and pushing the lace below her bouncy tits. The air hit her nipple, and her swift intake of breath had me pushing my hips into her hands.

"You're so fucking perfect, doll. I can't even believe you're here with me." My words tumbled over themselves as I tried to express how I felt to have her pliant and willing in my bed.

"Stop," she breathed. I immediately stilled and waited for her next words. "I need you in my mouth. Get up here." Honey pulled up at my arms and slid her body under mine.

My hips thrust forward as she shimmied her body lower on the bed.

Straddling her precious face, I stilled. Honey's eyes went wild as she wound one hand around the base of my cock as I tipped my hips forward. Her full pink lips brushed over the head of my cock, and it jerked in response. Her tongue moved over my shaft and licked me from base to tip. A shiver of desire wound down my spine as I sucked in a breath. "Oh, fuck."

A small satisfied laugh escaped her just before she opened and took my length the entire way down her throat. I stilled my hips—I didn't want to hurt her—but she grabbed my ass, pumping me into her mouth. I braced myself on the headboard and rocked my hips as she sucked my cock.

My mind went hazy and white. This fiercely independent woman was surrendering herself to me, allowing me to take control and have her. Tension swirled and built at the base of my spine, and if I wasn't careful, I would have come in her mouth like a two-pump chump. I hissed out a breath and gripped the headboard harder.

"If you don't stop, I'm going to come," I warned.

Honey cupped my balls and teased my sensitive skin before she licked up the base of my cock. "I want you to come," she said with her voice low. She licked the sides of my dick, and I had to clench my thighs to keep from shooting my load all over her.

"Not before I get to taste you, sweetheart."

I backed my legs down the bed and found Honey hot and wet. I gently slid her thong down her legs, letting my fingertips glide across her smooth skin. Gripping under her knees, I spread her thighs apart and appreciated her slick, wet folds as they opened for me.

"I want to taste you," I warned as I lowered my head

and dragged my tongue across her center. She moaned deeply and her hips pushed upward toward my face. Her taste was as intoxicating as her perfume, and I devoured her pussy. A tightness pinched in my chest as I thought about how good, how deeply satisfying it was to make Honey feel this worshipped.

She laced her fingers in my hair and tugged, and I liked the sharp pain that shot down my scalp. My tongue dipped into her pussy, and I felt her pulse around me. I pushed my face harder into her, feeling her pussy cover me as I lapped and sucked.

My dick throbbed with need. I wanted to be surrounded by her. She felt the need too and pulled on my shoulders to lift me up to her.

"Fill me, Colin. Now," She begged with a raspy breath.

Moving over her, I reached for a condom in the night-stand. After rolling it down my aching shaft, I lifted her hips. My hard cock pulsed with anticipation as her pussy glistened in the low lighting of my room. I watched as the head of my cock teased her opening. I found her tight entrance and pushed my hips forward, watching her pussy swallow the head of my cock.

I watched as I slid through her wet folds. I moved achingly slow, savoring the feel of her walls squeezing me. A guttural grunt escaped me with each thrust as I increased the pace. My hands stroked and teased her nipples as I brought us both closer and closer to the release we were chasing. As my balls tightened and I knew I was close, I tipped my hips forward and ground the base of my cock against her swollen clit. My hand found the side of her face, and she leaned into me. I moved my hand under her jaw, lifting her eyes to meet mine.

"You," I ground out. "I always needed you."

On my words she exploded around me. Hot, rhythmic pulses massaged my cock and I stilled. My release pushed thick ropes of desire into her, and with every lift of her hips, she milked more from me.

My arms felt weak and shaky, and I lowered my body onto her. I eased to the side, careful not to crush her beneath me.

"How can you do this to me?" she asked.

"I only want to make you feel good, baby."

She hummed and raked a hand down my chest and abs. "I feel like I could float away on a cloud."

Hot and sticky but not giving a *fuck*, I bundled her up and pulled her closer to me. Nothing could take that moment from us.

TWENTY-SEVEN

CHIKALU CHATTER

COLIN MCCOY PROFESSES HIS AFFECTIONS

COLIN MCCOY SERENADED *his way into Honey James's heart. For many, the highlight of our annual Sagebrush festival came during an onstage musical set, Mr. Colin McCoy professed his affections by performing an original ballad dedicated to Honey James. While we are used to the crooner's velvet voice, a song dedicated to a specific woman is a first for our talented musician. Female hearts were broken across the county, to be sure.*

After months of speculation, the heartfelt song ended, and the pair rushed toward each other in a romantic embrace. Cheers erupted from the crowd as they shared a passionate kiss better suited behind closed doors. Those who participated in the "Are They or Aren't They" betting pool may collect your winnings from Jared Lifton on Sunday after church.

TWENTY-EIGHT

HONEY

"I THINK I'm in love with you." I whispered the words so low, so quietly, they could barely be considered real. Colin's deep, heavy breathing assured me that he was asleep, and in that moment I felt brave enough to give voice to the incessant loop running in my head.

I leaned my head to the right, and the corner of my eye caught the blue glow of the clock on his nightstand. 11:50 p.m. Snuggling back into him, I breathed in his rich, earthy scent. That stupid fucking candle didn't even come close to how good he smelled. Colin lay spent and warm beneath me. His large, muscled arm draped across my back, and I had one leg flung across his torso, my arm across his chest. He was warm and the slow *tha-thunk* of his heartbeat was the exact opposite of the galloping in my own chest.

I lifted one hand and traced the hard lines of his chest, moving down over his abs. Even in sleep they had cut lines, and I dipped my fingers low to the spot below his hip where he was ticklish. His lower abs clenched at my touch, and a small smile played on my lips.

I'm the only one that knows he's ticklish there.

I thought back to all the times I had sex and immediately found a reason to exit stage left—as quickly as humanly possible. Staying meant sharing intimate moments, secrets, and offering a deeper part of myself. After throwing my dreams away on the notion that love meant sacrifice, I'd guarded my heart so fiercely that staying after sex was too dangerous. But in that moment, wrapped in Colin McCoy's arms, there wasn't any other place I could imagine being.

I thought back on the list of rules that I'd made for myself. The folded paper was tucked away in my panty drawer at the cottage.

HONEY'S RULES FOR A BETTER LIFE:
No fake, shallow friends
~~No hookups (no matter how hot)~~ *Well, shit.*
~~No swooning~~ *Damn him.*
~~Definitely no falling in love~~ *Clearly I'm not very good at this*
. . .
~~No deviating from the plan~~ *Fuck the plan.*

Well, one out of five isn't so bad.

What's a girl to do when she's up against the likes of Colin McCoy? I glanced up at him and appreciated the way his dark lashes swept down over the tops of his cheeks. Men always got the good eyelashes—totally unfair. Too keyed up for sleep, I carefully unpeeled myself from his side and slid out of bed. My little red lingerie from the Blush Boutique had worked wonders and were in happy little scraps on the bedroom floor. As I recalled the carnal look on Colin's face when I stepped out of the bathroom, I reminded myself to send Ms. Trina a special box of her favorite blueberry scones. That woman had a gift for pairing a woman with the perfect set of lingerie.

I crept into the bathroom and tugged a dark blue robe off the hook on the back of the linen closet door. It could nearly wrap around me twice, but I belted it and tiptoed downstairs. Quietly I pulled bacon from the fridge and started placing the rest of the ingredients for midnight BLTs on the stone island.

"I was worried you'd left."

I jumped and my breath caught when Colin's deep voice rumbled through the darkness. I turned and admired him as he stood in the doorway. His boxer briefs were tight to his thighs and left nothing to the imagination. His hair was rumpled, and a frown teased at his full mouth.

"Of course not," I answered with a laugh. "I was just hungry."

A slow smile spread across his face, and he dragged a hand across the expanse of his chest. "What do ya got?"

"Midnight BLTs, of course." I smirked. "Wanna help?"

Colin came up behind me and dragged a hand from my shoulder to my hip. My heart twirled in my chest, and I had to clear my throat. The simple, intimate gesture had me feeling completely unraveled. If he wasn't careful, I would never want to leave.

"What if she hates me?" I stared at Joanna through the mirror in my tiny cottage. Nothing about the cottage felt like home—I'd spent more nights at Colin's house than I had here, but I was going to meet his family tonight, and I needed time and space to fully prepare.

"She could never hate you. You're amazing!" Joanna

cheerfully moved through the small closet, pushing blouses from one side to the other. "This is cute." She held up a soft, silk dress with a deep V. Its kaftan-style sleeves and sheer material gave it a 1930s, old-Hollywood vibe.

"I don't know." I chewed my lip. "It's probably too much."

"I think you should go with something that makes you feel good, but I still think you should be *you*."

"I know but this is meeting his parents. I want to make a good impression, and a lot of these clothes I haven't even touched since moving here." I frowned at the thousands of dollars hanging, unworn, in the cedar closet.

What a waste.

I ran the smooth sleeve through my fingers. "So much of this doesn't even feel like *me* anymore, Jo. Did you know that I wore flannel yesterday? Flannel!"

Joanna laughed at my dramatic disregard for her favorite material, and I hated to admit that it was really fucking comfortable. I tucked away the gnawing thought that Chikalu Falls was changing me.

Is it Chikalu that's changing you or Colin? Wouldn't be the first time you upended your life for a man.

"What about this one?" Joanna interrupted my thoughts by holding up a cream cashmere sweater that felt like a cloud. It was thin enough to work for the oddly warm September we seemed to be having.

"Hell, yes! It's perfect—cute, comfy, and fits like a dream." I pulled the fabric to my face and enjoyed the luxurious, downy softness. I tossed the sweater over my gray tank top and slipped on a pair of slim jeans that made my ass look fantastic. A pair of long necklaces and I was set.

I fluffed my hair in the mirror and dabbed on a little perfume. When I finished, Jo wrapped her arms around my shoulders and looked at me in the mirror. "Be you. That's more than good enough."

I squeezed her arms, and my eyes shut at the same time —thankful that I had found my way back to Jo and hoping I would stay.

I TOOK the last step up to the porch, and when I looked up, I stopped abruptly, wobbling the homemade pecan pie in my hands.

My brain stumbled and couldn't quite reconcile what I was seeing. In the doorway stood a handsome older man— Colin was going to age beautifully if his father was any indication—and Jean. My wonderful, loving, gentle Jean stood tucked under his arm, looking almost as confused as I felt. The only difference was the small smile that played at the corners of her mouth while I was quite sure my jaw was scraping the floor.

"Jean?" I finally asked.

"Mom?" Colin asked at the same time, clearly just as confounded as I was.

"Honey! Oh." she clapped her hands together. "I was so hopeful!" Her shy smile broke into a wide grin as she opened her arms and stepped toward me. Jean pulled me into a tight hug and rocked me into a circle. On the trip around, I faced Colin and looked into his deep hazel eyes.

How could I not see it before? The beautiful voice. The same deep green-brown hazel eyes. I am such a dumbass.

"Do you two know each other?" Colin asked.

"Honey, I'm Keith. It's nice to finally meet you." Colin's dad took the pie plate from me. He then reached for my hand, and I shook it absently, still trying to clear the cobwebs from my brain.

Colin scrubbed a wide palm across the back of his neck. "You know my mom?" he asked me.

"Um, I . . . I mean, I know Jean." I laughed because what the fuck else could I do?

"Well, Mom, Dad. This is Honey, my girlfriend." Colin opened his arm in my direction, and I tucked myself underneath him as he squeezed my shoulder. We hadn't exactly talked about *what we were,* but the sound of him calling me his girlfriend had my skin tingling under my shirt.

"Come in, please!" Jean bubbled with excitement. "Oh, this is just too much!"

I hadn't seen her this effervescent in all the time we'd gotten coffee or taken a walk on the path that wound around the library. She seemed lighter somehow.

As we walked through the front door, Colin whispered in my ear, "This is so fucking weird."

I looked up at him and smiled tightly. I whispered through my gritted smile, "You have no idea . . ."

We walked into a small, cozy foyer that reminded me of old home movies. It smelled clean and warm and a little spicy—like apple pie—and I smiled to myself as I thought about Colin growing up in such a lovely home.

"Jean, I have to say, this is unexpected!" I decided that my directness could help break the ice.

Jean handed me a cold glass of lemonade. "Isn't it though? A week or so ago I heard Margie at the beauty parlor trying to dish the dirt. Lord knows only half of what she spills is the truth . . . but I was hopeful."

"No, no, no. Your son is Artie. You said so on the phone . . ."

"Jesus, mom. Really?" Colin laughed and a splotchy red

patch bloomed up his neck from under the collar of his shirt.

Jean swatted a hand in his direction. "Oh, stop. Artie is a nickname." She moved toward a small table against the wall and grabbed a picture frame. "Nate loved to play Knights of the Round Table, and Colin was such a good sport about it. He was Arthur and Nate was his Lancelot." Her delicate fingers smoothed over the glass and lingered a beat on the gap-toothed grins of the little boys. She handed the photo to me.

I took the frame and couldn't help but laugh. Colin looked about nine with sandy, cowlicked hair and gangly limbs. The photo was similar to the one Colin had framed at his house. This time the boys were dressed in cardboard armor and wooden swords. His younger brother stood tall, hands on his hips and laughter on his lips. My heart ached for the loss of Colin's little brother.

When I looked at him, the embarrassment was replaced with an empty stare, and I realized I wasn't the only one who built walls to protect my heart. My heartbeat pounded in my ears as I waded through uncharted territory. I reached for Colin's hand and found strength in his strong, wide palm. Gently gripping Jean's forearm with my other hand, I said, "That's such a happy memory. Thank you for sharing that with me."

Jean's eyes misted and her husband pulled her into a hug. Colin stiffened at my side.

TWENTY-NINE

COLIN

HONEY BEING friends with my mom was a total mindfuck. Standing with her in my parents' entryway with my mother on the brink of a meltdown was not how I imagined them meeting. I hadn't truly opened up to Honey about Nate or the circumstances around his death, and tension wound up my back and settled in my jaw.

How much had Mom shared about Nate's death?

Does Honey know it's my fault?

What other embarrassing shit has Mom shared about me?

To her credit, Honey seemed unfazed by the sudden heaviness that settled in the room. The air was thick, and for a beat we were all quiet.

Finally my dad cleared his throat. "Well, sweetheart, let's get these two settled in, and we can get started on dinner."

Watching my father rub small, slow circles across my mother's back, I realized how devoted he was to her—how in tune to her moods he truly was. In light of everything they had been through, he stood by her. Their love was the real thing, and it hit me that it was a large reason I had never wanted or been able to settle for less.

One look at Honey and I felt a deep tug in my chest. She glanced at me through long lashes, and I could see a thousand questions tumbling through her mind. Talking about Nate was still tender for everyone, like a bruise blooming just below the surface, but you couldn't help but push on it, or a thousand paper cuts you couldn't see, but the sting burned across your skin.

My parents moved silently to the kitchen, and Honey wound her arms around me in the quiet foyer of my parents' home. I tipped her head with both hands and stroked a thumb across her cheekbone. "I'm sorry. I should have warned you that things can get . . . intense."

She leaned her face into my hands like she always did. "There's nothing to be sorry for. I like hearing about Nate."

Her one-dimpled smile was genuine and pure, and I had to stop myself from dropping to my knees and worshipping her. The want I felt for her was unfamiliar and strangely exciting. Instead of crumbling in front of her, I placed a kiss on her lips and pulled her into my arms. I wanted to share things with her—more than just my bed. I wanted to laugh with her, bring her coffee every morning, teach her to play cards, be the man who got to show her off on the dance floor, all of the small, everyday moments that meant she was mine. I wanted to tell her everything about that night with Nate and what came after, but the words clogged in my throat.

"Fuck." I cleared my throat. "I'm a mess."

Honey's chin lifted and she met my eyes. "You're not a mess." She placed a kiss on my cheek. "Well . . . maybe you're a little bit of a mess. But right now you're my mess."

Right now.

Her words burned a path through my veins. Honey was talking like this relationship was temporary when I was having very *not* temporary feelings. It was the kind of thing I needed to keep in check if I was going to figure out a way to keep her.

"Dinner's ready if you two are hungry." Mom's soft voice floated out into the foyer. She'd lost a little of her sparkle, and darkness had seeped in just under her eyes. She was still teetering on the edge of collapse. I could feel it.

"It smells delicious." Honey kept her voice bright as she stepped toward the kitchen.

"We're having salad and homemade spaghetti and meatballs. It was Nate's favorite. I hope you're hungry."

My body went rigid. My mother was always doing that since Nate died—claiming something was his favorite when in fact, spaghetti was *my* favorite. Once she told Ms. Trina that a clay flower vase I had made in seventh grade art class was Nate's. I'd blown up at her and pointed to my initials carved in the bottom, and she *still* claimed that she distinctly remembered Nate making that at school. It baffled me but more, it enraged me.

"Sounds amazing!" Honey said. She looked at me like I was losing my goddamn mind as I stood there with clenched fists and flared nostrils. Her hand on my back was the only thing keeping me from flying off the fucking handle.

Honey kept a constant stream of pleasant chatter throughout dinner though she eyed me warily. She charmed my dad with funny stories about the old men at the coffee shop, and it was clear that she and Mom had a deeper friendship than I'd realized. Her eyes flicked to me, and she placed a hand over mine, but I couldn't shake the foul mood that dampened the evening. I felt like a petulant child and not like the man Honey deserved.

I will never be enough for her. For either of them.

My father's voice broke through my dark thoughts. "Colin, have you decided what you'll do about the expansion? I ran into Ray Shaw last week, and he was excited about the possibilities."

Fuck, fuck, fuck.

Panic swirled in my gut. "Oh, uh . . . " I cleared my throat. "No. That's not going to happen. Mom, did you get a good turnout for the Women's Club raffle?"

"Well, that's strange. I swear he said that you'd settled on it," Dad continued, despite my attempt to talk about something—anything—else.

Honey slanted me a look, and her eyes narrowed slightly. I didn't have the balls to even look her in the eyes.

"No, that can't be right, darling," Mom added. "Honey's bakery, Biscuits & Honey, is right next door. You know that."

Honey's body was now turned toward me, and her head tipped slightly. A cold prickle crept down my arm.

"He must be mistaken." It wasn't a complete lie—I had no intention of taking Honey's bakery from her, despite the fact I would eventually own the space once Mr. Stevens was ready. It was a temporary lie of omission, and I planned to clear that up as soon as I could explain it to her in a way that didn't make me feel like such an asshole.

I managed to turn the conversation to safer ground, and we got through dessert only having to ignore the thinly veiled layer of guilt that came along with a visit home. Tucking Honey into the cab of my truck, I released a sigh as I rounded the hood and climbed in. An ache between my shoulder blades pinched at the base of my neck and threatened to settle deep in my bones. I climbed into the truck and rubbed my palms up and down my thighs.

Honey had her arm propped up on the window and her head resting on her hand. She reached her left hand across the cab to knead the bundle of knots that formed in my neck. Her face was tipped toward me, and it struck me again just how lucky I was to share these tiny moments with her. I didn't deserve any of the kindness she was giving me. If she knew the truth, she would recoil from me instead of trying to make me feel better.

"That didn't go exactly as planned." I started.

"Hey. It was good. You dad is so nice, and I already know your mom—which is surprising but kind of awesome. I don't have to worry about impressing her because we're already friends."

I shook my head as I pulled the truck out of the driveway. "That's still so fucking weird."

"Right? I had no idea, I swear." Honey held her hands up in front of her to prove her innocence.

"I know, babe."

We sat in silence as her hand found my neck again, and she continued to knead the tension out of my tight muscles. Country music played low on the radio, and I headed back toward my house without even asking. It had been a while since I'd stopped thinking of it at *my place* and started thinking of it as *our place,* and I wasn't altogether sure what to do with those feelings.

HOT WATER POUNDED the aching muscles in my back. Once we'd gotten back home, Honey slipped out to the front porch to make a phone call, and I stripped down and headed into the shower. I needed to wash this day off of me.

My forehead was pressed against the tile as the heat of

the water spread across my back. When the shower door opened and Honey slipped in with me, the warmth spread lower, settling between my thighs. She stood behind me, wrapping her small body around my torso. Her tits pressed against my back, and I held her arms against me. She pressed soft kisses into my back.

"Fuck, Honey. You feel so good." I moaned and her kisses turned hungry. A scrape of her teeth against my side had my growing cock twitching in response.

"I want to make you feel good." She raked her nails across my abs, and I turned to face her.

"You do," I said, looking deeply into her sea blue eyes.

Those eyes flicked down, then up to mine, and a wicked grin flashed across her face. Honey licked, then bit her full lip. She moved her hands down, tracing my abs again as they traveled lower. My stomach tightened as she came dangerously close to my cock. Her hands brushed down my thighs, teasing me—I wanted her to wrap her fist around my cock and pump me hard, but she continued her torturous caress, up and down my thighs and around my torso.

Honey kissed my chest, and her tongue swirled around my nipple. I hissed in a breath and dragged my fingers down her slick back. She lowered herself, kneeling down in front of me, and my heart thundered in my chest.

I grunted as her hand wrapped around my hard cock. She squeezed the base and ran her tongue up the underside and looped her tongue around the crown. I pushed the shower head so the water ran in rivulets down her slender back and out of her eyes. She looked at me and smiled as she pulled the swollen head of my cock between her full lips.

"Oh, fuck."

Her throaty chuckle rumbled through her, and heat shot up my back as the vibrations moved over my sensitive skin.

In this position it would have been so easy for me to push my hips forward, claiming her mouth, and every inch of me wanted to do it. I loved how this woman could cut you down with a raised eyebrow, and yet she was on her knees, surrendering herself to me. She trusted me with her vulnerability, and that thought alone pulled me dangerously close to the edge.

I moved a piece of hair from her face as she pulled me to the back of her throat. Her lashes were low as I watched her full lips stretch around my thick shaft. With one hand holding the base, she pumped and sucked my length. I gently pumped my hips forward, and with a moan of approval, I fucked her mouth. Over and over, I pumped into her as my body coiled and begged for release.

"Baby, I'm close. You need to stop if—"

"No," she said, dragging her tongue along the ridge of my cock. "I want it. I want you to come right here." Honey slid one hand down her chest and across her hard nipple.

At her words, I was unleashed. Honey placed her hand on my hip and pulled my cock back into her warm mouth. The tightness of her mouth and throat had the edges of my vision turning spotty. Reaching my breaking point, I fisted my cock as she pushed both of her round, wet tits together and up. I stroked harder. When she pinched her nipples and moaned, my orgasm broke free. Hot and thick, I painted her flawless body, claiming it as my own. The intensity slammed into me, and my legs felt shaky and weak.

"Yes, Colin." Honey's voice was laced with indulgent pleasure. The warm water washed her chest as her head tipped back. Once I regained my bearings, I reached down to help her to her feet.

Fire burned in my throat as a fresh, unexpected wave of emotion crashed into me. The center of my chest felt hollowed out as the pressure and tension of the evening tingled down my limbs. Holding Honey, I reached behind her and shut off the water.

As I held her in silence, my nose burned and my eyes pricked, and I willed the sudden tears away.

What the fuck, dude? Get it together. Stop crying all over her, with your dick in your hands just because she gave you the most intense blowjob of your life.

I was used to burying my emotions and stuffing them down whenever they threatened to resurface, but in the confines of the shower with Honey in my arms, I felt stripped bare. In that moment I shed my armor and the overwhelming emotions that swirled just beneath the surface.

"I'm sorry, I just . . . " I didn't know how to finish the sentence.

"Hey." Her hand lifted to my face, but if I looked her in the eye, I knew I would completely lose my shit.

I dropped my forehead to hers, and when she wrapped her arms fiercely around me, a hot tear tumbled down my cheek. I blew out a breath to steady myself and cleared my throat.

I swiped my thumb and finger across my eyes and tried to steel myself against whatever shit had dredged up to the surface. These big feelings for her, the visit with my parents, guilt for Nate, guilt for not telling Honey about the shop, all stacked on top of each other, crushing me under the weight of it all, and it just felt like too much.

Honey moved quietly out of the shower, grabbed a towel, and pulled it around my body. "Hey, cowboy. Let's get you some rest."

I wanted to argue, but my eyes felt gritty and my body drained.

"I don't deserve you. All I want at this moment is to keep you."

With a kiss and a gentle shove toward the bed, she smiled, and a flicker of some unknown emotion passed over her face before she turned.

She's not the keeping kind. She hasn't talked about staying or even attempted to find a permanent residence in Chikalu yet.

A lump formed in my chest, but like the lovesick asshole I was, I followed her to the bed.

THIRTY

HONEY

IN THE DARK we lay facing each other, sharing the same breath. I stroked the hair away from his forehead and searched his eyes for answers. His unexpected swell of emotions in the shower was more than just a physical response from a blowjob—I knew that I was good but not that good. Something was definitely up, and if he didn't deal with whatever it was that was eating at him, things were going to get messy.

I realized before I ever got involved with Colin that he could be complicated and intense, and I tramped down the skittering of panic that rippled in my chest. I placed one hand under my pillow and let the heavy silence blanket us in the darkness.

"There's something I have to tell you," Colin started. Gooseflesh erupted on my skin, and a trickle of panic coursed through my veins. "How much did my mom tell you about me or Nate's death?" he asked.

"Not much," I answered truthfully. "I know that Jean has a son that passed away, but her emotions are too raw to ever get into it. Mostly we talk about books or cooking, things like that. I don't ask much because I know it's painful to talk about."

Colin closed his eyes, and his brow furrowed slightly. His voice was raspy and laced with pain when he spoke. "Nate got wrapped up in some shady shit, but he's dead because of me."

I searched his troubled, hazel eyes, unable to formulate a response. They were haunted in the way only people who've experienced something truly traumatic look wary and lost. Instinctively I said, "No, I'm sure that's not—"

"It's true," he said, cutting my argument short. His voice turned hard as he continued. "He always kind of struggled with fitting in and finding his place. Making friends, decent grades, staying out of trouble—It was always easier for Avery and me. It's not really advertised on the tourism brochures but with the heavy Irish immigrant population, sometimes there's rumblings of mob activity. After he died I paid off a bunch of gambling debts. I don't know . . ."

My eyes widened. It was known that the Irish mob had quietly settled in parts of Montana, but near a place like Chikalu? It was a lot to take in.

My stunned silence allowed Colin to continue. "Whenever Nate needed me, he called. Usually, I could talk him down and help him find a way to solve the latest problem he'd found himself in. But that night, instead of answering and talking him through whatever recent breakdown he was having, I ignored the call."

My lip quivered and I bit the inside of my cheek to keep my emotions in check. I stayed silent, allowing him to finish.

"The difference was that night, he went home and shot himself. So yeah, it's my fault."

"Oh, Colin," I said quietly. "You can't possibly believe that."

"Believe what? The truth?" Colin worked his jaw as darkness shadowed his hazel eyes.

I traced my fingers over his angry brow. "He made a choice that I wish he never made, but you can't carry that weight."

"It's my weight to carry." My heart ached at the sadness in his voice. A swell pinched in my chest and nerves crept up my back.

With a deep breath, I whispered the only words that tumbled through my mind. "Then let me carry it with you."

WITH COLIN OPENING UP to me about his brother, I felt a deep, intertwined connectedness that I had never experienced with anyone else, and I wasn't sure how to untangle those feelings. Part of me wanted to wrap myself around him and feel the warmth of his body seep into me. The other part wanted to hop in the Chevelle and get the hell out of there because I had *zero* fucking clue how to be the actual girlfriend he deserved.

There were moments when it felt like he was on the brink of saying something big, but he would shake his head and turn. I couldn't figure out what his deal was, and it made me jumpy as fuck. The words *I love you too!* almost tumbled out of me over dinner when Colin said, "I love comfort food," and I had to shove an extra-large forkful of macaroni and cheese in my mouth to keep quiet and hide my reddening cheeks.

Between the online business classes I had started, and diving headfirst into planning a grand opening, I kept myself busy and distracted from dealing with my feelings for Colin. If we could keep everything status quo, I would be fine.

Joanna had been just as busy with guided fishing tours, and I missed my sister, so we had decided to plan a girls' night out. Chikalu Falls was a small town, but there were a few places I'd yet to try. On the outskirts of town was a newer brewery owned by one of Maggie's brothers. She was coming too, along with some of the friends that Jo had made since moving to town. We decided to go to the brewery for a few appetizers and some drinks, though we all figured at some point we'd end up back at The Pidge.

"Are you for real right now?" Jo looked me up and down before dropping her hands against the outside of her thighs.

"What?" I said innocently as I did a slow twirl.

"I didn't realize girls' night out meant getting so fancy." She toyed with the inside of her lip as she glanced at her casual jeans and black top. Joanna was pretty but she never really did much in terms of jewelry or fancy shoes.

I, on the other hand, had missed having a reason to go out and get dolled up so I'd gone all out with my outfit tonight. Hair curled, lashes blackened, lips red. I wore a tight black bodycon dress that I'd paired with a distressed denim jacket and cuffed sleeves. My heels were sky high and sparkly. I felt like a badass rock star, and the thought made me think of Colin. A sexy little zing danced up my spine—I couldn't wait for him to see me in it.

And peel it off me.

"Well I think you look perfect," I said, "but if you want to add a little sparkle, I have a chunky necklace that would look great with the black." I pulled a long double strand necklace from my dresser drawer at the cottage and held it up for her. She played with its placement, swiped on an extra layer of mascara, and we were set.

"Let's roll, baby girl," I said. Jo laughed as we left my cottage and walked toward the driveway.

True to form, Lincoln was sitting on the front porch, nursing a beer. As we walked up, he stood—his massive frame ambling slowly toward us. The hard lines of his face softened when his gaze raked over Jo. My chest tightened at how openly and fully this man loved my sister.

"You look amazing," he said.

Jo blushed and went up on her tiptoes to kiss Linc. She whispered something in his ear, and though I could hardly believe it, the man actually blushed.

Lincoln looked at me smiling at him, and he cleared his throat. "I can drive you ladies."

"No way, man." I flipped my curled blond hair over one shoulder. "This is girls' night out, and we look fine as hell. We're taking the Chevelle."

PRONGHORN BREWERY WAS FAR ENOUGH out of town that when we arrived, I only recognized a handful of faces. Maggie wound through the crowd toward the back to find her brother, Hayes. The bar was upscale, with heavy wood and iron accents, and a nice change of pace from the small-town charm of Chikalu. The entire back wall opened up like garage doors during the summer and fall months and faced a breathtaking pine forest. Fire pits with cushy seating dotted the exterior. Hayes set us up with a reserved table, and we settled in with our drink orders.

After introductions the girls and I fell into easy conver-sation over draft beers and mixed drinks. Maggie's friends were from Chikalu or Canton Springs, the town over, and they were all personable and friendly. I hadn't felt so at ease in forever, and my mind flicked back to the friends I had left in Butte. We hadn't connected in a while, and I let the moment of guilt pass when I realized that I didn't really miss the shallow relationships of my former life.

"Okay gals, next round's on me, but first I'm going to hit the ladies'." I excused myself from the table.

In the quiet of the bathroom, my ears pricked at the entrance of a small, but vocal, group. The voices dripped with disgust at the sink.

Did they just say Colin McCoy?

"I thought so too, at first," one continued, "but there's no way it's serious."

I held my breath and leaned closer, as if that would help me hear every syllable.

"She is gorgeous, though," another said.

"Please," the first scoffed. "Sure, she's a pretty face, but she doesn't know anything about life in Chikalu."

"Maybe but they seem pretty serious to me."

"Serious until I show up again. Colin and I dated for a while and he doesn't know I'm back in town yet." Her laugh had my stomach filling with dread—I was now certain they were talking openly about my boyfriend.

"You know what I heard?" She continued, "He's only dating her because her little bakery is in the way of him expanding the bar. My cousin works in Ray Shaw's office, and she told me that Colin has a contract to *own* the bakery storefront."

My thoughts got hung up on her words.

What the actual fuck?

"Just goes to show, she's hanging on his coattails. She could never open it on her own. She clearly needs his money and reputation. But speaking of reputation—I bet I'll have his face between my thighs in less than a month."

Cold dread wound around my throat and my back stiffened. I had no clue what these bitches were talking about, but I was damn sure not going to hide in the toilet while they talked shit about me.

I tramped down the wave of frenzied emotions and slipped on the calmest expression I could manage. Ice surged through my veins as I walked out of the stall toward the sink. Washing my hands, I looked at the group through the mirror, hooking one eyebrow up at them.

"Anything you'd like to say to my face, ladies?" I asked as I slowly dried my hands.

The threesome glanced around at each other, their mouths popped open—each into a little O. They looked like scared guppies, and their surprise fanned the flames of my anger.

"No? Well next time you decide to talk shit about someone, I suggest you make sure you're actually alone." I set my shoulders and walked toward the door.

"Oh," I continued over my shoulder with a small laugh, "and if you ever order anything from *my* bakery, I suggest you eat with caution. I'm not above adding in a little something special for the three of you."

Their united gasps spread an evil smile across my face and kicked my adrenaline into high gear. I stalked toward the bar at the side of the brewery and leaned a hip against the heavy wood. A good-looking bartender with great biceps tipped his chin and headed in my direction. His broad shoulders made me think of Colin, and a trickle of desire pooled in my belly.

"What'll it be?"

"Another round for that table over there." I pointed to Jo and the girls around the fire pit on the patio. "And a double shot of Lagavulin."

"You got it." He tapped the bar top and pulled the expensive bottle from the top shelf. He poured the amber liquid and slid the glass toward me. I thought about the words those women spewed in the bathroom. Were they true or what is just vitriol from petty, jealous women? Shaking my head, I threw the shot back in one long, hard gulp.

"Another please," I croaked around the burn. The liquid made my throat feel tight as a wave of warmth spread through my chest. The bartender eyed me warily but silently filled my glass. As he looked at me, I paused and quirked an eyebrow at him. He turned to pour the rest of the drinks for our table, and I shot back the second glass and cleared my throat. The hot burn eased the ache that had settled in my chest.

I fluffed my hair and joined the rest of my group as the server brought over our drinks. I didn't plan on getting shit-faced, but every time I thought back to what I'd overheard, I tried to drown it with another sip. Anger had finally replaced the shock that thrummed through my veins, and pretty soon I knew I was in no shape to drive. Jo knew it too, so she grabbed my keys without even asking, and we drove toward The Pidge.

THIRTY-ONE

COLIN

I GLANCED at the clock for the seven hundredth time and cursed myself for not focusing on the conversation Isabel was trying to have with me.

"I'll need next Thursday off in order to go," she said.

"Yeah, Isabel. That's fine," I answered. "Just text it to me so I can put it on the calendar." I hoped like hell she couldn't tell I had no fucking clue what she was talking about. All night I was having trouble focusing on anything but Honey. I knew she was having a fun night out with the girls, but it was hard to shake the knot-in-the-pit-of-my-stomach feeling I carried around with me all day.

It also didn't help that Nate's ex, Jackie, was posted up on a stool on the outskirts of the dance floor. She was in my direct line of sight and had no qualms about sending scathing looks my way. I got it, her dirty looks were completely valid, but they still made me feel like a bigger piece of shit than I already knew I was.

"Here comes trouble." Isabel grinned over the beer taps and nodded her head in the direction of the door.

My eyes shot up, and the trickle of excitement that ran

up my arm was replaced with confusion. Jo pushed through the heavy door with a parade of girls behind her in varying states of intoxication. Jo was laughing and smiling along with them, but seemed pretty sober. A few other women I vaguely recognized whooped and hollered at the pumping bass of the band and headed straight toward the dance floor. Honey was the caboose, and one look at her and my heart stopped in my chest.

Her black dress hugged every inch of her lush curves, and my eyes shamelessly raked over her. The cropped denim jacket did little to hide her tight little body under-neath, and her normally short legs looked a million miles long in her spiked heels. She looked out of place—in the best way—and I had to take a second to discretely adjust my jeans. From the distance I couldn't tell how much she'd had to drink, but she followed the others onto the dance floor with a sway in her hips that told me she'd had more than a few.

"Go on out there. I've got this." Isabel tipped her chin toward Honey.

My grin spread slowly as I stalked toward Honey like a beast toward a gazelle. Hunger swam in my veins, and I watched her move and sway to the music. It was late enough that everyone gave up two-stepping and line dances and moved straight to dry humping and grinding. I slid in behind her, pressing my hips forward into her ass and skimming my hands over her hips.

Honey's head whipped around, and fire danced in her eyes until recognition had a grin splitting her gorgeous face. My heart skipped a beat—I loved she was ready to fight off someone other than me dancing up behind her.

She wound her arms around my neck and pulled me into a wet, moaning kiss. I could taste the smoky burn of expensive alcohol on her tongue, and it was both intoxi-cating and concerning. I pulled back to examine her face more carefully.

Honey's head tipped backward and rolled absently. Oh yeah, she was flirting with the edge of hammered.

"You all right, darlin?" I shout-whispered in her ear.

"Mmmm," was her only response.

My jaw ticked hard at her recklessness. I knew she drove to meet the girls. Anger flared in a hot wave up my spine, and I had to press my tongue to the roof of my mouth to keep myself from going ballistic. Just as I was about to railroad her for how fucking stupid it was to drink and drive, Jo chimed in, "We've been having fun but don't worry. She didn't drive."

I nodded my head in an unspoken thank-you. I had to spread my hand wide to unfurl my fist, and I willed my pulse to slow down.

Chill the fuck out, dude. She's just having a little fun. You can't always keep tabs on her.

As I tried to remain mature and rational, Honey continued to bounce and move with the music in my arms. Anger and protectiveness melted into a warm comfort as I concentrated on the way her body moved in time with mine.

A war raged inside me—I wanted to bundle her up and take her home, but the way the soft curves of her body pushed against the hard lines of mine made me want this moment to stretch on a while longer.

"I'm on the clock." I nibbled and kissed Honey's neck. "But we can continue this later. You ladies have yourself a good time."

"Thanks, Colin!" Jo shouted at me.

"I'm sending over some food. Anyone need a round?"

A collective cheer of "hell yeah" and "whoo" confirmed the group wasn't ready to call it a night quite yet.

"Thanks, babe!" Honey shouted and dismissed me with a wink. Some chump saw an opening and moved toward Honey and the group when I sidestepped and blocked his path.

"Think again." I stared down hard at him, my fist clenched and ready to go. A big part of me wanted him to do it too.

A tip of his flat-billed trucker hat and he moved back toward his group of *bros*. Jealousy wasn't an emotion I was used to feeling, but knowing Honey had a few too many cocktails tonight had my skin prickling and heartbeat hammering in my chest.

Two baskets of soft pretzel sticks, southwest egg roll bites, and burger sliders later, I felt much better about the situation. I knew greasy bar food soaking up alcohol was a myth, but taking care of my girl made me feel more at ease and settled some of the tension in my back. Plus, it gave me a chance to kill some time before I could leave Isabel alone behind the crowded bar and invade girls' night out.

Linc and Deck had found their way in and were taking up considerable space at the corner of the wooden bar.

"Dude," Isabel teased, "you're taking up, like, four seats. That eats into my tips!"

Lincoln grunted in her direction, but his mouth tipped up in a small smile. He was known for generously over-tipping, and the servers here usually had to fight over serving his table. Isabel had nothing to worry about.

Decker was leaning over, sipping on a cold one as he pretended not to eye the group of women shaking their asses on the dance floor.

"It's your night off. See anything you like?" I asked as I wiped down the scarred wood in front of them.

"Lots of pretty girls out there tonight, but I'm getting too old for this shit. I think I'm past the point where I can accurately decipher women's ages . . . and that's a problem."

It was a good enough cover, but we both knew that his academy training and keen eye wasn't the reason he wasn't interested in hooking up tonight. I glanced over at Honey who was looking significantly more stable on her heels. Maggie and her friends flanked her, and a warmth spread through me.

If she makes friends, deep connections to this town, maybe she won't want to leave us.

I lined up three shot glasses and filled them generously with dark liquor.

I raised my glass. "To getting older, but maybe not wiser."

Linc laughed as Deck mumbled something along the lines of, "Ain't that the truth."

With Honey back on the dance floor with Jo and company, I only briefly flicked a glance in Jackie's direction. As I watched her slide off the stool and move in Honey's direction, the muscles in my back clenched, and I tightened the grip on my beer. I paused and swallowed hard past the lump that formed in my throat as Honey and Jackie walked toward each other.

THIRTY-TWO

HONEY

I WAS DRUNK AS FUCK. At least, I was when we'd gotten to The Pidge. A few sweaty songs and a shameful number of southwest egg rolls later, I was past drunk and squarely back into happily buzzed territory.

"Feeling better?" Joanna asked.

"Yeah, it was touch and go for a minute. Thanks for riding it out with me."

Jo winked. "I got you."

"Well, Linc's here," I said as I motioned toward the three obscenely handsome men talking at the bar. "It's your turn to let loose."

She eyed the glass of water that replaced Lincoln's last beer and smiled. Our server, Marissa, brought another round of beers, and I couldn't help but notice the side-eye Maggie was giving the guys.

"What's the deal with you two?" My liquid courage was still lingering around the edges of my brain, dissolving all couth I may have had.

Maggie looked at me, confused. "With who?"

"Deck." I gestured openly at the bar again.

Maggie grabbed my hand and pulled it down. "Stop that! Don't point at him."

"Ah. See." I pointed at her. "I knew there was something going on." I grinned. Maggie's friends snuck sideways glances, and I knew I had hit a nerve.

"There's nothing going on with Cole and me."

"I call bullshit. You both go all moon-eyed over each other when you think no one is watching."

"Honey!" Jo chided.

A hot flare of embarrassment hit Maggie's cheeks, but as a good-looking guy walked past our table toward the dance floor, she grabbed his arm and twirled underneath it and smiled. "I have no idea what you're talking about."

My new friends cheered her on as she danced, and one by one they filtered back onto the dance floor and found someone to two-step with.

Jo and I stuck together, dancing with each other in the protective center of our friend circle. It wasn't until I caught the death stare, clearly aimed at me, of the woman Colin had pointed out as Nate's girlfriend that I stopped and my smile faded.

Knowing I hadn't personally earned any of her dirty looks, I walked toward her as she slid off her barstool.

"Hey. I'd like to introduce myself. I'm new in town. My name is Honey."

She glared at me through the thick black lines of her smudged eyeliner. "I know exactly who you are."

Unfazed, I pressed on. "Well I've been looking over my shoulder all night trying to figure out who's the unlucky recipient of your stank eye. I couldn't find anyone, so I figured it was me. What's up with that?"

She blinked once at my directness but recovered quickly. "I guess I'm just trying to figure out why a smart woman who owns her own business would settle for a piece of shit like Colin."

"Excuse me?" I bristled and my voice rose an octave.

"But then I realized," she pressed on, "that you're just as clueless as the rest of the skanks around here. You're so obsessed with a sharp jawline and a guitar that you don't even see what's right in front of you. You wouldn't make it a day without Colin's money or reputation, and *everyone's* talking about it." Jackie barked out a laugh. "You're a laughing stock, and we all know it."

Heat flared in my cheeks, and my chest puffed out, ready to throw down, when a strong arm wrapped around my waist and practically lifted me off the ground.

"Woah, woah." Maggie's voice cut above the music from the speakers. "Stop stirring up shit, Jackie. We're all just here for a good time."

I stood to the side of the group of women and admired the protective semi-circle they'd formed around me. I was so used to defending myself that I was momentarily dumbstruck.

"Don't give me shit," Jackie spat the words in my direction. "I'm doing her a favor since everyone else in this town has their heads so far up Colin's ass they can't see the truth." Her eyes flared and met mine. "Did he tell you? Did he tell you how the only reason Nate is dead is because he's a selfish prick?"

Maggie took one step forward. "Stop talking about shit you know nothing about—" Maggie paused and shook her head, dismissing her own rant and calmness took over. "No. We're done here."

I jumped in and practically snarled. "If you've got such a problem with Colin, you shouldn't be supporting him with your hard-earned money. Maybe it's time you drink somewhere else."

Jackie huffed and sneered in disgust but grabbed the jacket hanging over the seat of her barstool. The sharp movement had the jacket swinging, sending a half-full beer bottle clanking to the floor.

Before she turned for the door, Jackie pointed a long, stilettoed fingernail in my direction. "He uses people to get what he wants. Just remember that."

I ground the enamel from my teeth to hold back a scathing response as she stomped out the door. Her friends threw crumpled bills on the table and scurried behind her.

"What did she say to you?" Colin slid a protective arm around my shoulders, but his voice was hard. My heartbeat hammered at the base of my throat as my body struggled to come down from the spike in adrenaline.

"Nothing important. It's fine." I took a steadying breath but couldn't shake the thunderous clouds that hung around my thoughts. Jackie's words nagged at me—they mirrored what I'd overheard at the brewery, and it wasn't sitting right with me.

"It's getting late," Maggie said. "Anyone else wanna call it a night?"

The small group of women murmured in agreement, and just like that girls' night out came to a screeching halt.

"Yeah, I'm bushed," Jo added with a yawn.

"Hang around with me while I finish up." Colin's voice was rich and low in my ear. A wave of desire moved through my belly, but the pang that settled behind my eyes grew stronger. I needed to think through everything that unfolded tonight.

"I think I'm going to leave with the girls. Catch up with me later?"

Disappointment—anger maybe?—briefly flashed over his face, but he hid it well. "Of course," he said, clearing his throat. "But why don't you have Linc drop you off at my place? I want to see you when I get off work."

"See you there." I faked a tight smile as best as I could given my foul mood and planted a kiss firmly against his lips.

The sense of dread and unease at the left turn this night had taken followed me all the way back to Colin's house.

In the two hours since Jo and Linc dropped my car and me off at Colin's house, every irrational and confusing emotion tumbled through me. Jo asked if I wanted her to stay and keep me company, but I could tell she was itching to get Lincoln alone, and I wasn't going to subject her to my pissy mood any longer.

Something just felt so *off* about Jackie, the way Colin reacted to me talking with her, and the women at the brewery that I let it all crawl under my skin and fester. I showered, scrubbing my skin raw in an attempt to erase the bitter feelings that burned in my chest.

I thought of Colin and my hot, insatiable desire to lick and suck every part of him while he did the same to me. Up to this point things had been fun and easy. Once I let my guard down, everything had been going so well, and now it felt like we were completely off-kilter, and I hated thinking that things were going to shit. I may have loved him, but there were still things about him I didn't really know, and panic bubbled just below the surface as I thought of the endless possibilities.

By the time Colin got home, I was confused about my

feelings, horny as fuck, and white-hot mad that I couldn't pinpoint *why* I was feeling so off. There was something going on with him, and he wasn't telling me, that—I had decided—was a fact.

Handling complicated matters of the heart in the only way I knew how, I was standing at his kitchen island wearing only a strappy black thong and my sparkly stilettos when he walked through the door. I looked over my shoulder at him, and the darkness in his eyes matched my own.

I pushed my long blond hair over one shoulder and quirked an eyebrow in his direction. Without a word, Colin slammed the door closed and stalked in my direction, his long strides swallowing up the distance between us. I pushed my ass out, just slightly, and pinned him with my stare.

Colin came up behind me, his rough, wide palms moving up my back. He thrust his hips into me, pushing my hip bones until they bit into the edge of the granite countertop. Every solid inch of him was warm and hard against me. Colin tipped me forward as he ran wet, hot kisses up my neck and pushed my naked breasts into the cold surface of the counter.

My nipples pinched hard at the coolness of the counter, and an ache pulsed between my legs. Colin grunted a low, hungry growl in my ear as his teeth scraped the sides of my neck. Heat and tension were rolling off him in waves, and I wanted them to crash into me and make me forget the shit show of a night.

"You are so fucking hot." Colin ran his thumb across my nipple, and I bit down on my lip to keep from moaning. I was still holding tightly to the unexplained anger inside of me and refused to give him the satisfaction of a whimper.

Despite the rosiness that bloomed in my cheeks, I steadied by breath and pushed my ass against the steel rod I felt through the denim of his jeans.

I lifted my torso and twisted to face him. Colin planted his arms beside me, caging me between the island and his hard, muscled body. Defiance flared in my eyes as I tipped my chin. I placed my hands on his broad chest and pushed back on him gently. He took one step back, and his eyes roamed over my half-naked body. I pushed myself up on the countertop and crossed one leg over the other, leaning back on my hands.

"Take off your shirt," I demanded. My gaze was steady, daring him to defy me.

His nostrils flared once, but he did as he was told. His fingers moved over the buttons, popping each open, one by one. My hungry eyes followed the line of bare skin and enjoyed the thin trail of hair that dipped below the waistband of his jeans.

He stepped forward, curling one hand around the back of my neck and resting his thumb against my bottom lip. He brushed my lip softly, but when I pulled his thumb into my mouth, swirled my tongue around it and bit gently, he knew I wasn't fucking around.

"On your knees, cowboy."

As Colin sank to the floor, I uncrossed my legs and spread my knees wide for him.

"Fuck," he breathed. I felt his heated gaze all over me, and I was drunk with power.

"You like that?" I asked, teasing the edge of my thong and brushing my hand gently over my center. My pussy throbbed with anticipation when he licked his lower lip.

Colin moved forward, pushing my knees farther apart as I leaned backward. Like a starving man, Colin licked the sides of my thong, teasing the lips of my pussy until he tore my panties to the side and devoured me. Deep strokes of his tongue had me gripping his hair and tipping my hips forward.

He's using you.

You're a flake and everyone knows it.

You gave up everything for a man. Again.

Dark, angry thoughts wound themselves around the aching need I had for him. Sex usually helped to make things clearer, but the fact that I couldn't tease out my feelings had the anger blossoming in my chest.

"More. Fuck, yes." My breath came out in spurts as he nipped and teased at my clit. Gone was the Colin that gently teased and played. But when he purposely wasn't giving me enough friction or pressure to put me over the edge, I realized that he was hate-fucking me just as fiercely as I was.

My head snapped up, and I glared at him. "Get up here," I demanded.

Colin stood, yanking me closer by the back of the neck and kissed me hard. I could taste my arousal on his tongue, and a hot trickle seeped between my legs. Our kiss was frenzied, and our teeth clashed as we both sought control.

I moaned and traced my hands down the hard planes of his abs before I dipped lower, grabbing his cock through his jeans. His hips pressed into me, and I pressed my hand against him, hard and torturously slow.

Colin lifted his head and pulled me off the countertop. He turned, pinning me hard against the kitchen wall. He kept trying to take control from me, and I wasn't about to let him. I grabbed at his belt and unfastened it with a steady hand. He took a step back, his chest rising and falling rapidly.

Grabbing the buckle, Colin yanked his belt out of the loops and dropped it. The clatter of the buckle hitting the floor snapped my gaze to his face. He was dangerously handsome, and this undiscovered angry side of him had my inner walls clenching in anticipation. I trusted him but I was mad as hell and didn't know if it was the latent alcohol or my unresolved feelings summering just under the surface. Regardless, I wanted to unleash all of my pent-up feelings on him.

Despite my heels, I still had to tip my chin to meet his eyes. "On the couch. Now."

Colin unbuttoned and unzipped his jeans, dropping them and his boxer briefs to the floor as he moved toward the couch. He grabbed a condom from our stash in the end table and tossed it on the seat next to him. Standing in front of him, I propped one high-heeled leg on the couch beside him.

"Now," I said, "no more fucking around. Eat this pussy like you mean it."

A slow grin spread across his face. "Yes, ma'am."

Reaching around me, Colin grabbed my ass and pulled me toward him. Within seconds the pressure between my thighs was building. With every suck on my clit and swirl of his tongue, he was hunting my orgasm just as intensely as I was. Gripping his shoulders, I came undone—pulsing and moaning as he grunted in approval and lapped up every drop of my come.

As the waves subsided, I still hadn't felt the anger in me release its hold. The overwhelming need to feel his cock inside me was unbearable. I moved to my knees, admiring the drop of wetness that had formed at the tip of his cock. He was so hard and thick that his skin strained and pulled taut as the vein beneath it pulsed in anticipation.

I circled my tongue around his crown and gripped the base. He twitched once and on a sharp inhale of breath, his hands balled into fists. Colin tipped his hips forward, urging me deeper. I obliged, taking him to the deepest parts of my throat and humming against him.

"I love watching you suck my cock," Colin said on a moan.

I was dizzy with pleasure at the control I had over him in that moment, and his words had me taking him in deep, long strokes.

The stress of opening the bakery, worry that the town gossip held a grain of truth, unease over the big feelings I had for Colin, all came bubbling up to the surface as I sucked and teased his thick cock. I needed to drown out all those emotions. I lifted my head and watched the heat flare and dance in his hazel eyes.

I reached for the condom and tore open the package to roll it down his shaft. He shifted to change our position, but I pressed my hands on his shoulders. I straddled his hips, and they settled perfectly between my thighs, like the space was made for him. I carefully lined him up to my entrance but dragged his swollen head up to my clit and far back to the tight bundle of nerves of my ass. His eyes widened once as I gently pressed. On a throaty laugh, I teased him again and again with my seam before slowly pressing down. Achingly slow, my pussy stretched open for him, the walls squeezing around him. His arms wound around my back and pulled me closer as his hips thrust upward.

I ground my clit against the base of his cock, desperate to forget the complicated feelings that I was having. If I could focus solely on him, I didn't have to think about whether our relationship was based on lies or secrets. What I felt when he was inside me was simple and pure.

Furiously he pumped up into me as I angled myself over him. My nails raked across his shoulders and chest, and I didn't give a fuck. He was close too, and I was damn sure going to have another orgasm before this was over. Colin reached up to pinch my nipple, and the taut rope holding me together snapped. I shouted his name once and felt his dick pulse inside me as we both fell hard over the edge.

When the last waves subsided, I pushed off and plopped myself on the couch next to him. I had lost one shoe but had officially fucked the angry right out of myself and couldn't help but take in our ridiculous state. Colin's breath was hard and fast, but he slowly rubbed his hand along the edge of my thigh. He looked at me, breathless and chuckling, and I started to laugh too—apparently, I wasn't the only one who needed it rough and dirty tonight.

THIRTY-THREE

COLIN

Goddamn.

I had no idea I was walking into angry, hot-as-fuck Honey when I'd ended my night at the bar. I knew something was off when she'd left, and I wrestled with the unsettling feelings that Jackie always managed to kick up.

But *fuck.*

Honey's hair was a mess, and her full lips were swollen from our frantic kisses. I had no intention of being rough with her, but once she'd gone down that path, it was game on. Sated and spent, she blew out a breath of air that lifted the front strands of her hair. I lifted my hand to smooth the flyaways from her face and try to get a handle on what just happened. In the past, I could maintain control—It was the only way I knew how to fuck. Tonight I was completely and thoroughly *used.*

My mind ticked back to the band bunnies who happily sought their claim to fame by using any band member they could, but I quickly tried to dismiss the troublesome thought. Honey was different but I didn't entirely understand why she was mad.

Was it something Jackie said to her? Did she know about the bakery? Had she somehow found out I have been keeping that information from her?

I dismissed the errant thoughts with a stretch and chose to focus on my sex-endorphins-soaked brain. Whatever this was tonight, it was what we both needed.

Just looking at her heavy-lidded eyes and satisfied smile, my heart skipped a beat and took off in a sprint. Before getting cleaned up, I leaned over Honey and let my lips touch her warm skin.

"I'm not sure what that was about but damn, baby. Remind me to piss you off more often."

Honey chuckled lightly and ran her fingertips through my hair. Right then I almost told her about the real estate deal with the bakery space. I wanted to tell her that I'd made the arrangement before *we* had become an *us*—that it didn't even matter anymore because whatever I had was hers. The words were right there but died on my lips when she nuzzled into me. I inhaled a deep lungful of her apricot and spice scent and focused on the sound of our labored breathing. Despite the sharp bite of guilt, I still couldn't bring myself to ruin the moment.

We both got up and showered. There, the mood shifted from angry and frenetic to tender and unhurried. I let my hands slip down her smooth skin and caress the knots that had formed between her shoulders. Honey allowed me to run my hands down her soapy thighs and tease her love-swollen pussy.

After, we made slow, intimate love. When I whispered her name against her lips, I only hoped that she could feel what I did in that moment. We were so good together, and somewhere along the line, she had taken up permanent residency in my soul. I fell asleep stroking the wet strands of

Honey's hair and believing, for the first time in a long while, that I may be able to keep—maybe even deserve—something as precious and staggering as Honey James in my life.

I WAS JOLTED awake by an incensed Honey. Confusion clung to my brain like cobwebs as she kicked her foot at the bed to rattle me awake and yelled, "What the fuck is *this*, Colin?"

In her hand, she held a crumbled bit of paper over her head. I had no fucking clue what was going on, and she wasn't about to let me catch up.

"Well?" she demanded. "What is it?"

"What the fuck?" I yelled.

"Don't you raise your voice at me, asshole!" she fumed. "I want to know exactly what this is. Why does this piece of paper with *my* bakery's address on it show an acceptance of an offer to purchase with *your* name on it?"

Oh, fuck. No. No. No. No. Not now. Not like this.

"Well?!"

I put one hand up and gathered the sheet around my waist with the other to hold together any scrap of dignity I could manage. I never planned on having this conversation with a bare ass and morning wood.

"Honey, I can explain."

"I sure fucking hope so!" She wasn't letting me get a word in edgewise, and with every word she got louder and louder.

"Mr. Stevens was only going to sell the bakery to me after they leased it—when he was ready to sell. Ray Shaw was taking care of it, and I assumed it would be years before it went through. Shaw worked out a deal with Stevens's son that was lucrative for the family and allowed me to expand the bar." Fury rose in her eyes and her cheeks reddened. "But," I continued before she should cut me off again, "that agreement was made before I knew it was you he agreed to rent the storefront to. I swear I had no idea."

"Months, Colin. Months! How many opportunities did you have to tell me, and you chose not to?" Tears sprung in her eyes and the hitch in her voice shredded my insides.

"Look, I know. I fucked up." Knots cinched in my gut and I felt sick.

"Fucked up doesn't even begin to cover it. What were you going to do? Fuck me for a year, and when my lease was up, send me off with a pat on the ass and a 'nice to know you'?"

I stood and pulled on a pair of gray sweatpants as panic pulsed through my veins. I didn't give a flying fuck what I had to do, she needed to understand.

"No, of course not." I dragged a hand through my hair. "Look, I didn't have it all planned out. I had no idea how long Mr. Stevens planned to lease, and I never expected us to be a thing—you'd made it pretty clear you wanted nothing to do with me."

"How dare you blame this on me?"

"I'm not. That's not what I—all I'm saying is that I didn't see this coming. Then when we *did* become more, I convinced myself that me buying him out wasn't necessarily a bad thing. Just because I will own the space doesn't mean that you have to leave it. I'll give it to you, for fuck's sake!"

"You kept this from me—made the decision *for* me. Is that what you meant when you said you wanted to keep me? Take away any choice I had? Don't you see how fucked up that is?"

I felt nauseated and pain radiated from my chest down

my arms. I *had* made the decision—thousands of times—to keep this from her because I was afraid of her reaction. Any time I could have told her, either something came up, or I found some bullshit reason to wait. I was too afraid to change what we had because it was the best thing in my whole life. I thought that if I held on tighter, I could find a good way and a good time to tell her. I was epically stupid, and my deeply ingrained self-hatred overflowed.

You're a fuckup. When it comes down to it, you'll always make the wrong choice.

A sob wracked out of Honey, and my chest cracked wide open. I took a step toward her, willing her to let me wrap her in my arms and find a way to make this right. Honey countered my advance and swiftly moved around me and out our bedroom door, gathering anything of hers she could hold as she walked.

I followed her down the hallway to the front door, where she paused with her hand on the knob. Honey took a long, shaky breath but didn't turn to look at me.

"Let me make this right," I pleaded. I would do anything to fix this, and she had to see that.

A heavy moment hung in the air before she turned to look at me, the light gone in her blue eyes, and destroyed me. "You broke my trust. You can't fix this."

I sank to my knees as the door slammed closed behind her.

THIRTY-FOUR
HONEY

THE VISION of Colin's eyes shifting from shock and anger to desperation and pain looped through my mind on an endless repeat. The morning after our intensely angry fuck-fest, I snuck out of bed early to start making him breakfast. Realizing his fridge still resembled that of a rock star bachelor—literally nothing fresh—I pulled a scrap of paper from the pile of junk mail on his counter to write a quick note and tell him I was running to the cafe for donuts and coffee.

It was then that I saw the letterhead from Ray Shaw's real estate company—the letterhead that had *my* bakery address stamped across the top and outlined an accepted offer for the parlor space. Colin's masculine signature was scrawled across the bottom. Confusion was quickly replaced by anger as realization flowed over me.

Somehow in the midst of all his charming gifts and dates and declarations of love, I had been fooled into believing it was real so he could get what he wanted.

He uses people to get what he wants.

You're a laughing stock, and we all know it.

Jackie's words burned in my gut, and bile rose at the back of my throat. I was mad as hell but not just at him.

Isn't this what always happens? If you get close to someone, you get hurt.

Tears flooded my vision, making me grip my steering wheel harder. I grunted to clear the thickness in my throat and angrily swiped at my eyes.

How could I have been so fucking stupid?

"Good morning!" I chirped as I pushed open the back door to Joanna's house. I had seen Lincoln on his morning run, so I decided it was safe to pop over and see my sister before heading into the bakery.

"Honey!" Joanna's head popped up from behind the counter, and her eyes were wide with shock. "What's up?"

I eyed her warily. She had a giant fruit plate on the counter and what looked like twenty-seven bowls covered in batter in the sink. There was flour dusting the cabinet and the floor. The kitchen looked like a war zone. "What the hell are you doing?"

Jo blew a strand of hair away from her face and looked around guiltily as I smelled something burning coming from the oven. "Me? No. Um, nothing."

I raised an eyebrow.

Joanna rolled her eyes. "Fine. I'm making you misery cookies . . . kind of."

"What the fuck are misery cookies?" I forced a laugh. "And you're definitely burning something."

I moved around the counter to inspect the travesty in the oven. Sure enough, she was attempting to bake *something,* but it neither looked nor smelled like a cookie.

"Misery cookies—because you're sad? Colin called Lincoln."

My spine straightened but I took a deep breath and squared my shoulders to Jo. "Oh?"

"Honey, he told Lincoln what happened. Are you okay? Why didn't you call me?" She moved forward but I glanced away and popped a grape from the fruit plate in my mouth.

I shrugged a shoulder and tried my best to hide any trace of emotion. "I'm fine." I smiled at her to prove just how very *fine* I was.

Jo crossed her arms and pinned me with a stare.

"We had a fight. I don't really want to talk about it." I had to bury it if I had any chance of survival.

"I just can't believe he bought the store and didn't tell you. It doesn't make any sense . . ."

"It makes perfect sense," I interrupted, anger simmering through my veins. "He wants to expand the bar. That's not news. He saw an opportunity and he took it." The ice in my voice helped to cool the fire charring my throat.

"Honey . . . Lincoln said Colin was a total mess. Really torn up about it. He said he hadn't seen him that upset since . . ." Jo trailed off and looked at the floor.

Heat rose in my cheeks, and a pinch in my chest grew to a sharp, stabbing pain as it constricted.

Am I too young to have a heart attack? Am I having a fucking heart attack?

Panic flooded my system—a sharp prickle tingled at the base of my skull, and my hands felt numb. I couldn't do this. I could not fall apart over a man when I knew from the beginning that dating him was a mistake.

Jo cast me a questioning glance as I successfully steadied my breathing.

"Look," I said as cheerfully as I could manage, "we got

into a fight but it's fine. The bakery opens in a couple of weeks, and I have a ton of work to do. I appreciate the misery cookies but they're not necessary." I wrapped Jo in a hug. If I could find a way to comfort her, I could squash the need for comfort myself. It usually worked that way.

"That's probably a good thing," she chuckled. "I tried a new recipe, and it looks nothing like the picture ... and they smell *awful*."

"Let's leave the baking to me." I squeezed Jo's waist. "How about we get this place cleaned up and have breakfast at the cafe instead?"

Jo looked around at her disastrous kitchen. "That's a deal."

PRETENDING that I wasn't dying was surprisingly difficult in Chikalu Falls. In a city like Butte, a fake smile and chirpy hello were all you needed to keep people moving and out of your fucking business.

In Chikalu? That wasn't happening.

I knew Jo was onto my bullshit, but she was giving me space ... for now. It was only a matter of time before she sat me down with a bottle of wine and expected me to share every detail. I would too but I loved her all the more for giving me a little distance and letting that happen on my own time.

The rest of Chikalu seemed to think it was their personal mission to either dig up some more dirt or treat whatever happened between Colin and me like they were mourning a death. In reality I much preferred dealing with the busybodies—the mourners were particularly difficult because that felt a little too close to the truth.

I avoided the bakery.

I avoided the bar.

I avoided the running trail.

I avoided the right turn toward the Dairy Palace and the entire block leading to the Blush Boutique.

In an effort to remain totally unaffected, the town shrank smaller and smaller. Colin's presence had seeped into every facet of my life, and it was considerably hindering my post-breakup rebound.

I quickly looked down the street as I crossed to slip into the post office. Earlier I had gotten a notice saying that I had several packages waiting for me, and my stomach filled with dread.

Annette, the world's slowest postal worker, retrieved my packages—five large rectangular boxes. I had to creatively maneuver them into my Chevelle, and as I drove toward the bakery, my eyes kept flicking in the rearview at the boxes.

Once inside, I carefully cut the packaging and peeled back the paper. Large matte black and white photos in sleek black frames caused my chest to constrict. A few weeks ago, I had spent an afternoon with Maggie and Jean at the Chikalu Women's Club digging through old photographs of the residents of Chikalu.

Jean and a few other women shared laughter and stories as we rummaged through an endless number of photo boxes. I had selected my four favorites to hang in the bakery —a young Mr. Bailey and his wife Charlotte in front of his motorcycle. Mrs. Coulson wearing a beehive hairdo pouring steaming mugs of coffee to the old men in the cafe. Ms. Trina in a crowd of people laughing and two-stepping at a long-ago held Sagebrush festival. I also included a gorgeous silhouette of Jo fly fishing on the river by her home.

When the collection felt incomplete, I went on a limb

and asked Jean for a favor. One by one, I unboxed the framed prints, and the ache in my heart burned brightly. The last box—of course it was—contained the photograph I had asked Jean to include. It was a copy of the same photograph Colin had framed in his living room—him and Nate, their dirty, happy faces smiling back at me. I ran my hand gently across the forehead of Colin's picture and swallowed down the sob that threatened to consume me.

Late into the night, I measured and leveled and rearranged the frames until they felt right. They were a reflection of the heart and soul of the residents of Chikalu Falls. It was a weird little town of people who loved each other. I remember my grandmother once saying that there were no strangers in Chilaku, just friends you hadn't met yet.

As I flipped the lights off and locked the back door, I couldn't help but think how the entire town had wrapped its hands around my heart, and my stomach roiled at the thought of how close I had been to becoming one of them.

THIRTY-FIVE

CHIKALU CHATTER

PHALLUS EMERGES AFTER WEEKS IN HIDING

FOR THE PAST SEVERAL MONTHS, *Chikalu has been plagued by a mysterious vandal. Police continue to search for those responsible for spray painting immature and degrading representations of a phallus wearing a top hat. Several businesses have been affected, but the latest building to be tagged was the much-anticipated bakery, Biscuits & Honey.*

Honey James, the bakery's owner has been noticeably absent around town, sparking rumors of a possible falling out between her and next-door neighbor beau, Colin McCoy. Despite her recent absence in town, when seen scrubbing the paint from the brick building, helping hands emerged, and the offensive picture was quickly removed.

When asked if police were close to apprehending the parties responsible, Detective Sergeant Cole Decker assured that they are working tirelessly to identify the suspects.

THIRTY-SIX
HONEY

Sitting outside of my tiny little cottage, I wrapped a blanket around my shoulders and stared out onto the river-bank. I hated that it felt more like a stopover, and not at all like *home*.

That's because home was with Colin.

I tramped down the annoyingly intrusive thought of him and wrapped my blanket tighter. The cool September air had a bite in it, and I shivered against the breeze.

"You trying to die out here? You'll have better luck just walking into the woods."

I turned my head to see old man Bailey walking in stiff but purposeful strides out of his cottage toward me. I laughed at the ridiculousness of his words.

"I'm not trying to die, Mr. Bailey. I'm just watching the sunset."

"Well you ain't wearing a jacket, so just assumed you wanted to freeze to death."

"I appreciate your kindness and concern, but I think I'll be okay," I said as he stepped closer. In his hands, he carried two small coffee cups. He passed one to me as he sat beside me on the small bench.

"Haven't seen you around here much. Thought maybe you moved out."

I sipped the hot black coffee and blinked away the tears that stung the corners of my eyes. "No," I smiled at him. "You're not that lucky." I gently bumped my shoulder into his.

"Ah, you're all right as far as neighbors go." Mr. Bailey looked out onto the water, and we sat in silence and sipped our coffee. Long after it turned cold, I rested my head against his strong, broad shoulders.

A lump had lodged in my throat, making it impossible to speak, but I didn't need to. Mr. Bailey sat with me while I watched the geese swoop low over the water. One tear tumbled down my cheek, and a ripple effect caused all the others flowing after it. Silent, wracking sobs took over my body as the overwhelming stress of bottling everything up and pretending I was fine came crashing in around me.

Mr. Bailey shifted, moving his arm along my back and pulling me in close to him. He didn't offer any words of encouragement or reassurance—hell, I wasn't sure he even knew why I was having a total meltdown—but he stayed with me until my sobs subsided and my breathing slowed.

I leveled my breathing and rubbed the sleeve of my sweater across my swollen eyelids.

"Thank you," I whispered.

"Sometimes you just have to let it out, darlin'. You're a strong woman, but it's not always the smart move to bottle it all up." His strong hand squeezed my shoulder.

"What am I going to do?" I asked, unsure if I wanted to know the answer.

"Whatever it is that needs to be done."

~

"Whatever it is that needs to be done." I spoke Mr. Bailey's words to my reflection in the bathroom mirror.

I was heartsick and trying to put on a brave face and pretend that I wasn't dying inside was draining any last reserves of spark I had left in me. My eyes looked hollowed, and even my most expensive makeup couldn't cover the dark shadows that never seemed to go away. I tossed a look at the misery nest of blankets piled on my bed and sighed.

I had always been honest with Colin, and I thought we had shared an understanding. Together we made perfect sense, and no one should have gotten hurt . . . but his lie of omission cut me deeper than I could have expected. The power someone had over you when you handed over your heart was the very reason I had kept men at a distance for most of my adult life. Despite knowing this, the hollow space behind my ribs still ached for him. I needed to be honest with myself about who I was and exactly what I wanted.

"Get your head out of your ass," I said to myself. With a deep breath, I pushed my hair from my face. I couldn't lose the bakery. In a desperate panic, Colin had said he would just give it to me, but I could never accept that—It would only prove that I didn't do any of this on my own, that I wasn't capable.

Fuck. That.

I considered all my options.

Cut and run back to Butte. Ugh, no.

Be a mature adult and talk to Colin. Fuck no.

Fight like hell.

With a satisfied nod, I pulled my phone from my pocket and searched my contacts. When the number I pulled up appeared on the screen, my finger hesitated only a fraction of a second before hitting *Call* and waiting while it rang.

"Well, this is a surprise." The familiar voice was warm and friendly.

"Hey, Chad. What do you have going on this weekend? I need to see you."

THIRTY-SEVEN

COLIN

I WAS DYING. Of that, I was absolutely certain. In the eight days since Honey and I imploded, I walked around feeling like I couldn't breathe. Honey had been skirting me all week —ignoring my calls and texts, which I expected, but she'd also been a ghost around town. The few times I saw a light on at the bakery, it was only a contractor doing work or Jo dropping something off.

I couldn't keep her—a simple fact I knew since the night I met her and tried like hell to disprove in the last months of our relationship.

I have no idea how long I sat on the desk in my cramped office, listening intently for any sounds coming from the bakery and wanting to ram my fists through the drywall when I heard a hard knock at my door.

"It's me." Avery's singsong greeting was muffled by the walls. Without missing a beat, she peeked her head around the heavy wooden door.

Word about Honey and my breakup spread like wildfire around Chikalu so it was only a matter of time before she found me.

"Hey Artie Fartie. You busy?" she asked.

I rolled my eyes at the nickname. "Just working."

I was being a prick, but I couldn't muster the energy to fake it in front of her. I stared at the laptop and stack of papers in front of me without knowing exactly what I had been working on. An hour had passed since I sat down, and I couldn't manage to stay focused on anything but Honey and my colossal fuckup.

"I saw Honey at the cafe today. Hadn't seen her in a while."

"Yeah," I said, refusing to let the questions about her tumble out of me. *Did she seem okay? What was she wearing? Did she ask about me?* I didn't have the right to ask about her—not anymore. I still couldn't believe what I had done.

I tried to work, but my brain was a complete disaster. I was angry, exhausted, miserable, irritable, and suffocating with guilt. I had hurt the woman I loved.

I was supposed to be a solid businessman making solid business decisions, and I couldn't even manage a simple booking schedule. I stared angrily at my laptop, refusing to look at my twin sister.

"We gonna talk about this"—she gestured at all of me —"or are you just gonna bury it?" She settled her hands on her hips and waited.

I blew out a hard breath. "I don't know what you want me to say. I fucked up."

"Yeah, I figured."

My head snapped up. "What the fuck's that supposed to mean?"

Avery's eyes narrowed at my tone, and she raised both palms to me. "Okay, fine," she said, slapping her palms on her thighs. "Consider this a twin-tervention."

I tossed her a bland look. Avery was always making up weird words about us being twins, and apparently my need for an intervention was amusing to her.

"Listen, dude." She pressed on. "I've got your back. I always have. But whatever's going on with her, it's actually getting to you. If it had been her fault, you'd be angry, but since you're imploding, I think it's safe to assume you're blaming yourself for something. So spill."

Over the next forty minutes, I word-vomited all over Avery. I explained what I could to her—most of which she already knew, but it felt good to get it off my chest. Our hookup after Jo's event. Honey coming back to town. Taking her advice to woo Honey the best I could. Pursuing her, hooking up again, and hurling my heart at her with blind abandon. Honey being friends with Mom. I also explained the things she didn't know. The deal with Mr. Stevens. Falling completely and totally in love with her.

Avery listened quietly with little more than a few solemn nods. When I finished, she blew out a breath and fluffed her wild, curly hair. "Shit."

"Yeah," I said quietly.

"I wish I could offer you better advice, but I think I'm just as bad at this as you are." We both shared a humorless laugh. "But I do think there's something that might help."

I raised my eyebrows in question.

"You need to talk to Mom."

"Mom?" I bristled.

"Yes, Mom. Look, I know you don't always see it, but she's really good with this kind of thing. Plus, she knows Honey. Maybe it could help."

～

I CLIMBED the steps to my parents' house deliberately slowly. I never knew what kind of mood I would be walking into when I came home, so there was nothing I could do but hope for the best. When I reached the top of the stairs, I ran my hand against my pant leg to dry the dampness on my palm. I flexed my hand once and lifted it to knock.

God, I hope Avery's right about this.

After a beat, my mother opened the door. Surprise crossed over her hazel eyes, but she immediately moved through the door and wrapped me in a hug. Her frame was small, but her arms were strong as they squeezed my middle.

"Hey, Mom." I choked out.

"Come on in, baby. I've been hoping you'd come."

We made small talk for a bit while she poured some iced tea and put a small plate of Nate's favorite cookies in front of me. I stared at the snickerdoodle cookies and took a bite—they really were delicious.

When we ran out of small talk, she said simply, "I heard about you and Honey. Do you want to talk about it?"

Despite the fact that I took Avery's suggestion to come here and talk, I couldn't find the words. "There's not much to talk about, I guess. We broke up."

Her eyes misted and my gut churned. Deep down, I knew this was a mistake.

"That's such a shame," she said quietly.

"Yeah, well, bringing her home to meet you was a mistake." I said bitterly. Self-loathing flared in my chest, and I couldn't look my mother in the eyes for fear she'd see how easily I had ruined yet another good thing in my life.

"What exactly is that supposed to mean?" The pain laced in her voice surprised me, and I looked up, confused.

Her shoulders were set, eyes wide, and her lips were trembling.

Confusion caused her words to tumble and crash inside my head.

"I just—" I blew out a breath and tried to explain this to her despite my embarrassment. "I mean I shouldn't have brought her to meet you if it wasn't going to last . . . If I couldn't make it work."

"Colin," she said on a shaky breath, "I need to ask you something." Mom took a deep breath but didn't raise her eyes from the floor. "Are you ashamed of me?" Her voice was barely above a whisper, and my throat grew thick with emotion.

"What? Mom, no."

How could she ask me that?

"It's okay, dear. I understand. I'm a mess and I get confused and . . ."

"I'm not ashamed of you." The words rushed out of me as a prickle settled at the base of my skull. So much more— words I felt but couldn't choke out, were caught in my throat.

Finally I said, "I'm ashamed of myself."

The unspoken truth crackled out of me and released a dam of emotions I had built after Nate's death. My mother's hand paused as she rubbed a small circle on my back, and I felt like I was eleven again. For three years, I've struggled for her approval and to make up for what I'd done.

"I can't imagine what you have to be ashamed of," she said quietly. "But I can see that this is my fault, Colin. After Nate died, you came back and took care of me—took care of all of us. I was too selfish to tell you to go back to your music. I needed to keep you close. Once the bar started to take off, I told myself that you were happier here."

"I am happier here, Mom. Chikalu Falls is my home. But I just can't walk around pretending that I didn't completely ruin your life."

Her hand stopped on the side of my face and tilted my head so our eyes could meet. "Ruin *my* life? How could you ever think that? You and Avery are the most precious things in the world to me."

I had to look away when I told her the truth. "There are things you don't know. Things I did the night he died that I wish I could take back but can't. It would all be different."

"Oh, Colin." She ran a hand over my hair as she had done thousands of times since my childhood. "I know Nate tried to call you that night. I've always known."

My chest squeezed and a rhythm pounded in my head. "I . . . I don't understand."

"Your father told me not long after—we don't keep secrets. Not like those anyway."

"I—" A quiet sob wracked out of me. "I'm sorry Mom. I should have answered the phone."

Her tiny frame wrapped me in a hug as I buried my face in my hands. "Nate made his choices, Colin. So many over the years I wish he hadn't, but never once have I *ever* thought any of it was your fault."

"I just want to be a good man," I admitted quietly.

"You are," she said. Before I could argue, she added, "I know you are for so many reasons, but mainly because you've carried this and feel bad. Good people feel bad for things, even when they're not at fault."

The years of heartache and regret felt pulsing and raw. I had carried the burden of Nate's death for so long that it was both overwhelming and relieving to know the truth of that night was out there.

My mother shushed and comforted me in a way I didn't

realize I had craved from her. For three years, I buried myself in work, breaking my back to build the business and prove to her that I wasn't a total fuckup—that I was worthy of her love. I had failed to see that through her grief, she had never stopped loving me at all. She was fragile and she had changed, but her love was always there.

"I'm sorry I get frustrated with you," I said softly.

She shook her head. "I know it's hard for you too. Things like his favorite foods help me feel close to him, but I know I mess that up sometimes. I get confused and I want him back so badly."

"I know."

"He loved you so much," she continued. "I know a piece of you died with him. But he's here." She placed her hand across my chest, and my heart thumped hard beneath it. "You help me feel close to him."

Drained and exposed, I inhaled a deep, cleansing breath. My eyes were gritty and raw. I swallowed down the rocky lump in my throat.

"So," she said softly, "what are we going to do about this girl of yours?"

"I'm not sure what I *can* do. I wasn't completely honest with her." Shame caused my cheeks to flame.

"Oh, Colin." She sighed. "Sometimes we make decisions in the moment that we think are for the best," she reassured me. "I'm sure it's nothing that can't be fixed."

"Well, if you've got any ideas, I'm all ears."

"It may be a betrayal of her friendship and trust, but you're my son so I don't care." She thought for a moment. "You know you can't just give the bakery space to her, right?"

"I thought about that. I know she'd never accept that. She's too proud and too hard-headed for a gift like that." I stood to pace across the soft beige tile of my childhood kitchen.

Mom stood in front of me. "She may be stubborn as the day is long, but it's more than that."

I shook my head. "I know. She's earned this."

"Damn right. So whatever it is you do, make sure that it comes from here." She patted a hand across the hollow, aching space in my chest that used to contain my heart. "Show her that you value her as an *equal*."

THIRTY-EIGHT

HONEY

"Well, you are a sight." Chad sat across from me in an expertly tailored navy blue suit. His eyes raked over me, but I ignored his uncomfortable stare and continued scanning the menu at Chikalu Falls' only upscale restaurant, Francesca's. I decided on wearing my kaftan-style silk wrap dress—the one I had tried on with Jo. This was a serious business meeting, and I was determined to dress the part of a successful, capable businesswoman.

"Thank you," I responded and toyed with the plunging neckline of the dress, pulling the two sides a little closer together. Suddenly I felt self-conscious and uncomfortable. Somewhere between the cottage and the restaurant, my dress went from feeling chic and elegant to overtly sexy and inappropriate. For a brief moment, the urge to change into jeans and a soft Henley crossed my mind.

Who even are you?

Squashing the thought, I settled my nerves by taking a healthy sip of lemon water.

"Hi, I'm Nia, I'll be your server tonight . . . " Her voice trailed off as she looked from Chad to me. I recognized Nia from around town, and her raised eyebrow let me know she'd recognized me too and was surprised to see me sitting across from someone other than Colin. Heat flared in my cheeks as my thoughts briefly shifted to Colin.

"Thank you, Nia. We'll take a bottle of the Spring Mountain Cabernet."

Nia's eyes blinked briefly as I glanced down to see he'd just ordered the most expensive bottle on the menu. Before I could interject to assure Chad I wasn't interested in sharing a bottle with him, Nia's lips were pressed in a thin line, and she turned to walk away.

Clearing my throat, I breathed through the skittering of nerves that swept through my system.

"Chad," I began. "Thank you for meeting me. As I explained on the phone, I need your real estate expertise. There's the . . . situation with the bakery space, and I could really use your advice."

"Of course. I'm happy to help an old friend." Chad's million-dollar smile shone brightly in the dim lighting of the restaurant. In all honesty, I had chosen the place in town where we had the lowest chance of running into any of the gossip mongers lurking around. It was a weeknight and Francesca's was typically a Friday or Saturday date-night place around Chikalu. It was for the best; Colin and I needed to keep our distance from each other.

Say it a few more times. Maybe then you'll start to believe it.

I grumbled at my heartsick ego.

"So," he continued, completely unfazed by my lack of attention, "here's my proposal for your next steps." Chad slid a file folder across the table. "I included my recommendations for contesting the sale of the bakery, but I have to tell you . . . unfortunately as a lessee you don't have many options. I'd suggest you talk to Mr. Stevens. He may not be aware of your desire to purchase the space prior to making the agreement with the bar owner. As the current legal owner, he should be made aware of your intentions."

I nodded grimly. I appreciated him looking into it and giving me honest feedback. I reached down to slide the folder into the bag at my feet. When I turned, I looked above Chad's right shoulder. "Oh, fuck."

Chad's eyes squinted in question as he turned. Standing at the entryway of Francesca's was a very tense, very angry looking Colin. My heart leapt through my rib cage toward him, and a tingle shot straight between my legs as my eyes took in the tension in his stance and the veins running down his corded forearms. I hated that my body still reacted to his, but I couldn't help it. My hand paused with the folder midway to my bag, and I was frozen in place.

It's fine. This is fine.

Emotion flared across Colin's face as he squared his shoulders. Chad cast me another questioning glance before he turned to see Colin stalking toward our table.

"Well, this isn't fucking happening." Colin's fists were balled at his sides, and tension rolled off him as he stood beside the table.

Chad stood, nearly nose-to-nose with Colin, and a heavy beat lingered in the air. Finally he reached out a hand to Colin. "Hi, there. I'm Chad, Honey's friend." He paused slightly before the word *friend,* and I did not appreciate what it insinuated, however true it may have once been.

Colin looked down at his hand without shaking it. Anger rolled off him in waves. "What the hell is this, Honey?"

Defiance flared in my eyes. He's the one who betrayed *my* trust. He didn't get to think he called the shots anymore.

My eyes shot to Nia who withered under my stare. Her guilty expression gave away exactly how Colin knew to find us here.

"I'm having dinner with a friend," I said coolly. "What does it look like?"

My nerves were going haywire, but I was still steaming mad and refused to allow myself to appreciate how ruggedly handsome Colin looked when he was royally pissed off or what that primal attraction said about me as a person. I stood but took a sip of water to cool the fire searing my throat.

"That's it? You just flip it off that quickly?" Hurt crossed his face, and my damn traitorous heart squeezed in my chest. I was mad at him—fucking furious—but avoiding him was one thing. Seeing him hurt and angry had my heart ripping at the seams all over again.

I set my glass down with a *clack*. "*Now?* You really want to do this right here?"

Chad cleared his throat and silently signaled to Nia as I locked eyes with Colin. She hurriedly placed a sleek, black billfold on the table, and Chad tucked in several bills.

"I'm sorry, Chad, but you'll have to excuse me." My temper was dangerously close to making a scene.

That's what you do. Make a scene because you're a hothead with poor judgement.

No. Not anymore, I wasn't. With a small breath, I turned to leave.

"I'll walk you out," Chad started.

"The fuck you will." Colin spat his words at Chad, and as Colin took one step forward, Chad sank back into his seat.

I turned my back on them both and stormed toward the door.

What right? What right does he have to be upset? This wasn't even a date, but if his immature ass wanted to go ahead and think that, then fine.

Fuming, my black stiletto heels clacked down the sidewalk as I stomped toward my car. Yes, seeing Colin blind with jealous rage ignited some deeply primal part in me. My inner goddess threatened to swoon, but I was still too mad to enjoy it. In a huff, I tore the shoes from my feet. When I straightened, Colin's wide palm gently gripped my upper arm, and my head whipped up to meet the fire in his eyes.

"How dare you!" I seethed.

"I just wanted to talk to you."

"You took it from me, Colin, without me even realizing it, you took the bakery from me. Before I even really ever had it." Tears sprung at the corners of my eyes and I lifted my chin. I refused to cry in front of him, barefoot, on the side of the road.

"I told you that I had no intention of taking anything from you." Colin stood toe-to-toe with me and heat radiated off him. "Besides, you haven't been a saint either. I saw the photographs you hung in the bakery."

I was taken aback. "What about them?"

"You didn't think to ask me if I was okay with it? You took the most horrible experience of my life and hung it on the walls for everyone to see. Did you stop to think about how seeing it every fucking day would make me feel?"

A searing coal settled in my stomach. I *hadn't* thought about that. I had seen the pictures as a way to honor Nate and his relationship with Colin. With Jean's blessing, it never occurred to me that Colin wouldn't see it that way.

Heat bloomed across my chest, and butterflies skittered in my stomach. "I'm sorry Colin. You're right, I didn't think of it that way. But is that why you came here tonight? To make me feel like shit because you feel guilty about the shop?"

"Jesus, Honey, no! We had one argument—granted, I fucked up, I get that—but instead of talking to me about it, you ran. You owed me more than packing up and leaving."

"I don't need an explanation or an accusation from you."

"Well I *am* going to explain it to you! Because that's what you do when you're in a relationship—you hear the other person out, even when you don't want to. And you definitely don't go on dates with someone new!"

"Honey, are you okay?" Chad's voice was laced with concern as his long strides carried him across the sidewalk toward Colin and me.

Sweet baby Jesus, not right now, Chad.

I looked up at him, and a dull sting was forming behind my right eye. I raised one hand. "Yes, Chad. I'm sorry our dinner was interrupted but I'm fine."

The vein that ran down Colin's throat pulsed as he flexed his fist at his side. I placed my body between the men, not wanting to see poor Chad get the shit beat out of him over a misunderstanding.

I looked at Colin. "This was not a date. Chad is leaving and we can talk about this later."

Chad must have had a death wish because his bravado outweighed his will to live when he leaned forward to place a chaste kiss across my cheek.

Colin stepped forward and I instinctively put my hand on his chest. His heartbeat hammered beneath my hand, and fire shot up my arm and straight to my chest at the contact. His jaw ticked as he glared at Chad. When Colin placed his hand over mine, it was nearly my undoing.

My eyes met his as Chad walked away, and the sizzle of electricity in the air was palpable. A streak of lightning blazed across the sky, turning his hazel eyes an electric shade of green. His chest rose and fell with heavy breaths, and the familiar pull of desire pooled between my legs.

Thick raindrops slowly hit our shoulders with a *plunk,* but neither of us acknowledged them. Colin took one step toward me, his hips meeting mine.

"Honey," he started. His voice was low and gravelly and spread over me like caramel. Colin's hand wound around my neck as he stared into my eyes. On a deep inhale, my breasts brushed his muscular chest, and the breath caught in a hitch.

"Colin," I whispered. I wanted to stand my ground, but with my chin tipped up to him, I knew it was a losing battle.

"You can run from me, Honey, but I will always come for you."

With that, Colin's mouth crashed into mine. Emotion poured from him into me. A squeak escaped my throat as he ravaged my mouth. My hands tugged at his shirt, his muscles bunching under my touch and sending a fresh wave of desire through me. I wanted to be consumed by him.

Rain pelted us as I wound myself around his thighs and clung to him—lost in the sensation of every pent-up emotion pouring out of me. His hips moved forward, and the steel length of his cock had me moaning in his mouth. I was about to climb that man like a tree in the middle of the street when he shifted and pulled me into the darkness of the alley.

Under the cloak of darkness, his hands snaked up my sides and across my breasts. The high slit of my skirt parted, and his rough hands raked across the sensitive skin of my inner thigh. I wanted him. I wanted to stop the ache in my chest and the jumble of uncertainty filling my brain.

"Honey, please."

His plea clouded my brain, but a crack of thunder had me jumping back.

Falling into bed with him will not fix this.

Colin's eyes met mine. "Marry me."

I stared, unable to reconcile the words that just fell out of his mouth.

What. The actual. Fuck.

Thick, dark clouds were rolling in, swirling and hanging dangerously low as Colin paced across the sidewalk. "Look, we're great together. I know what you need, and I can give that to you. So marry me."

My hands were trembling, and I swallowed hard to keep my voice from cracking. "There's a lot more to marriage than that, Colin."

"I understand that," he insisted, "and we'll figure it out." Colin stepped to me and gently wrapped his hands around my upper arms, pulling me close to him. "Just take the leap with me."

Just leap. That's what he was asking me to do—make another impulsive decision and trust that it would all work out. My heart pounded out a frenzied beat. If he could hear it beating, it was calling to him, but I was rooted in place.

"I'm sorry, Colin." I unpeeled myself from him and pushed gently against his chest before I cried in front of him again. "I have to go."

THIRTY-NINE

COLIN

So that did not go at all how it played out in my mind. I melted against the brick wall in the dark alleyway as rain pelted my back and soaked through my clothes. When I saw her car in the parking lot of Francesca's, I had every intention of politely asking her if we could find some time to talk tomorrow. I was fully prepared to grovel if it came to it.

I also didn't expect to see her in a dress that made her look like an old-Hollywood movie star—complete with a plunging neckline and a slit that rode high on her muscular thigh. Her eyes were smoky, and her lips were begging to be kissed. Just looking at her made it hard to breathe, like the air in the room had gone thick.

I felt unsettled and had a hard time sorting out the Honey I had come to love and the sophisticated city girl sitting at the table. A rogue thought tumbled through my mind. In the days we'd been apart, she was staying at her cottage on Joanna and Lincoln's property. Honey had spent the majority of her time at my place but never once talked about finding something more permanent in Chikalu. Come to think of it, she hadn't even mentioned it.

Was she planning to leave if the bakery didn't work out? Maybe she never planned to stay in the first place.

My back clenched and something akin to unease skittered through my gut when I saw her looking as gorgeous as ever, sitting across from that douchebag. I wasn't in any state to talk with her, but instead of making the smart move and turning around, I lost my goddamn mind. In reality the guy was nothing but polite, especially considering I broke up their date at Francesca's, but I wasn't about to give her up without a fight. I didn't know who he was, but I didn't give a shit—he wasn't me and Honey was mine.

Instead of apologizing I used the opportunity to pick another fight. I certainly hadn't thought I was going to demand she marry me, but in a panic the words flew out of my mouth. I meant them—I loved her and was ready to do anything to keep her, but she deserved so much more than that.

Why can't I get this shit right?

I felt the heavy blanket of overwhelming sadness settle across my shoulders. Cold and wet, I knew I couldn't keep sitting in a dark alleyway like a dipshit. I pulled myself up, shoulders hung low, and started walking toward the bar.

A quick *beep beep* of a car horn had me lifting my eyes. Through the rain I saw Lincoln rolling down the window of his truck.

Fuck. I guess now's as good a time as any to tell him I did the one thing he warned me against. I had hurt Honey.

"Get in."

I climbed into the cab of the truck and wiped the rain from my eyes. For a moment we sat in silence before Linc pulled his truck back onto the road and headed toward my truck.

"Thanks, man." I said and Lincoln just nodded. A man

of few words, I knew that I could sit in silence, and he wouldn't even ask why I was falling apart in an alley in the rain, but I was grasping at straws, and he seemed to be navigating a successful relationship despite his personal demons.

"I know asking you puts you in a bad spot, man, but how do I fix this?" I pleaded.

Linc blew out a hard breath. His grip tightened on the steering wheel but his eyes never left the dark road. "Joanna is my woman, and Honey may be her sister. But you will always be my brother. I'm not sure how we'll fix this but we will."

We.

"How bad is it?" he asked.

"I saw her car at Francesca's and went to apologize—ask her if we could meet for coffee tomorrow and talk through it. But then I saw her on a date and lost my fucking mind. I broke up their dinner and made an ass out of myself instead of groveling like I should have done. I also may have told her to marry me." I dragged a hand through my hair on a sigh.

"Yeah," he said, "that's pretty fucking dumb."

FORTY

COLIN

THE WALLS of my cramped office at The Pidge were closing in on me. Lincoln had dropped me off at my truck, and I drove straight here. The deep bass of the band playing outside my door mirrored the pounding in my skull. I sat with my head in my hands.

I'm too old to be this fucking dumb.

Staring at the nearly drained glass of whiskey between my elbows, I was empty as a drum. I was never going to be able to make it right with Honey. It was over. I blew my chance.

For the past three years I had done what I could to prove—to my family, my friends, this town—that I was more than a musician living a reckless lifestyle. But one thing I learned a long time ago—when you're on the road, the line between right and wrong blurs. Sometimes it all but disappears. How had I justified not telling Honey about Ray brokering a deal with Mr. Stevens?

The final pull of my whiskey burned a trail down my throat, and I set the glass down with a snap.

Without notice, the door to my office swung open, and

Deck's large frame darkened the doorway. I barely grunted in his direction before I went searching through my desk for another bottle.

"Lincoln wasn't kidding. You look like absolute dog shit."

"I thought you had work?" Aha, thirteen-year-old single-malt Irish whiskey would do. I grabbed the bottle and unscrewed the top.

"Had something better to do." Deck pulled a chair over, and I slid him a glass. He eyed me warily but didn't speak.

I stared at the amber liquid, my vision already going blurry at the edges. "You know, I found two long blond hairs on the passenger seat of my truck today."

"Yep."

"I just—I need to know what the hell happened. How could I have royally fucked up?"

Decker took a deep pull of his whiskey. "Well, that's easy. You're a schmuck like the rest of us."

My bones were slowly melting, and the pain that had taken up residence in my chest dulled at the edges.

"I just thought we had something. How could she let it go so easily?"

"You had to have missed something. You're sure she was on a date?" Deck propped his legs up on the chair next to him.

"Sure as hell looked like one to me . . . but I don't know what to believe anymore." I dragged my hands down my face, and both eyes felt gritty and raw.

Deck thought carefully for a beat before setting his glass down. "Think of it like a crime scene."

"I'm not a cop, dude." I said, frustrated that this wasn't helping.

"I can help you. You had to have missed something," he said calmly.

Taking a deep breath, I closed my eyes and let my mind click back to seeing Honey at Francesca's. At first all I could picture was her clear blue eyes, the way her dress hugged her curves and made me want to murder the man sitting across from her. But then little details I had disregarded became slightly clearer.

Beside her wasn't her usual date-night purse that was too small to carry much more than some cash and her lipstick. Instead, she carried a briefcase. I also momentarily recalled the look of shock on her face when she saw me standing in the doorway. Something was in her hand but what was it? A folder maybe?

I leaned back in my chair and looked at Deck who was patiently waiting for me to work it all out. "I think it may have been a business meeting of some kind. I think she had documents with her—a file folder or something?"

Deck's voice was calm and reassuring. If I wasn't so desperate, I would've given him shit about using his cop voice on me, but I had to admit, it did help.

"Okay, so maybe she wasn't on a date," he said, "but you're missing the point."

I looked at him, trying to understand what he was getting at.

"The point," he continued, "is this—does it even matter if she *was* on a date? Does her being on a date mean that you aren't batshit crazy in love with her? Does it mean that you'll *stop* loving her?"

"Fuck no." Anger bubbled under the surface of my skin at the mere thought of giving up on us.

"All right, then. Stop glorifying the problem and start figuring out what we're going to do about it."

We.

There it was again. Lincoln had said the same thing when he pulled up on my soaking wet ass in the alleyway beside Francesca's. It helped, knowing I wasn't facing one of the biggest fuckups of my life alone.

I eyed my best friend. We'd known each other a long time, and there were still moments when he surprised me. Deck never opened up, especially about his relationships with women, but if I was going to find a way back to Honey, I was going to take all the help I could get.

Deck pocketed the phone I hadn't realized he was holding. "Reinforcements are here."

A moment later Linc pushed open my office door, and music flooded my office. Finn followed right behind him. Both stood, staring at me like the sad sack of shit I was.

"So what's the plan?" My voice sounded thick in my ears, and I briefly wondered if I was slurring my words.

"We're gonna do what any man needs to do in this situation," Finn said plainly.

I tipped an eyebrow up in question.

"We're getting shit-faced tonight." Lincoln set a fresh bottle of whiskey on the desk. "Jo's on call to cart our sorry asses home when we need it, but for now we're drinking."

Finn shot both fists in the air, breaking the tension and we all laughed. His hand clamped on my shoulder and squeezed. "I've had most of my brilliant ideas on the far side of hammered. We'll think of something."

"Shit, between the four of us, we're bound to come up with at least one good idea," Deck reassured.

Linc pulled a deck of cards from the side pocket of his pants and started shuffling. "I'll deal us in."

∿

"Just like that? You just said, 'marry me'? No asking or taking a knee or anything, and you thought she'd what? Bat her lashes and say yes?" Finn's look of disdain was well deserved, but the words still stung.

My vision was hazy at the edges, and I was pretty sure one eye may have been closed. "Pretty much."

Deck just shook his head and took another swallow of whiskey. Poker had been forgotten mid-game, and the cards were in hapless piles on my desk.

"She could see it too," I said. "She knew it was a desperate plea, and instead of getting mad or arguing with me, she just walked away."

"I've known Honey for a long time," Finn added. "Being close with Jo, I've seen that she's always been carefree and fun and a wild card to Jo's steady nature. But there's more to it than that. She's underestimated a lot."

I went to rub my eyelids and missed. My brain was soaked in alcohol, but it didn't prevent me from immediately feeling defensive for her. "Honey is the most incredible woman I have ever known. She's generous and funny and kind and creative. There's nothing she can't do. I'm so in love with her I feel like my heart is missing from my chest because she's walking around with it in that expensive fucking purse of hers."

Lincoln leaned forward in his chair, having stayed silent for much of our conversation. "Does she know that? Besides a shitty proposal, have you told her that you love her?"

I shook my head. Instead of following my heart, I followed my fear and made an absolute mess of this.

Lincoln pulled his phone from his pocket and tapped out a quick text. "Fine then. You know what to do. Get up, get sober, and get your fucking girl."

FORTY-ONE

CHIKALU CHATTER

CARBONARA WITH A SIDE OF CONFLICT AT FRANCESCA'S

*H*AVE *Honey and Colin called it quits? Residents noted a suspicious distance between the couple in the past few days; however, trouble in paradise has been confirmed. Several residents reported seeing Honey at the popular date location, Francesca's, with a mysterious man. While few believe that Ms. James was on an actual date, the lover's heart believes what it sees. Colin reportedly burst into the restaurant in a jealous rage to break up what some thought to be a business meeting.*

"I'm not speaking out of turn, but it definitely wasn't a date." Nia Titan, who was the server on duty the night of the dispute, stated. "Besides," she continued, "there's no way Honey would date a guy like that. He's not one of us."

Despite the reported grace under pressure of Ms. Honey, the disagreement escalated outside the restaurant where the mysterious outsider placed a kiss on her cheek and left in a sleek black Mercedes. As if out of a movie, rain cloaked the former couple during their tense discussion, and a forlorn looking Colin was left standing in the rain. Minutes later, he accepted a ride from close friend Lincoln Scott—yes, the very fiancé of Honey's sister Joanna. Will this cause more family drama, or can our town's newest couple survive this spat?

FORTY-TWO

HONEY

"This is all so surreal." I set down the last of the tools and stood with Joanna at the entrance of the bakery. Her arm wrapped around me and squeezed as my eyes took in the transformed ice cream parlor.

I had kept the high stools along the wall for people to sit but replaced the chipped laminate countertops with smooth white quartz. The display cases gleamed and were ready for me to fill with whatever delicious treats I could concoct. I even had interviews set up to hire—I was hoping a couple of high school kids looking for a job could help run the register and deliver orders. The rough-hewn wood floor was original, and everything had a fresh coat of bright paint. The oversized prints on the wall showed life in a small town and fit perfectly into the modern farmhouse vibe of Biscuits & Honey.

My eyes settled on the framed portrait of a young Colin and his brother, Nate. My breath hitched and I willed the sting in my nose to go away. Joanna saw my gaze land on Colin, and she gave me another squeeze.

"Have you talked to him yet?" she asked.

"No." I shook my head. "Things are just so fucked up right now. I'm having all these thoughts and feelings, and I don't know what to do with them."

I thought back to the unanswered text on my phone.

Chad: It was really great seeing you. I hope we can finish our date soon.

It would be so easy to go back to casual sex with detached men who didn't demand quite so much emotional real estate from me. My stomach rolled as I stared, again, at the words on the screen. First of all, it was *never* a date. Second of all, no. Just . . . no. I was done with that version of my life.

"Linc has been pretty close-lipped about it, but I can tell he's worried about Colin."

My heart ached in my chest. "Seeing him the other night caught me completely off guard. He saw me with Chad, assumed it was a date, and then all but demanded we get married."

Jo nodded like she already knew, which likely meant Colin told Lincoln his version of what happened at Francesca's. "So he proposed? Like, actual marriage?"

"Not really. Mostly he just blurted out 'marry me' without much else to go with it. It was the least romantic thing he's ever done for me."

Jo's lips were in a firm line as she nodded. "And you said no, obviously."

"I was so shocked I didn't really say anything. But all I wanted to do was throw myself at him and scream, 'yes!' What does that say about me?"

"I think it says that the man you love asked you to marry him, and you wanted to say yes. Granted, I think you deserve an actual proposal, but that's between you two."

"But, Jo, he couldn't have been serious. I think he only said it because he thought I was on a date with Chad."

"I don't know. Colin isn't one to screw around. The guys in this town are fiercely loyal and men of their word. I think if he said he wanted to marry you, he meant it."

I pressed my fingers into my eyes and let out the breath I was holding. "I am miserable and I don't even know who I am anymore. How could I be ready to marry someone? Six months ago I was completely content living my life with my fancy clothes and an apartment that overlooked the city. Colin had to come along and screw all that up."

Jo perched herself on one of the high-top stools. "Were you really happy back in Butte? In all fairness, you kind of burned your own life in Butte to the ground. Colin was just here to help pick you up—along with the rest of us."

I blew out a hard breath. I was annoyed that she was calling me out but she wasn't wrong. The decision to leave my life in a gloriously impulsive way had been my own.

"I never expected this. I honestly thought I could bake for people and that maybe someday it could turn into something more. But I can never seem to do anything half-assed, and I went full steam ahead. Plus, I never expected to fall for this weird little town and the people in it."

"Including Colin?" she asked.

"Of course, including him." I glanced at the wall that separated his bar from the bakery, wondering if he was there today and if he could hear me. I lowered my voice slightly. "I love him. I fell hard and fast without me even realizing it. What's worse is that I'm *in* love with everything about him. But this bakery is my chance at a new life—one that's better than I imagined and allows me to be close to you. When I really think about it, I have needed this for so long."

"What's stopping you from having both? Just because he made a mistake doesn't make him a bad guy. And there's no one saying that you can't have the bakery *and* a life with Colin. He made a business decision with the real estate space—a smart one, if you ask me. Yes, he should have talked to you about it when Mr. Stevens was ready to sell, but he didn't, and that was a mistake."

I blinked at her. Joanna tapped her foot against the stool. "When I came back to Chikalu, all I wanted was to open my own guide service," she continued. "I was so focused on that one goal that I completely lost sight of any other possibilities. Then Lincoln came along, and I realized that shifting my goals to include him didn't mean that I compromised what I wanted. It made it better. You need to let your pride go."

My toe found a groove in the floor as her words tumbled over me. "Is that what I'm doing? Punishing him because of my wounded pride? That I feel like I couldn't do it on my own?" I wasn't really asking her, I knew it was the truth.

"That seems to be a major part of it. But you need to ask yourself a few things."

I looked at her expectantly.

"Can you forgive him?"

That was an easy one, deep down I knew I already had. "Yes, but—"

"Can you trust him moving forward?"

That was harder. I knew in my bones he was a good man, but I needed a promise. To hear the words that he would never lie to me again. "I think so—"

"Do you want Colin to be in your life?"

More than anything.

Truly. I wanted a lifetime of cookies in the oven, a home we made together, dancing in the kitchen, watching him sing along with the guitar shirtless in our bed. And it was the sadness of realizing I may have lost that chance that scared me the most. He had come to me, wanting to talk, and I threw his apology in his face before he even had the chance to explain his side of things.

My throat grew tight, and I didn't trust my voice, so I nodded at my sister. Her eyes softened.

"It's time you stopped letting your past dictate your future. Stop trying to make up for the decisions you made when you were young and dumb. Take a breath. Think about what you really want, and use up all that zest for life that makes you so *you* and go get it."

Embarrassment burned at my ears. Joanna had definitely called me out, and I knew she was right. "I think I got into my own head and didn't know the way out," I admitted. "But I tried . . . I even made a fucking list."

"A list?"

I dug into my purse and pulled a folded piece of paper from the pocket. It was rumpled and deep lines had been scored across the words until it tore. I handed it to Jo.

"What's this?" she asked.

"It was my guide to a better life."

Her eyes moved over the scrap of paper and read. "No fake, shallow friends. No hookups. No swooning. Definitely no falling in love. No deviating from the plan."

I shrugged my shoulders. "Clearly I failed." I gestured to the paper.

"I don't think so," she said. "Since you've been here, you've made friends. Deep, caring relationships with everyone from Maggie to Ms. Jean. People in this town care about you, Honey. Plus, I would hardly call Colin just a hookup. And no swooning? Well, that's just dumb. Swooning is half the fun." A slow smile spread across her pretty face. "So you deviated from the plan. I think that's a hell of a thing—your plan sucked. And maybe listening to your heart and marrying Colin is exactly the right thing."

Warmth spread through me as I thought about what she said. I *had* found something more than a boyfriend in Chikalu Falls. I found friends and neighbors—a sense of belonging and value. A hometown. I found the love of my life.

Now I just had to figure out a way to keep all of it—my bakery, a sense of hard work and accomplishment, and Colin McCoy in my life.

You can figure this out.

I eyed the small pile of tools I had borrowed from Lincoln. When my eye caught the sledgehammer, excitement fluttered in my belly.

"Jo . . . I have an idea."

FORTY-THREE

CHIKALU CHATTER

TOWN HALL MEETING DETERMINES THE FATE OF BISCUITS & HONEY

O*N THE HEELS of the reported breakup of Honey James and Colin McCoy, the fate of Biscuits & Honey hangs in the balance. In recent days it has come to light that the youngest Stevens boy, Charles, fast-tracked a deal with Realtor Ray Shaw for the purchase of the parlor space in Colin McCoy's name. Concerned citizens now wonder what this means, and if the pending ownership will damage his budding relationship with Honey further. Others expressed concern that the much-anticipated bakery, Biscuits & Honey, may not open at all despite Honey's rental agreement with Mr. Stevens.*

There will be a town hall meeting in the high school gymnasium to discuss the legal and local ordinances regarding ownership of the parlor space. Public commentary is welcomed at the meeting.

FORTY-FOUR

HONEY

THE BUZZ of the oven timer jolted me back to the present and away from the incessant loop of memories of Colin. A pinch in my chest still tightened when I thought of quiet mornings waking beside him. I missed so much about him, but it was the smallest things that crept into my thoughts—the little hum he made when he woke up and pulled me closer to him, the smell of his T-shirts I still used as pajamas, the way his fingertips dragged along the side of my neck and had my skin tingling beneath his touch.

I peeked inside the oven and with a satisfied nod, pulled out the large tray of french macarons. Crispy with smooth tops, perfectly tall feet, uniform sizes—all signs of a perfectly baked macaron. After cooling, I would pipe the filling and assemble the delicate and fickle sandwich cookies. While they cooled, I started piling pecan rolls into the white cardboard bakery boxes.

"Damn, Honey." I turned, only briefly, at the sound of Maggie's voice.

"Yeah, I know." I hurried past her as she stared into the kitchen of Biscuits & Honey. "It's a lot."

Maggie moved forward, grabbed another empty box and started packing them next to me. We settled into comfortable silence, though I knew she was waiting for me to say something. A low thrum of anxiety buzzed through me. I tried taking deep breaths to settle my nerves.

"I want to bring some sweets to the town hall meeting. I need to show everyone that I'm not going anywhere. Despite everything that's happened, I'm staying put this time."

"It all looks delicious." She lifted a scone—raspberry with pink peppercorn—and raised an eyebrow in question. I rolled my eyes and nodded as she took a bite with a soul-satisfying "mmmm". I loved making people happy with my desserts, and that was the exact reason it felt right to stay in Chikalu.

That, and Colin McCoy.

I looked around at the long metal island that was covered with macarons, Butte Pasties, pecan rolls, magic layer bars, six different types of cookies, and small fruit hand-pies. I willed away the memories of all the delicious things Colin and I had done on that island in order to concentrate. My hand tapped anxiously against my thigh.

"I may have slightly overdone it with the stress baking," I admitted with a huff.

Maggie bumped her shoulder to mine.

"The meeting is just small-town chatter. It doesn't really *mean* anything. You have a signed lease. No one can take that away from you."

I squared my shoulders. Though I knew she was right, I didn't want to keep my bakery because it was a formality. I wanted to *belong*—even if I had to do it one damn cookie at a time.

∼

THE NEED TO see Colin was overwhelming, but first I had to get through this insane town hall meeting. Every second away from him was agonizing, so before I headed to the high school, I tried to find him. I wanted to run up to him and tell him how I felt so that we could finally get on with our lives, together.

I didn't see his truck parked out front, but I still banged on the locked door to the bar, to be sure. He wasn't at his house when I crept past either.

Where the hell is he hiding?

I was filled with a sense of urgency, but the clock was ticking closer and closer to when I needed to be at the meeting. To stand in front of the town with my head held high.

I hammered the accelerator, and the boxes piled in the trunk and back seat shifted precariously. I eyed them in the rearview mirror and hoped I had packed them tightly enough to keep them mostly intact. Playing with the inside of my lower lip, I considered heading to Jean's house to see if Colin was with his mom but realized I would never make it back in time.

"Colin, you better be here." I grumbled to myself and made the right turn toward Chikalu Falls high school where half the baseball team was waiting to help me unload.

FORTY-FIVE
COLIN

I DIDN'T EXACTLY HAVE a plan, but I knew that Honey wouldn't miss the town hall meeting. She was too damn stubborn. I looked out into the gathering crowd to see my dad with an arm wrapped around my mom. She gave me a small, encouraging smile and nod. Together they were the picture of a happy marriage—one that had been through hell and back. I think I had always taken their relationship for granted and never put much thought into what made it so special. I probably didn't even realize that it was truly something special. Thinking of Honey, it seemed like such an odd and selfish thing to miss. She deserved that kind of devotion.

There was no doubt in my mind that I could give that to her. I had learned so much about that gorgeous, complicated woman. I knew from the first night we met that she would give me a run for my money. There was something about her that seemed to be waiting for things to go bad, and she held a piece of herself back just in case she needed to run. It was something I was prepared to work around every day of my life if that meant keeping Honey close to me.

I half expected Honey to cut and run after what I put her through these last few months. She didn't know it, but I was going to do everything I could do to not only make it up to her but prove to her that she could count on me to be the best thing in her life.

But rather than running, she blew through the high school gymnasium doors—all sass and spitfire. When I saw her, my breath caught in my chest, and my heart hammered against my ribs. Her blond hair was curled and cascaded over her shoulders. I ached to feel its silky softness slide through my fingers again. With fire in her eyes, she directed the teenage boys she had carrying armfuls of pastry boxes to the refreshments table.

I couldn't help but smile at the way she directed those boys, and they followed behind her like lovesick puppies. I was up and heading in her direction when Mayor Thompson cleared her throat into the microphone.

"Thank you, folks, for attending tonight's town hall meeting." Mayor Thompson adjusted the slim frames of her glasses and glanced at her notes. She looked out over the crowd—it looked like the entire town had shown up. The rows of chairs were filled, and people stood along the back of the gymnasium. "On tonight's agenda we have Ms. Rebecca Coulson. She would like a formal apology from the Chikalu Chatter for the recent comments that her french crullers are dry and overbaked."

Ms. Coulson sat up straighter in the front row and gave Mayor Thompson a curt nod. The mayor continued, "We will also be reviewing the proposed zoning regulations upon the completion of the interstate. But first we will open for public commentary. Please form an orderly line behind the microphone in the aisle if you wish to speak."

One by one citizens of Chikalu Falls lined up behind

the microphone. I risked a glance at Honey and saw her shoulders squared, head held high. If she had noticed me, I couldn't tell. The line wound to the back of the gym—the town had come out in droves, and apparently they had something to say.

"Howja do, Mayor. You all know I'm Trina, and I own the Blush Boutique. I came out tonight to show my support for Ms. Honey and her bakery. Another strong, female entrepreneur is just what this town needs. Also, Mayor Thompson, your order came in last week. Pick it up any time." She ended her speech with a wink, and a blush crept across the mayor's face.

Ray Shaw stepped up the microphone. He was calm and assertive. "I just want everyone to know that the deal brokered between my client, Mr. McCoy, and Mr. Stevens was agreed upon months ago. No ill will was meant for Ms. James, but the facts remain. We brokered an honest deal, and Colin McCoy is within his rights to purchase the space." Murmurs spread through the crowd, and I saw some nods in agreement and some shaking their heads in disbelief.

"Colin has been my boss and friend for the past two years," Isabel's dark eyes met mine as she spoke. "I care about my job, and I care about this town. Despite my loyalties to my boss, I believe the bar and dance hall is big enough to meet our needs, and there's room in this town for both businesses." Isabel's eyes pleaded with me to understand, and I nodded my head at her.

Next to step up was Mr. Bailey whose slow, steady steps toward the microphone had a silence sweeping over the crowd. "You all know who I am. Alls I've got to say is that woman," he pointed at Honey, "is tough as nails. She makes a damn fine biscuit. She's stepped up for us and our town by helping at Sagebrush, and she deserves to be here. Any one of you feel like running her out, you can answer to me." With that, he walked over to Honey, took a seat behind her and laid his hand on her shoulder.

One by one the townsfolk spoke their piece. Most in favor of Honey continuing to open her bakery. Some spoke in their support of me and the bar, but I couldn't care less. I was on the side of everyone who stood behind our girl. Pride for her and for our town swelled in my chest.

They had shown up for her—welcomed her as one of our own.

As the line dwindled down, Mayor Thompson rose and stood in front of her microphone again. "Well, thank you all for sharing your thoughts. We will get on with the rest of the agenda if there are no other comments."

As she spoke the words, I walked up to the microphone. "Excuse me, Mayor." A collective genteel gasp echoed in the gym. "I do have one more comment to make, if that's all right with you."

A warm smile spread across the mayor's face. "Of course, dear. The mic is yours."

Nerves danced in my belly. I had sung in front of tens of thousands of people, but I had never been more nervous than I was to see Honey's wide blue eyes looking at me. Mr. Bailey glared in my direction, and next to him, Jo flashed a secret thumbs up and nodded in encouragement.

I cleared my throat. "First, I'd like to say thank you to everyone who came out tonight. While I appreciate those who spoke in support of the bar expanding, I can assure you, that's unnecessary. While it was my original intention to expand, things have changed. I have changed."

At that, Honey stood. I continued, despite the lump

lodged in my chest, "I will not be expanding The Dirty Pigeon at the time. I—"

"Stop!" Honey shouted above the murmurs of the crowd. She was pushing her way through the aisle toward me. "Colin, I said stop!"

I watched with an amused twitch of my lips as she *excuse me'd* and *pardon me'd* her way through the crowd. "Yes, ma'am," I answered her.

Honey was breathless by the time she reached me. She blew a strand of straw-blond hair from her face. "Fuck! Annabeth Hayes is slower than dirt," she huffed. "That was out loud. Sorry, Ms. Annabeth."

I chuckled. "Hey, darlin'."

"Don't you 'hey, darlin' me." She pointed one finger in my direction. Though she radiated white-hot anger, I couldn't help but be amused at how quickly she tried to reach me. "Before you go and do something epically stupid, you need to know a few things. Here's the deal—you hurt my feelings when you lied to me, you're kind of being a prick about the photographs, and I'm in love with you. So figure your shit out and let's get on with it."

I sucked in a breath and reached for her hand. "There's something you need to know too." This was my chance to explain things to her, to make it right, and I hoped to god I could find the right words. "I will be purchasing the bakery. But only because Mr. Stevens needs to sell it, and I have the means to buy it right now. I don't want to see it go to someone other than you or a developer from the city. Whenever you're ready, you can purchase it from me outright. The space is yours. I would never, *ever* take that from you."

Honey's blue eyes were wild as my words settled in. Finally she said. "Well, I'm paying you rent."

I reached out and touched her face. "That's fine, baby. I know that's important to you. But what I am saying is this— the bakery will always be yours. You have my word." I brought her hand to my chest. "And I love you. I knew it on some level since we met at Jo's event and couldn't shake you. You're it for me."

Honey surged forward and I lifted her into a deeply passionate kiss. The entire town erupted in applause around us. My kiss was insistent, and I didn't give a *fuck* who was watching. I was not letting her go until she felt how deeply I loved her.

I set Honey down and ran my nose along her face, whispering into her ear. "Look around, Honey. The whole damn town's in love with you."

FORTY-SIX

HONEY

When Colin set me on my toes, and I glanced around, the joyous faces of my friends and neighbors surrounded me. The whole town may be in love with me, but I was in love with them too.

Tiny flutters of happiness surged through my body. I looked into Colin's hazel eyes and breathed in his lemon cedar scent and I knew. Colin was it for me. One day soon I was going to convince him to ask me again, and I was going to marry the fuck out of that man. That day couldn't come soon enough.

"Ask me," I said a little breathlessly.

Colin lifted an eyebrow, but as understanding took hold, his lopsided grin spread across his face. "Right now? You're sure?"

"Ask me again, or I'll ask you first," I teased.

Colin looked around and took one step back. With a hand on his chest, he cleared his throat. He caught the eyes of Deck and Linc and nodded once before dropping to one knee.

"Honey James, I've got something to ask you."

The crowd went silent as tears sprang to the corners of my eyes and I nodded. We were standing in a high school gymnasium that smelled like basketballs, stale coffee, and too many baked goods, surrounded by the town that had accepted me as one of their own. Nothing about this was traditional. I had tried to keep our relationship a secret, and we'd only dated openly for a few weeks, but I knew it in my bones. Colin was right and I wanted nothing more than to spend my life with him in this weird little town.

Colin reached for my hand, and I held my breath. "Honey James, will you marry me?"

I lifted my face to the ceiling and shouted, "Yes!" I laughed and felt more confident than I ever had in my life. I looked into his eyes that sparkled with browns and greens. "Yes, Colin McCoy, I will marry you."

Whoops and hollers echoed off the gymnasium walls as Colin rose from his knee and held me in a tight embrace.

His deep, gravelly voice danced over my skin. "This is the best day of my entire life. I don't deserve you, but I will spend every day trying." He kissed my neck and held my face between his hands. "I love you so much."

I laughed as he rained kisses across my skin. "I love you too."

The crowd descended on us, and before I knew it, I was pulled into tight hugs and was swaying back and forth with nearly every woman in town. Colin endured back slaps, handshakes, and hugs from the men.

Jo rushed forward and squealed, and we hugged and danced in a circle. Lincoln wrapped Colin into a fierce hug. "Glad you got your head out of your ass, brother."

Colin grinned. "Couldn't have done it without you. Thanks for everything."

"Have you told him yet?" Joanna asked.

"Told me what?"

It was my turn to get nervous. "Well, we should head over to the bakery. I have something to show you."

"WHAT THE FUCK IS THIS?" Colin's mouth was agape. Standing in the back office of the bakery, he was staring, slack-jawed at the gigantic hole in the drywall into his own office.

"Well," I started, "I decided that we were both being morons. You needed a bigger office, and I wanted to be close to you. So now, we get both." With a satisfied grin, I planted both hands on my hips.

His eyes were still wide. "You busted a fucking hole in the wall."

"I did." I grinned.

Colin put me in a playful headlock and mussed my hair. "You are one crazy hellcat. I love you."

"I love you too. And I'm glad you love me back because I did this before I even knew for sure you felt the same. It would have gotten real awkward if this didn't work out."

We both laughed. When Colin pulled me into an embrace, all playfulness fizzled from the air as I wiggled my ass against him. He nuzzled my neck, and his lips moved down as I squirmed. I let out a soft moan as Colin's hands moved up my sides to pinch my nipples.

I gasped lightly and let my head fall back against his shoulder, arching my back and reveling in the feel of his steel erection pushing against me. Colin nipped at my neck.

"You know what I like?" Colin expertly undid the top buttons on my dress and slipped a hand inside, cupping my breast over the thin lacy material of my bra. He licked the sensitive skin behind my ear, and I could hardly concentrate on anything but the warm wetness spreading between my thighs.

Colin dragged his other hand up my leg, sliding his fingers along the inside of my right thigh.

Yes. More. Please. More.

"What do you like?" My voice was heady and thick with desire.

"Your sweet pussy." His fingers teased my seam over my panties, stopping to feel the wetness soaking through the fabric. I expelled a hot breath, unable to speak.

As he stroked my folds, he moved the fabric aside and ran a thick finger through it. "You're warm and wet. I fucking love that."

"I love what you're doing to me. Keep talking." I turned to face him, but instead of allowing it, Colin moved me forward toward his desk.

"Yeah?" he asked as he placed my hands on the desk. "Do you like knowing I've fantasized about you? Here in my office? Across my desk as I licked and sucked every part of you?"

I moaned in approval and swiveled my ass, needing his touch. Colin dipped his head lower, brushing his lips against the outer shell of my ear, sending a deep shiver up my back. He hiked my skirt up, exposing my backside, and his hands roamed over my round curves. His fingers hooked over the sides of my panties, and he dragged them to my knees. Brushing his fingertips up the backs of my thighs, my core clenched in anticipation.

Colin moved his fingers through my folds again, teasing me. "So many times," he continued. "I'd think of you propped on this desk, legs spread open for me. I'd take my cock in my hands and make myself come just thinking about you."

Colin pushed inside me and continued his demanding assault between my legs—stroking and teasing as I bucked against his hand.

"But I don't need the fantasy. You're a fantasy come to fucking life."

At his words and his touch, I spasmed around his fingers, the rhythmic pulses at war with my ragged breaths. I looked at Colin over my shoulder to see him place one finger into his mouth, tasting my wetness.

"Not enough," he growled as he sank to his knees behind me. Before I could protest and demand his cock, Colin's mouth was on me. My arms shook and he dragged the rough flat of his tongue against me. "You taste so fucking good," he moaned.

"Now, Colin. I need that dick." I was breathless and panting, on the verge of coming again.

He stood. His fingers toyed with his belt buckle as I turned to face him. "You need this?" he asked

I moved my hands down the hard ridges of his stomach as the muscles bunched and flexed. I teased the sensitive skin below his belly button as I unbuttoned and unzipped his jeans. Colin pulled off his shirt as I pushed his pants and boxers down, freeing his thick, hard cock. I licked my lower lip at the sight of it.

Colin moved to get a condom from his pocket when I placed my hand on his arm, stopping him. "I want to feel you."

His eyes bore into mine as they grew darker with wild desire. I stepped out of my thong and leaned back against Colin's desk. Setting my bottom on the edge, I opened my legs, exposing myself to him. Colin fisted his cock and lined the thick tip to my entrance.

"You want to feel this?"

"Yes, Colin. I want to feel nothing but you."

Colin's cock pushed inside me, achingly slow, and my body stretched to accommodate him. Feeling nothing between us was intensely erotic, and my heart ticked up a beat as my breaths came out in soft pants. Colin moved devastatingly slow, and he watched himself slide through my center.

"Nothing feels as good as you feel," he ground out. His hips moved faster, and his hands grabbed my sides, his fingers dimpling the soft skin. Pumping into me, Colin captured my lips in a deep, wet kiss. My tongue slid over his, and a soft grunt vibrated between us. Colin's arms wrapped around me, pulling me closer to him and rubbing my clit against the base of him, exactly where I needed it.

My pussy tightened around him, and I felt myself exploding into bliss, and his back stiffened, and I felt his cock throb inside me. Over and over, he emptied himself inside me. Colin's forehead was against mine as our breathing slowed, but my heartbeat still pounded in my ears.

"That was probably really fucking dumb but I don't care. I love having you bare."

I smoothed his hair away from his forehead and bit my lip as I got lost in the swirling greens and browns of his eyes.

"Actually," I said, "I started birth control last month. I wanted you like this too. We're safe."

"I didn't think I could love you more, but knowing I can have you with nothing between us was incredible." Colin kissed me gently as he slipped from me, and I instantly missed him. Our breath mixed and we both worked to steady ourselves.

When our pulses returned to normal, we cleaned ourselves, and I did my best to rearrange my lopsided dress and mussed hair. Swiping any stray mascara from below my eye, I asked, "How do I look?"

He crossed to me and brushed a thumb across my cheekbones. "You're gorgeous." A blush warmed my cheeks beneath his hand. "Now let's get you home."

Home.

FORTY-SEVEN

COLIN

THE STAGE LIGHTS were low as we waited for our set to begin. The familiar thrum of nerves ran down my arm, and I adjusted the guitar across my thighs. I enjoyed the fact that I still got a little nervous every time I sat on stage—it kept me on my toes and forced me to practice, even when I didn't feel like it.

It was showtime.

Technically I wasn't supposed to be playing tonight, but when a band canceled at the last minute, the house band and I stepped up to fill the time slot. The bar was crowded, and they expected a night of good food, great music, and I was determined to help make their night on the town worth it.

As the lights went up, I nodded to the band and strummed the first notes of our opening song. Couples filtered out onto the floor, spinning and two-stepping as we started with country classics. Through the crowd, I kept an eye on my girl. Every chance I got, I would catch her eye and nod or throw her a wink. Honey was perched on a high-top barstool, surrounded by my best friends. When she wanted to dance, Finn would twirl her around the dance floor. Once or twice she even convinced Deck to get off his grumpy ass and enjoy a song or two.

Honey would swing her hips to my music, and she always cheered the loudest when we finished each song. My heart swelled for her every time I heard her above the crowd. At the table, Jo and Lincoln kept her company, enjoying the absolutely sinful desserts she started baking for the bar. Every weekend, Honey baked up various confections around a specific theme. Given the band lineup, this week was Bayou Blues, and it included beignets, mini Cajun cakes, and a ridiculously decadent praline bread pudding—one of which I had Isa hide deep in our kitchen fridge so there'd be one left for me at the end of the night.

On the heels of our engagement, I half expected Linc and Deck to lecture me on rushing in or being sure we were both ready, but all they had to offer me were strong hugs, congratulations, and words of encouragement. When Avery and I had talked after my proposal at the town hall meeting, she burst into tears and told me that while I was a fantastic brother, she'd always secretly wanted a sister. It only took one coffee date with Avery and Mom, and Honey had been volunteered for more sisterly outings than I think she'd bargained for.

My whole family—while we'd never truly be whole again—felt at peace. Without secrets and me learning to lower the walls I had built, it was easy for them to see that Honey was it for me. There was nothing simpler than that.

As had become tradition, I ended our set with Honey's song. It had become somewhat of a town anthem —a symbol of finding love. It moved me to see couples pairing off to glide and sway on the dance floor. Despite friends and neighbors asking Honey to dance, she always politely refused. This was our song and even when my throat got thick with emotion, I did my best to pour all that intensity into the song with her eyes locked with mine.

After wrapping the set, I wound my way through the handshakes and hugs of the crowd to find our table. "Amazing as always, babe!" Honey wrapped me in a fierce hug, and I took a deep pull of the apricots and spice scent on her skin.

"I'm glad you still like it." I looked deeply into her blue eyes. "Almost ready to call it a night?" I asked.

Her eyes danced playfully. "Wanna sneak off somewhere? I heard someone's brand new office desk was delivered today."

I laughed and a pull of desire hit my belly. Before I could throw her over my shoulder like a fucking caveman, Decker—phone pressed to his ear and sporting a serious scowl—walked over, and his hand clamped on my shoulder.

"Bad news, man." He was radiating serious cop vibes, and my back went stiff as my thoughts instinctively flicked to my mother. "Dick bandits."

Honey's bubble of laughter pierced through his serious demeanor, and even he cracked the slightest of smiles.

"No shit. The bakery or the bar?" I asked.

"The bar," he blew out an irritated sigh. "A big, veiny fucker, right on the front . . . this one's smiling and waving the top hat."

The collective howl of laughter from our table eased the tension rolling off Decker's shoulders. I was smart enough to know that a little harmless graffiti wasn't enough to put him in such a pissy mood. When I scanned the crowd, I saw Maggie O'Brien accepting a fresh beer from a rancher in town, and his mood made a lot more sense.

"All right. Thanks for the heads up." I shook his hand. "I'm sure we'll get it taken care of."

"These fucking kids, man." Deck shook his head. "Enjoy the rest of your night. I gotta run," he said as he walked away but not before casting one last glance at the bar toward Maggie.

I wound my arm around Honey's shoulders, and she radiated happiness up at me. I was going to take my woman home—to *our home*—and it was going to be the best thing I did all day. Hands down it was better than a great night onstage, booking an unbookable band, or serving up drinks to my friends and neighbors. There was nothing better than sharing my life with Honey.

FORTY-EIGHT

CHIKALU CHATTER

GRAND RE-OPENING OF BISCUITS & HONEY
SET FOR SATURDAY NIGHT

CHIKALU FALLS' *own Biscuits & Honey will celebrate a Grand Re-Opening of sorts on Saturday night. After only six months since its original opening, the beloved bakery will celebrate the newly expanded space. Co-owners, and fiancés, Honey James and Colin McCoy recently purchased Ed Morton's waning hardware store. Mr. Morton stated, "With the new interstate and the big box hardware store opening up, it's time I retire. I'm happy the store's going to our own people." It looks as though the couple is turning into Chikalu's very own real estate moguls.*

FORTY-NINE

EPILOGUE

HONEY

CHIKALU FALLS KNEW how to throw a great party, I would give them that. The town had gone all out in celebration of the expansion of Biscuits & Honey. Colin's kitchen and the bakery catered, there was a fully stocked bar, balloons, and an enormous *Grand Re-Opening* sign. They had even planned for live music and, because it wasn't a Chikalu Falls party without dancing, there was even a plywood dance floor for two-stepping.

When Jean and the rest of the Chikalu Women's Club approached me with the idea of a re-opening celebration, I had told them it wasn't necessary. I quickly learned that trying to dissuade that particular group of hard-headed women was all but impossible. Truth be told, excitement bloomed across my chest any time I thought about it. The bakery had grown and evolved into something more than I could have imagined, and it was a symbol of two people coming together. Old and new finding their place in this small town.

Within the first few months of officially opening, I was

having a hard time keeping up with the demand. Between all-day bakery orders, I was getting more requests for my desserts and pastries for birthday parties, sorority parties, baby showers, and even weddings. I was shocked that so many people wanted my food to be a part of their most special occasions.

It felt like some kind of magic, but I knew the real magic of it all was the acceptance of a town I'd known and loved since my childhood. In Chikalu, I could bottle up all my me-ness and not be afraid to live my life out loud—crass and sass and big hair included.

Even back when I tried to pretend that what I was feeling for Colin was nothing more than attraction to his killer body and the tingles his deep voice caused every time he spoke, I knew in my heart that it was so much more.

With his arm wrapped around my shoulder, he leaned in and brushed a kiss across my hair. "I am so fucking proud of you."

He planted a kiss firmly on my mouth and peeled away from me to mingle. I looked around. The entire town had shown up in support, and I sighed a deep, satisfied breath.

Mr. Bailey sat with the other senior men—the Coffee Clutch—sharing old war stories. The youngest by at least two decades, Lincoln had been brought into the fold, and while he only looked mildly uncomfortable, I knew it was only a matter of time until those crazy old bastards wore him down.

Even Ms. Coulson had shown up. She peered down her straight nose at the side table that was bursting with donuts and other breakfast pastries—including my french crullers. Despite her visible, outward disgust, it remained our little secret that we exchanged notes and found the reason she had trouble with her crullers. I shared my recipe with her, and despite the fact the recipes were now identical, the town remained divided over which crullers reigned supreme. In all honesty, it cracked me up thinking that the town argued over it, and I was happy to lose a customer or two if that meant they'd still eat a cruller over coffee and pick a side.

Walking past me, Ms. Trina waved hello and shot me a quick, not-so-subtle wink. Earlier that week, I had made a very special order, and Colin was in for quite the surprise tonight. I carefully brushed the outside of my thigh, feeling the sexy bow on the strap of the garter belt I wore beneath my flowy dress.

"What's with that sly smile?" Jo asked as she walked up and hugged me fiercely.

"Ms. Trina strikes again."

"Ah." She laughed. "That woman has a talent, that's for sure."

"That she does," I laughed, clinking my nearly empty glass to Jo's.

Jo squeezed me again. "My heart is so happy."

She wrapped her arms around Lincoln as he stepped up beside us. Colin followed and lifted a fresh, tall, bubbly glass of champagne. "Yes," my greedy eyes went wide. "You are a lifesaver."

"Can we call it a night?" Linc asked Joanna.

"We sure can, big guy." Turning to us, Jo said, "Linc's all peopled out for the day. Breakfast tomorrow?" she asked.

I nodded and gave her one last hug before they ambled down the sidewalk, entangled in each other's arms.

Colin brushed a strand of hair from my eyes before brushing his thumb across my jaw. "You deserve to relax and enjoy this party." His arm swept gently toward the crowd that was spilling out of the bakery and into the closed-off section of Main Street. "This is all for you. I'll be sure to get you back home tonight." His wink sent heat straight between my legs. Fanning my warm cheeks, I scanned the street again.

Decker was standing on the edges of the crowd in plain clothes, watching for any unsupervised youths with spray paint cans. It had been months since anyone had been tagged, but Deck was convinced the Dick Bandit was still out there. He stood, watching the crowd and taking sips of something dark from his glass. Colin saw my gaze settle on him.

"He's off duty and apparently using whiskey to deal with his forced proximity to Maggie and her new boyfriend tonight." Colin's head nodded toward Maggie and the same rancher she'd been dating for the last few months.

"I can never figure those two out," I said, taking a sip of my champagne. The bubbles tickled my throat, and I leaned my head onto Colin's shoulder as we watched the scene unfold in front of us—Maggie pretending not to shoot Decker heated looks over her date's shoulder, and Decker pretending not to follow her every move.

"You got me. He won't admit a thing," Colin said with a shrug. I slanted a look at Colin. I had a feeling he knew a little more than he let on, but I could respect his loyalty to his best friend. My fingers twirled the diamond ring on my left hand and my chest warmed. We had thought about going into Butte to have something custom made, but after a minute we both realized that just didn't feel right. Mitzy Pointus, Chikalu's favorite jeweler, was able to find something truly unique. She had several heirloom rings from an old estate sale, and we were able to rework one of them into the most gorgeous engagement ring I could ask for. It, too, was a symbol of something old and new coming together in Chikalu—just like us.

"You are the most incredible woman, Honey McCoy." Colin kissed my ring as if he knew exactly where my thoughts had wandered.

"*Shh.* Keep your voice down. I haven't told Jo yet." A smile played on my lips. A week ago, Colin and I had woken up tangled in each other when he'd suggested we not wait a minute longer to get married. Nothing sounded better than waking up as Mrs. McCoy, so we found a flight out of Montana and flew down to a white sand beach in Mexico to get married under the stars. Our cover was a lone, romantic getaway, but no one but the two of us knew the truth. Apparently, we weren't doing anything traditionally in this relationship.

Unlike the first time I tried keeping Colin a secret, I couldn't wait to scream it from the top of my lungs and backflip down Main Street until everyone knew Colin was my man—forever. I just had to disappoint my older sister at her missing the wedding. I knew she'd understand, but her feelings would be hurt if she wasn't the first to know. Tomorrow at breakfast I'd break the news.

"Is this really our life?" I asked as I scanned the crowd again. Old Ms. Gertie was half in the bag, dancing with any young stud that ventured too close, and I secretly hoped to be witness to her drunken striptease.

"It sure is, baby. And I couldn't ask for anything more."

Colin settled in behind me, wrapping me in his thick, protective arms. "I just wish Nate could have seen what you've done with the bar," he sighed. Colin had taken the bakery's theme of old photographs and included more inside the bar—friends and neighbors living a vibrant life in and around Chikalu. Many had pictures of his little brother. It transformed the bar and dance hall from a college hang out into a place where people gathered to make more happy memories in their hometown.

"He'd probably give me shit about it but yeah. I think he'd be proud." His voice was thick with emotion, but more and more he talked openly about Nate, and slowly his wounds were healing. Colin and Jean's relationship was flourishing, and the heaviness he'd carried for so long seemed to be lifting.

It seemed like a lifetime ago that I drove into Chikalu Falls with zero plan and a trunk full of irresponsible shoes. But now all this was real. I was a successful business owner and a member of a community that loved fiercely. I was married to Colin McCoy, and it was only a matter of time before we started our own family and raised our babies right here in Chikalu. This life in Chikalu was crazy and messy and all mine.

"Hey, darlin'?" he whispered in my ear. "Can I keep you?"

"Always."

$\sim$

WANT a peek into Colin and Honey's first rendezvous? Get instant access to a KEEPING YOU bonus scene at:

https://lenahendrix.com/get-honey-and-colins-bonus-scene/

. . .

IF YOU'D LIKE to try your hand at some of the recipes featured in this book, keep reading!

NEXT UP IN the Chikalu Falls series is Maggie and Deck's story, PROTECTING YOU. Continue reading for a sneak peek!

FIFTY

IRISH BUTTE PASTY

FOR THE PASTRY:

- 2 cups flour
- 1/2 cup shortening
- 1/2 stick butter
- 1/3 cup cold water
- 1/2 teaspoon salt

For the filling:

- 8 ounces high quality beef, I use ground sirloin
- 1 cup diced potato
- 2/3 cup diced root vegetables, I like carrots and rutabaga
- 1/3 cup chopped onion
- 2 cloves garlic
- 1 teaspoon salt
- 1/2 teaspoon pepper
- 1 egg

Add the flour, salt, lard and butter to a food mixer and bring together.

Pour in the water and mix until a ball is formed.

Wrap in cling film and chill for at least 3 hours.

Dice the potato, root vegetables, onion, and garlic into small pieces.

Combine all of the ingredients for the filling with the exception of the egg.

Divide the pastry into four pieces and then roll out so that you can cut out four small discs.

Place a quarter of the filling on each disc and then fold over sealing with water.

Crimp the pasties by pinching the fold between your thumb and fore finger.

Then fold over and continue until the entire edge is crimped.

Brush over with the beaten egg and bake at 350°F for 50-55 minutes.

FIFTY-ONE

MIDNIGHT BLTS

- 4 slices of bread
- 4 slices of thick cut bacon, cooked
- 1 tomato, sliced
- 3 leaves of romaine lettuce, white spine removed, divided use
- 1/4 cup of mayo
- 1-2 teaspoons of chili garlic paste (found in the international aisle of most grocery stores)

LIGHTLY TOAST BREAD, cook the bacon, slice the tomato, and remove the bitter spine of the lettuce. In a small bowl, combine the mayo and chili garlic paste.

Lightly spread the mayo-chili garlic paste on all four pieces of toast. Build your BLT.

Our preferred order: Bread, mayo mixture, lettuce, bacon, tomato, lettuce, bacon, tomato, lettuce, mayo mixture, bread

Best enjoyed at midnight.

FIFTY-TWO

SAGEBRUSH COCKTAIL

SERVES ONE

- 3 large sage leaves
- 1 teaspoon sugar (plus extra for rim)
- 1 lemon wedge
- 2 ounces gin
- 2 ounces freshly squeezed grapefruit juice
- Garnish: grapefruit twist, fresh sage leaf

SELECT YOUR GLASS. If using the coup, rim the glass with a bit of lemon, then roll into a bit of sugar.

Set the glass aside.

Into a cocktail shaker, add 1/4 section of lemon, skin and all with 1 teaspoon sugar and 3 fresh sage leaves.

Muddle until very broken down. This will release the oils from the skin of the lemon as well as release all the lovely sage flavor.

Into the shaker, add 2 ounces of gin with 2 ounces of freshly squeezed grapefruit juice.

Fill the shaker 1/2 way with ice then shake and shake, at least 20 seconds.

Strain into your prepared glass.

Add a giant square cube, the garnish the top of the ice cube with very thin pieces of the grapefruit skin and a small leaf of fresh sage.

SNEAK PEEK AT PROTECTING YOU

Maggie—Now

Fᴜᴄᴋ ᴛʜᴇ ʙᴀᴋᴇ ꜱᴀʟᴇ.

Blowing the hairs that had escaped from my sagging ponytail out of my eyes, I quickly looked both ways before crossing Main Street and barreling out of my flower shop toward Biscuits & Honey. The local bakery had been open about a year and was owned by Honey McCoy. In the short time she'd lived here, she became one of my best friends. She had swiftly become a leader among the busiest shops in town. She and the bar owner, Colin, had gotten married and shared the offices that joined their two spaces. Honey was an outsider who had successfully integrated herself into life in Chikalu Falls, Montana.

As I hustled across the street, I pulled my chunky sweater tighter across my chest. I'd left my heavy coat in the car after leaving my flower shop, and that was a mistake. Autumn had settled into our little town, and as the cold evening wind slapped at my skin, I blew out a quick breath.

Outside the glass door of the shop, I glanced back down

at the text that had come from my daughter just as I was wrapping up a long day at the shop.

Lottie: I need something for the bake sale tomorrow.

Me: Well, did you bake something?

Lottie: Seriously? Mom.

Irritation rolled through me as I nodded and gave a tight smile to the couple walking into The Dirty Pigeon, the bar and dance hall next to the bakery. I swallowed down the wave of humiliation at having to ask for help—something I was sure the other mothers didn't have to do. Thank god for Honey, because there was no way I could muster the energy to bake something tonight for Lottie's Halloween school fundraiser. I figured it was typical for a fourteen-year-old not to tell her mom *in advance* that she needed something as time-consuming as a baked good.

With all the pity glances I got from the other mothers at school, I couldn't flake on the fundraiser. Most of the other moms were older, stylishly coiffed, and ready to judge. I was seventeen when I had Lottie and, save for *one night* of recklessness, I had always been the most responsible teen I knew. A pie from Biscuits & Honey would still receive judgment from the other mothers, since it wasn't technically homemade, but at least it would be the most delicious item on the table.

Maybe I'll buy two, just in case . . .

The dusky fall sky was losing its last streaks of pinks and oranges, but inside the airy and bright shop, patrons sat along the wall, chatting and sipping coffee while enjoying pastries and pumpkin-spiced dessert. Cinnamon and brown sugar aromas wafted from the kitchen, and pride for my friend's success swelled in my chest. I offered smiles and nods to friends and neighbors dotting the small interior.

As I took one step toward the counter, I saw *him*.

Cole Decker was three customers ahead of me in line, and I lowered my head a bit, hoping he wouldn't notice me. That man was fucking infuriating—always finding ways to make my life a little more miserable. Sometimes I didn't know if he did it on purpose or if he was just wired to make my body hum and inconvenience me in as many ways as possible.

He still looks delicious, though.

I steeled against my traitorous thoughts. It may have been almost fifteen years since Cole and I had been best friends but my physical attraction had never died. In fact, as he aged annoyingly well with his gravelly voice, broad shoulders, and tiny smattering of gray in the dark brown at his temples, I only struggled to keep my hormones in check around him more.

I peeked around the person in front of me to watch the way his dark police uniform hugged the curves of his ass and clung to his muscular thighs. Despite his bulletproof vest, you couldn't mistake the expanse of his chest and taper of his waist. My body clenched with desire, and I felt hot in my cozy sweater.

Who the hell still has a six-pack at thirty-three?

Cole Decker, that was who.

The veins on the back of his hand entranced me as he pointed out pastries for the gal behind the counter to stuff into a white box. She plucked cinnamon buns, Italian wedding cookies, peanut butter and butterscotch scotcheroos—a wide assortment of treats that caused the box to bend under the weight.

"Leave some for the rest of us."

The words tumbled from my mouth, and before I realized my inside thought had become my outside thought, Cole turned his head to glare at me over his shoulder.

Damn it.

My spine stiffened, and I lifted my chin a notch. The icy stares he shot my way would not intimidate me. I knew that big, strong asshole had cried at the ending of *The Notebook.*

He muttered something under his breath and reached for his wallet. I sighed and looked at the sparse display case. A handful of cookies and a lonely cherry pie.

Sorry, Lottie, looks like we're only getting one pie. At least it's my favorite.

I tapped my foot, impatience buzzing down my leg. It was dark now, and I still had a lot to do for the weekend's upcoming wedding. Cole shot another look over his shoulder and paused with the cash in his hand.

"You know . . . ," he said. His voice was deep and commanding and definitely did *not* make my stomach flip-flop. "I'll take the cherry pie too."

"Wha—no!" I shouted before I could help myself.

Heads turned and heat rose from my chest to my cheeks.

A smirk danced across his face, but he paid for his order, gathered the boxes, and stepped out of line. It moved forward while he took one imposing step toward me.

"Is there a problem, Ms. O'Brien?" The dull, slightly bored tone of his voice only spurred my aggravation.

I clenched my jaw and swallowed past the pebble lodged in my throat. "Actually, yes. I was going to buy that pie."

He set the box of pastries on the empty high-top table next to us. "This pie?" he asked, gesturing to the package still in his grasp.

"Yeah. It's the last one." I planted my hands on my hips in an effort not to choke a police officer. Cole and I hardly ever spoke, and energy zapped under my skin. "You have enough treats, don't you think?"

"Guys at the station get hungry on the midnight shift." His eyes flicked down my body, and I felt my nipples pebble beneath the thin camisole I wore under my sweater.

"I need that pie. It's an emergency." I crossed my arms in an X over my chest to hide the splotchy red patches I could feel blooming under my collarbone.

Cole flipped open the box with one hand and grabbed a fork with the other. "A pie emergency?" he asked, pointing to the golden pastry with the fork.

I rolled my eyes at him. I did not have time for his shit tonight. "Yes," I hissed. "Just let me buy it from you."

He pressed his lips together in a *hmm* as if he were really considering helping me out. "Well"—his voice dipped low, and he leaned toward me slightly, the plastic tines plunging into the flaky crust as he pulled up a huge, gooey bite of tart cherry goodness—"this pie is mine."

The way his voice deepened on the word *mine* had my body screaming. I stared at the fullness of his lips as they closed around the warm pie, and I licked my own, imagining what his kiss would taste like—sweet and tangy and masculine.

I shook my head to clear the fog of desire.

He's cocky and an asshole, I reminded myself. *And he just stole your fucking pie.*

I pulled a blank expression over my face, allowing fire to seep into my eyes. "Real nice," I scoffed. I pushed past him and sailed toward the exit door without looking back.

"Wear a coat before you freeze to death."

Ignoring him completely, I kept moving. I didn't need

him to tell me what to do, no matter how logical it was. I hustled down the sidewalk and across the street to my car. Cole Decker was infuriating and, as usual, I let him get under my skin. Quite literally the only man who could make me angry and horny at the same time.

The frigid wind was biting, and my numb fingers fumbled with my car keys as I replayed the scene in my head. I could never seem to keep my cool when Cole was around, and as much as I tried to avoid running into our hot-as-sin local detective, he was popping up in my life more and more. To add inconvenience to irritation, now I had to figure out what the hell I was going to do about Lottie's bake sale tomorrow.

I typed out a frenzied text to Honey. I needed to call in a favor, because with my frazzled nerves, there was no way I could pull off something edible for the bake sale.

⌇

"You're a lifesaver." I sighed in relief as Honey slid a white box toward me.

"I got you, girlie." She winked and perched herself opposite me at the high-top table.

After I'd frantically texted her from my parking space, she had assured me she would take care of it and had told me to meet her at The Pidge, what everyone called The Dirty Pigeon.

"I seriously can't thank you enough. I came in to buy a pie, and he stole it out from under me!" I seemed irrationally pissed and childish, but I didn't give a fuck. He could have let me purchase it, and instead, he *ate it in front of me*. What a prick.

"I saw," she said with a smirk. "I was cleaning up in the back."

Embarrassment colored my cheeks. Honey needled me about Cole often enough, but I always brushed it off and claimed she was crazy to think there was ever anything between us.

"Someone liiiiiikes you," she teased.

I rolled my eyes. "Please. We aren't seven."

Honey laughed a little to herself as a waitress placed our usual drinks in front of us. There were definite perks to being close friends with the bar's owner.

"I don't care what you say, that man is stupid for you."

"Well, he's certainly stupid." I sipped my drink and tamped down the guilty feelings of name-calling Cole. He was many things, but stupid wasn't one of them, and even I realized I was the one being childish.

"Look, buying the last pie if he knew you were going to was a dick move. He may be Colin's best friend, but I can take care of it." A slow smile spread across her face, and mischief danced in her eyes. "His next order can have him shitting his pants for a week and not knowing why."

Honey was ruthless and the most loyal friend I'd ever had.

Feeling lighter than I had in weeks, I laughed. "No, don't do that. Who will keep this town safe if Captain America is out of commission?"

"That's true." Crestfallen, Honey swirled her drink. "It's too bad he's actually a decent human." Honey winked at me. "Mostly."

I simply rolled my eyes. It was common knowledge that Cole was the local golden boy, but for some reason he had a serious bone to pick with me. Rumors had spread far and wide through town as to why and ranged from a land dispute to high school drama to unrequited love—*ha*.

Honey pointed to the pie box and bumped my shoulder with hers. "So what's the deal?"

"Lottie informed me, *tonight*, she signed up for baked goods for the school fundraiser tomorrow."

Honey nodded as she sipped and swayed to the beat of the house band. "That sounds fun." She laughed.

"She's killing me. One minute she's the spawn of Satan, and the next she's begging to cuddle on the couch. I can't keep up."

"You're a great mom." Her hand covered mine. "She's lucky to have you."

I smiled at my friend. Being a single mother was never easy, and times like these, when your friends showed up for you with no questions asked, flooded my system with guilty feelings. It only served to remind me that I couldn't manage to do it on my own.

Our attention turned to the stage as Honey's husband, Colin, crooned into the microphone. A friend of his since high school, I felt nothing but platonic feelings for him, but it was undeniable that the man was handsome and could sing his heart out. Bluesy and warm, his voice was pure velvet.

Honey's blonde head swayed to the music, and her eyes filled with lust as she watched her man. A ping of jealousy shot me in the chest.

The soulful song faded, and I rubbed my hand against my thigh, willing the ache in my chest to release. "I should get going," I said to Honey. "I can't thank you enough for saving my ass tonight."

Her eyes softened. "I've always got your back. See you at the fundraiser?"

I lifted the pie box. "You know it." I kissed her on the cheek and left the bar, but not before letting my eyes flick past my favorite photo hanging on the wall. It was of Cole, Colin, and the third of their trio, Lincoln, dressed in football gear after a win, their youthful faces radiating charm and excitement. I had snapped the photo, and it always took me back to a time when life seemed full of promise, simpler.

The naive dreams of a young girl had been incinerated the moment I found out I had gotten pregnant on prom night by a boy who'd used me just for sex.

David had known how to charm me that night, and while he'd made a half-assed attempt at dating me after, he was never serious about a relationship with a shy girl who preferred books and country drives to field parties. A few weeks later, when my period was late, I drove twenty miles to a town where no one knew me and got a pregnancy test over the counter. I emptied my soul as I cried, alone in the smelly stall, and stared at the twin pink lines in the public bathroom.

When I tried to tell David, his response of "Is it even mine?" was a bullet to my chest. David was old money, and I was trailer trash who put out on prom night.

What a fucking cliché.

Mama wrapped me in a hug, and we talked about options. David's family offered me money to not have the baby, but I refused and steeled myself against the judgment that inevitably came my way.

After David's death, a large part of growing up had been letting the dreams of a younger me float away on the breeze. The chance at being Cole's girl had been one of those dreams.

The crisp air blew my hair back, and I gripped the box tightly. The whole town would turn out for the school fundraiser, and with Honey's help, I wouldn't show up empty-handed. Balancing the box in one hand, I fumbled for my keys.

A flash of yellow on my windshield caught my eye. "You have got to be kidding me."

I placed the pie on the front seat and reached to pull the paper from under the wiper. Stamped in dark ink was a parking ticket: multi-space, illegal parking. I glanced down at the white line beneath the wheel of my car. Sure, I was not *between* the lines, but illegal parking? No way.

I scanned the ticket and found exactly what I suspected —Cole Decker's signature scrawled across the bottom.

That fucking guy.

I sucked in a steadying breath to keep from coming completely unhinged. Deep down, I knew with a pretty bouquet arrangement and a sweet smile, I might get Arlene Johnson, the elderly secretary at the police station, to dismiss the ticket. Add it to the ever-growing list of things I needed to get done in the morning.

I looked over my shoulder in time to see Cole pass in a squad car. Not giving him the satisfaction of seeing how much he got to me, I ground my teeth together and slipped into my Honda. I pulled out of the parking space and wound up the dark mountain highway without allowing myself one last look at the infuriating boy who once held my heart.

FIND PROTECTING You on Amazon

A SPECIAL NOTE

BEING A SIBLING SURVIVOR OF SUICIDE, I fully understand the deeply difficult process of healing in the aftermath.

You are not alone.

If you are someone you know is struggling with depression and/or a mental health crisis, please contact the Suicide Prevention Hotline at 800-273-8255 or text TALK to 741741.

ALSO BY LENA HENDRIX

The Chikalu Falls Series

Finding You

Protecting You

Coming in 2022

The Badge and the Bad Boy

(Redemption Ranch Book 1)

ACKNOWLEDGMENTS

What a wild ride!

To my husband who never tires of random plot points that interrupt dinner or days I'm stressing over completely fictional problems. You also make a killer Midnight BLT. I'm sorry I shared your secret recipe with the world, but it's too good to keep to ourselves. I'll make it up to you somehow.

To my parents who not only survived the loss of their oldest child, but taught the rest of us what it looks like to lean on one another. You two have the strongest bond I have ever seen and I am proud to be your daughter. But seriously Mom, do *not* let Pop read my books. Yikes.

To my fabulous editor Nancy. Thank you for calling me out when I write nonsense. Kim, thanks for your patience when looking for cover models and I just don't like his "vibe." Laetitia, you are my comma queen. Thank you for proofing this story and making it the best it can be!

My Three Amigals! You continue to be the most amazing beta-turned-alpha readers a gal could ask for. If it weren't for you, I would probably be stuck a third of the way through, hating life. Jenn, your keen eye for editing and creatively working through plot is second-to-none. Ariel, I love that I can bounce the craziest ideas off you and somehow we find a way to come out better on the other side! Our book-talk-wine-dates are my favorite.

To my Golden Girls. How did I get so lucky?! Thank you for plucking me out of obscurity and forming the most kick-ass girl gang on the planet. I can't wait to see where this sisterhood is taking us!